Praise for

INVASIVE SPECIES

"Cost me a perfectly good night's sleep . . . I hope Wallace carries a screenplay of *Invasive Species* in his hip pocket; he's going to need it."   —Bill Ransom, author of *Burn*

"Wallace's unsettling, mind-bending apocalyptic novel chillingly dives into what happens when the balance of the world is disrupted and an invasive species grabs the reins. Terrifying and, yes, poetic, this is a novel that gets under your skin with an 'it could happen here' kind of chilling grace."

—Caroline Leavitt, *New York Times* bestselling author of *Is This Tomorrow*

"A vivid detour into hell . . . Scary good."

—Luis Alberto Urrea, author of *The Water Museum* and *Queen of America*

"Unbelievably engrossing and mildly terrifying, *Invasive Species* is impossible to set down."

—*San Francisco Book Review*

"Wallace has crafted a truly believable tale of invasion in this book . . . This one is deserving of every bit of the hype it has received and then some."   —Bookshelf Bombshells

"Wallace seems to have  page-turners in history Crichton, and has outd

D1041904

Titles by Joseph Wallace

INVASIVE SPECIES
SLAVEMAKERS

SLAVEMAKERS

JOSEPH WALLACE

ACE BOOKS, NEW YORK

ACE

An imprint of Penguin Random House LLC
375 Hudson Street, New York, New York 10014

SLAVEMAKERS

An Ace Book / published by arrangement with the author

ISBN: 978-0-425-27718-8

PUBLISHING HISTORY
Ace premium edition / December 2015

PRINTED IN THE UNITED STATES OF AMERICA

10 9 8 7 6 5 4 3 2 1

Cover art by Nekro.
Cover design by George Long and Adam Auerbach.
Interior text design by Kelly Lipovich.

Penguin
Random
House

For Sharon, Shana, and Jacob. Always.

*And for Danielle, Emmalisa, Liana, Mike, Sophie Dora,
Stephanie, and Violet, whose boundless enthusiasm meant everything
to me as I was writing this book.*

ACKNOWLEDGMENTS

With this novel, as with all my books, I'm grateful to many people for their help . . . and their patience:

Sharon AvRutick, a superb editor and, as always, my first reader, who guided me through the process of making this complex story come clear.

Deborah Schneider, my brilliant literary agent and a marvelously insightful reader as well. This novel and I are both indebted to her.

Robin Barletta, Natalee Rosenstein, and the whole team at Berkley and Ace. I'm grateful for their faith in this book and the beautiful job they did turning it into a reality.

My brothers, Jonathan and Rich, who share my love of nature, not least the creepy-crawly parts.

Keith Bass, with memories of bug-filled tents with leopards snarling just outside; Danielle Tobias, who allowed me to distract her from work for lively conversations about parasitic wasps, zombie ants, and other cool creatures; and Carl Mehling and Fiona Brady, who provided timeless perspectives on the history of life on earth—as well as peerless company over delicious meals on Arthur Avenue.

And, crucially, Emmalisa Stangarone, my research assistant. During hours-long Skype sessions, Emma patiently and generously discussed her findings, experiences, and insights, helping me breathe life into some of the novel's most important characters and settings.

I'm also indebted to two books. Among the many (many!) postapocalyptic novels I've read, one that strikes deep is John Wyndham's haunting *The Day of the Triffids* (1951), with its indelible exploration of the concept of a "soft apocalypse." And, for a fearless portrayal of black widow spiders, tarantula hawk wasps, rattlesnakes, and other ferocious hunters, Gordon Grice's 1998 *The Red Hourglass: Lives of the Predators* can't be topped. My slavemakers—and the universe they inhabit—wouldn't exist without it.

To learn more about *Slavemakers*, my other books and stories, and me, check out josephwallace.com. (You can get in touch with me there as well.) The website links to my YouTube channel, where I've uploaded short films to accompany my novels. I'm also on Twitter @Joe_Wallace and at facebook.com/JoeWallaceWriter. Hope to hear from you.

PROLOGUE

THE HELICOPTER ROSE from the black, blood-soaked grass, slewing sideways as its rotors spilled air. Malcolm Granger fought with the stick and the throttle, but even though he was the best pilot he'd ever met, he knew that his chances of wrestling this overloaded Schweizer S-333 over the trees were god-awful—and of getting himself and his passengers to safety, even worse.

Thirty seconds earlier, Malcolm had been sure he was about to die. He'd seen the instrument of his death approaching, coming at him from all directions, and had known there was nothing he could do to prevent it. He'd known he was helpless.

This pissed him off. He fucking hated being helpless. He'd done the best he could, gotten further already than anyone else would have, he was sure of that. And death had never scared him. Losing, failing, that gutted him, but dying itself? No worries.

But then, just like that, the threat had disappeared. In a blink. The thieves were coming, they were inside the helicopter with him, then they were . . . gone. The moment of his death passed, and he was still alive.

He couldn't understand it. But understanding didn't matter. The S-333 bucked in his hands, fell twenty feet, threatened to roll. He was still alive, and if the bugs hadn't killed him, this fucking machine wasn't going to be the thing that did.

Down on the ground, too close once again, he saw the pale smudges of faces in the darkness, flickering white in the light of the immense flames consuming the buildings to the south. That was where the jet had gone down, the passenger plane that, screaming upside down a hundred feet above them, had come close to turning the helicopter—and Malcolm—into a smear of metal and flesh.

Smudges of faces. Not human faces, though. The faces of whatever humans became in the last stage. The faces of monsters reaching for him as he regained control and hovered for an instant just above their grasp.

The humans who were still alive weren't looking up. They were running. Or rolling on the ground. Or clutching at their eyes. Or they were already lying still.

Soon enough, all of them would be dead. Dead or worse. There was no room for them on the Schweizer, nor time.

Once more, Malcolm regained control, and the helicopter roared upward to safety. Temporary safety. At his feet, Trey Gilliard writhed and spasmed. Malcolm had no idea what had possessed him, but you didn't have to be a devil-worshipper to see that he was possessed.

Or: Half of Trey writhed. The other half was hanging out of the hatch. The way the S-333 was slipping and sliding, he would have been long gone, plummeted to the blood-soaked ground into the grasp of the monsters, if not for Sheila.

Malcolm had barely met Sheila, and she hadn't made much of an impression on him. A serious young woman who rarely smiled and sometimes seemed overwhelmed by the speed with which things were falling apart.

But now, watching her hang on to Trey, risking her own life to save his, Malcolm was changing his opinion. As they skimmed just above the trees that lined the park—feeling the heat from the airplane crash and a dozen, a hundred, other fires already beginning to consume the city—he saw her pull Trey fully inside and to safety.

Well. Shit. Safety by its current definition.

In his life on the edges of civilization, Malcolm, clear-eyed and fearless, had been witness to war and famine and acts of terrorism, to human suffering and death in all its variety and abundance. But as he took the little helicopter higher and aimed it north, the sights that greeted him were almost unendurable.

He wanted to close his eyes. Yet he forced himself to look because already he knew that someone had to see it. Had to watch the destruction of the civilization, the world, they'd all thought could not be breached.

On the floor near Malcolm's feet, Trey was finally still. Sheila was huddled over him, her face close to his.

So Malcolm was the only witness. No, that wasn't true. There were others. Millions. Billions. But they were all dead already, even if they didn't realize it yet.

He would be the only one to see and live to remember. The only one left to tell the story.

If they reached their destination, the little airport where the others waited for them. If he survived this night.

He piloted the S-333 over and around countless burning buildings. Orange and red and pure blinding white, spreading, flooding like a tsunami's wake down avenues snarled with cars that would never move again. Buildings collapsing, sending plumes of sparks and fountains of smoke erupting skyward.

On the streets below, some headlights were still gleaming. Brighter, and more hopeless, were the spinning red-and-white beacons of the fire engines. But no one was left to operate the hoses, and anyway, it was far too late. The city was beyond saving.

The cars and trucks were abandoned, but not the buildings that were still standing. He saw people perched on windowsills, outlined by fire. People jumping, choosing one kind of death over another. Small groups and big crowds huddled on rooftops, black smoke billowing past them, faces turned toward the helicopter, toward Malcolm, as if he were a vision from a future where they might survive. A dream of life.

A hopeless dream. Because everywhere, *everywhere*, was the whirlwind. Thieves in such numbers that even Malcolm's head spun. Vast spiraling clouds of them, the maestros of the city's destruction.

No. Not them. Not the whirlwind. It was the mind that had done this. The thieves were just the instruments of its plan.

* * *

THEY FLEW NORTH.

Finally leaving the conflagration behind and passing over the darkened suburbs. Some fires here as well, just beginning to spread, but all else dark except for the head-lights. The power grid gone, and gone for good.

The highways gone as well, blocked forever by crashed and wrecked cars. Yet not every route was closed off, and Malcolm glimpsed below them the weakly glowing firefly's trail of a car moving along some smaller road. A lone car cresting a hill, its headlights flashing like a lighthouse beacon.

No: like the ghostly lights on a ship, seen from the surface as it sinks into the depths.

Malcolm took one last look at the car, imagining its unseen driver hurtling from one certain death to another. Then he straightened. Ahead, through a scrim of bare trees, he could see the emergency lights illuminating the runway of Westchester County Airport. At the foot of the runway stood the Citation X private jet that he had retrofitted for this night. This night that had come too soon.

The little plane that held some of the few who would survive the destruction of the Last World.

IN ALL THE years that followed, Malcolm told only a few people about what he had seen that night. Only those few who were closest to him, who never passed on the details to anyone else.

But others let their imaginations run wild, and in doing so assumed that Malcolm would never want to venture back into the world whose final torments he'd witnessed. They assumed he'd be happy spending the rest of his life in the haven that Refugia, the village that was their home, provided.

So everyone was shocked when, even in the early years, Malcolm was already making plans to leave once again. And when, as soon as he could, he started building the three-masted, square-rigged ship that years later would be christened the *Trey Gilliard*. A ship designed for nothing but exploration. Escape.

People guessed, they psychoanalyzed, they speculated. But they couldn't understand why Malcolm couldn't stop wandering.

Or what—or who—he was so desperate to find.

ONE

Refugia

"DON'T GO," TREY said.

Looking into his eyes, Kait didn't reply. He'd made the same request, the same plea, many times, and she'd never replied.

Don't go. When Malcolm finishes building that ship, and it finally sails away from here, don't be on it.

No. It wasn't true. Sometimes she had answered the request. With a question.

"Why not?"

And then it had been his turn to be silent.

It was maddening.

This time, as usual, she planned not to answer, not even with a question. Nor did she intend to allow any expression to cross her face.

Yet even though she was the best she knew at remaining expressionless—she'd been good at that forever—she could tell from the glint in his eyes that he was seeing her frustration, her annoyance, anyway.

And that, on some level, her reaction amused him.

The longtime pattern between Trey Gilliard and Kaitlin Finneran Gilliard.

Father and daughter. Kind of. By temperament and paperwork and love, if not by blood.

So, without intending to, because he was her father, because he was ill, she found herself saying, "All right. I won't."

For a moment, his eyes went wide. He tilted his head and looked at her more closely, his large dark eyes prominent in his gaunt face.

Then, without saying anything, he turned away and looked out over the savanna again. After a moment, she did the same, and they sat side by side, but in silence.

KAIT AND TREY came often to this spot, the watchtower that stood where Refugia's northern wall met its eastern one. The sturdy walls, made of kapok and other local hardwoods, and the towers at each corner were designed to withstand an unnamed, unidentified danger. An onslaught that, once the terrible early months after the Fall had passed, seemed less and less likely ever to occur.

In the nearly twenty years since the colony had been established, there'd never been a warning given from any of the towers. No, that wasn't true: Twice the colonists—Malcolm had dubbed them "Fugians" early on, and the name had stuck—had been alerted to a monsoon rolling inland from the Atlantic Ocean three miles away.

But the kind of threats they'd guessed might be coming? The kind of invasion they couldn't even put into words, but feared anyway? No. Of course not.

Still, even now, someone was stationed in each of the watchtowers twenty-four hours a day. Because you never knew. Because people still had nightmares.

In those early weeks and months, some had feared a human invasion: desperate, starving people fleeing Dakar or Banjul or one of the other fallen cities to the north.

Clare Shapiro, Refugia's resident skeptic, had scoffed at the idea. "You all have read too many pulp novels and seen too many movies," she'd said. "Invading hordes? I think not."

And she'd been right. No one had come. Not once. Not ever.

Shapiro hadn't been done, though. "You know as well as I do," she'd said. "The attackers that will bring our walls tumbling down won't be anything we'll see coming. And a wall sure won't stop them."

Yes, they had known. But the logic of it didn't much matter. Kait had long since learned that humans did all sorts of things for no reason other than reassurance. Growing up in this vulnerable colony, seemingly the last human population on earth, she'd come to understand the value of being reassured.

So as soon as she'd been deemed old enough—fourteen—she'd taken her turn in the watch. It had been no burden, an eight-hour shift every ten days or so. She'd always been a solitary soul, so she enjoyed the chance to be alone, looking out over the savannas to the north or the rain forests that flanked Refugia's other three walls.

The forests, regenerating year by year, always a shocking, intense green, and the grasslands, ever-changing depending on the season and the time of day. Sometimes gray, sometimes a reddish brown, and sometimes the palest jade, as fragile as an eggshell.

Brown now as she and Trey looked out at them. Yet even so, in the midst of the dry season, the savanna was still beautiful, in its own subtle way. The green of the thorn trees, flat and jagged against the horizon. The warm gold of the grazing antelope, the bushbucks and kob. The enormous billowing clouds, white and slate gray, that built up on the horizon every afternoon, harbingers of the approaching rainy season.

Kait knew that Trey loved the diverse landscapes around Refugia. The rain forests, the mossy streams, the coastline with its endless miles of empty white-sand beaches.

He'd spent most of his life before the Fall escaping civilization and lighting out for the most remote and unpopulated territories he could find on a shrinking planet. Seeking out swamps and thorn forests and icy mountain páramos— all the places that people in their right mind avoided. With those as far from his reach as the moon, Kait thought he'd been most at peace when they sat together and looked out over the savanna.

At the water hole that lay across what had once been the red-dirt Massou-Djibo Road but was now just a grassy stripe a little lighter than the savanna beyond, six elephants were bathing. The elephants had returned just months before, yet another sign—and there were many—of an earth recovering from the contagion that had been the human species.

Anyone who had been part of the Last World, and had been paying even the slightest bit of attention, had known that elephants had been on their way out during those final, unstable years. The worldwide demand for ivory had become so insatiable that extinction was certain. When poachers were machine-gunning elephants from helicopters and poisoning water holes with cyanide, what possible other future did the species face?

There was just a single hope: that *Homo sapiens* would exit before the last elephants did the same. And, amazingly, that was what had happened.

Watching them, Trey smiled. But when he spoke, it wasn't about the elephants or anything else out on the savanna. It was the same old topic, the one that always made Kait feel like a child, as she'd been when they first met.

"I used to play poker with this guy," he said.

Poker was one of the games that had been carried over to the Next World, poker for money, even though the money itself was meaningless. They even had real playing cards, packs hoarded by the hundred, some before the Fall and others retrieved by Malcolm on his forays away from Refugia in the first months after.

Kait played sometimes, though she'd never seen Trey at a game.

"Guy named Greg," he went on. "You'd bluff him, and he'd always know. *Always*. If you had a real hand, he'd fold. But if you were bluffing, he'd stay in and beat you. Every damn time."

Kait stayed quiet and let him get to the point.

Trey shook his head at the memory. "He said it was easy to spot a bluff. He could always tell. 'Take you, for example,' he said to me. 'If you're planning to bluff, you always take a deep breath before you bet.'

"'I do?' I said. And he nodded. 'But don't feel bad. Everybody has something, or three things. Their pupils dilate. They get a little sweaty on the temples. They drum their fingers a certain way. Always something.'"

Trey turned his head to look at her, and Kait thought she might be blushing. "So it's that obvious?" she said. "That I'll be on board the ship?"

"Sure." He smiled at her expression. "I've never understood most people that well. But *you*? You I know."

Kait knew this was true. That didn't make it any less exasperating.

"But I don't understand—" The words were out before she even knew she was saying them.

He looked interested. "Don't understand what?"

She felt her chin lift. "Back before, you would have been the first one on that boat."

Kait saw him draw in a breath, like they were playing poker. But this time it was no bluff, and all at once his illness, that relentless, unstoppable thing, showed starkly in his pale skin, taut over his cheekbones.

When he spoke, his voice was quieter. "It's true," he said. "But the world was a different place back then."

"*More* dangerous, not less," she said.

Trey was silent.

She stared at him. "Dad, it *was* more dangerous, wasn't it?"

Still Trey did not speak.

HOW COULD IT not have been?

In the chaotic weeks and months that preceded the end of the Last World, the parasitic wasps they called thieves had both explosively extended their range and expanded the variety of species they used as hosts for their young. Though monkeys had been their preferred targets in the remote forests where they'd evolved, they'd soon found humans fertile territory as well.

The thieves were far from the first insects to parasitize *Homo sapiens.* Some species of botfly, for example, depended entirely on human flesh to raise their larvae. These flies still sometimes afflicted the Fugians, even the hardiest of whom didn't relish extracting a wiggling white worm from their scalps or the palms of their hands.

But the thieves were far more sophisticated than the primitive botflies. Both wasp adults and larvae poured drugs, toxins, into the hosts, to control their behavior— at first to make them forget they'd been infected and later to make them fiercely protective of the alien life growing inside them.

And, lastly, to guarantee that the host died if the larva was removed before hatching, and in any event died upon the emergence of the adult wasp.

Before the end, this all had been widely known. But Trey had understood far better than most what it meant because he'd been one of the earliest thief victims. He'd been infected, parasitized, had a thief larva growing inside him and pumping its poisons into his blood.

He'd barely survived the surgery to remove the larva from his belly, but although he had lived, he'd been condemned by the thieves. Destined for a long, slow, irreversible slide into weakness, decrepitude, early death.

Condemned in another way as well because of something else the thieves had done to him. The larva growing inside him had connected him to the wasps' hive mind. And not just Trey: others who'd been host to a thief larva but had somehow survived.

But what did that mean? Her whole life, Kait had been desperate to learn what it was like.

And now, sitting beside him on the edge of Refugia, the home she was ready to leave as soon as she could, she understood that something about Trey's condition—his curse—was the cause of his warning to her. His plea, because it *was* a plea, to stay behind when the ship left. To stay home. To stay safe.

"Dad," she said.

His eyes had been closed, but when he opened them to look at her, they were clear.

"Tell me *why* I shouldn't go," she said, "and maybe I'll understand."

Trey was silent.

Kait didn't relent. "When you close your eyes," she asked him, "what do you see?"

But still he would not say.

TWO

AND NOW SHE would never find out. Not from Trey, at least.

Because that conversation had been years ago, of course. The two of them had been sitting side by side, watching the elephants bathe and spar.

Year Six, it had been, or Seven. Back when Kait was young, a child still, and filled with a child's questions.

And Trey was still alive.

But he was long dead by now. And Kait was nearly thirty, not that much younger than he'd been when they first met. These days, she sometimes found it hard to remember what his face looked like, or the tone and timbre of his voice.

But not his words. Those she would never forget even as she prepared to ignore them.

Don't go.

* * *

KAIT STOOD AT the edge of the beach that lay three miles west of Refugia. The gleaming white-sand beach, largely free twenty years after the Fall even from plastic garbage spat up by the surf, that bordered the Atlantic Ocean.

Just offshore, the *Trey Gilliard*, the ship Trey had warned her against—and had been named for him, in honor and irony—was preparing for departure. The next day, it was going to set off on the first great scientific exploration of the Next World, and Kait, as both she and Trey had always known, was going to be on board.

The first great scientific exploration. At least, that was the reason everyone gave, and it was true that Refugia's chief biologist, Ross McKay, would be part of the crew of twenty-eight. Ross, who'd been a primatologist in the Last World, Clare Shapiro, and other scientists would be keeping journals, collecting specimens, and doing everything that the great scientific explorers of the nineteenth century, the last before aviation, had done.

But that was not the only reason, or even the main one.

The main reason was to discover if, in fact, Refugia was it: the last human colony on earth.

Another human trait that had carried over from the Last World to this one. The desire, need, obsession, to find out if you are alone.

DOWN THE BEACH, a caravan of rowboats was bringing the last shipments to the *Trey Gilliard*. Food: salted meat, fruits and vegetables, both fresh and pickled. Freshwater for the tanks belowdecks.

And medicines, including precious supplies of antibiotics. Kait thought that Shapiro was going on the expedition partly to keep a close eye on the pharmacy, which she'd done so much to develop and stock.

Including the vaccine, derived from the fruit and seeds of the n'te vine, which—when taken weekly—kept the people of Refugia safe from the thieves.

Kait recognized everyone hauling supplies. There was Fatou Konte, born not thirty miles from here, who would be ship physician. Brett and Darby Callahan, the odd twins, just a little older than Kait, who'd worked nearly as tirelessly as Malcolm had to make the *Trey Gilliard* seaworthy. Shapiro, supervising. Malcolm himself.

Of course she recognized all of them: When you lived in an isolated community of just 281 souls, you came to know every face—and every quirk, every fear, every strain of kindness and cruelty—as if they were your own.

You knew too much.

Kait had thought about that often, what it had been like to live in a world where you could know thousands— or millions—of others without much effort. Though she understood now that this had been an aberration, a sign of the sickness possessing the world in the century or so before the Fall.

Such a vast human population, so mobile and interconnected, was a blip that could never have endured. It had gone against Nature. Humans could build airplanes, satellites, computers, bombs, but they were still primates, and throughout million of years of evolution, no primates had ever lived in hordes of thousands, much less millions.

In fact, Refugia's structure and size, an isolated society with no interaction with any other, but a society nonetheless, was a lot more in line with the way primate societies had always existed than the cities of the Last World had ever been.

The problem, Kait thought, was that the colony's older residents sometimes missed the old ways too much. Life would be easier in a generation or two, when no one could remember the way things had once been.

She turned away from the beach. She'd go down to join them soon, but not quite yet. There was something she had to do first.

SHE'D TAKEN ONLY a few steps along the trail that led among the palm trees and scrubby beachside undergrowth when she stopped and tilted her head, waiting.

There it was: the familiar migrainous shimmering movement at the corner of her vision.

She'd known she'd find it somewhere around here. There was always a little thief colony near the beach. The sandy soil suited the wasps, and so did the distance from Refugia. Close enough to keep an eye on the humans there, far enough away to stay alive.

Maybe stay alive. Whenever Fugians came upon one of the colonies, they destroyed it. But no one worried much about the thieves' presence. For now, at least, the wasps posed no threat.

A thief rose on bloodred wings from the black hole

of its burrow and hovered in front of her face. Its triangular head tilted this way and that as it stared at her with its bulbous, multifaceted green eyes.

That's what thieves did. They looked you in the eyes.

Kait stood unmoving. The big wasp, three inches long at least, flew closer, its wings beating so rapidly they were invisible save for the characteristic bloody smear they left in the air. Kait saw its thin, black body arch. Its abdomen pulsed and extruded the stinger, a needle as white as ivory. A drop of black liquid—its deadly venom—danced on the needle's end.

Her heart thudded. Maybe this was the time. The time when her immunity would fail her. The moment when the thieves would first demonstrate that they'd evolved the ability to overcome the vaccine, as Shapiro had long predicted they eventually would.

If this was the case, Kait knew what would happen. The thief would rise, then stoop like a hawk toward her, too fast for even the sharpest eyes to follow. Its stinger would plunge like a hypodermic into the flesh of her neck. The injected venom would flood through her, and the thief would pull back and hover once again at a safe distance, watching as she fell to the ground in agony.

And then it, and any others in the vicinity—and there were always others—would attack her eyes. That was what the thieves always did: destroyed their victims' eyes.

Or at least, that's what they *used* to do.

The thief shifted position in midair. But in that moment's hesitation—a pause that she knew as well as her own breath—Kait thrust her right hand out and snatched the wasp from the air.

This was something she'd been doing for nearly two decades though everyone told her not to. In a place like Refugia, most people didn't believe in taking any unnecessary risks. Not when you were one of 281.

Kait understood that, but even so, she could never stop herself. She was always compelled to look closer, to see once again what had brought the Last World to ruin and killed so many people she'd loved.

She held the wasp between her thumb and forefinger, in that spot on its thorax that rendered it helpless. Where she was out of range of both its mandibles and its lethal stinger.

Not that it didn't try to reach her, twisting its head around, curving its abdomen up over its back like a scorpion, the black poison dripping from the stinger's end. The thieves' characteristic bitter smell rose more strongly from it, making her nose prickle.

She always wondered after she caught one: If she let it go, would this be the time it overcame the vaccine's prohibition and stung her?

All she knew was that it hadn't happened yet.

She looked at the wasp more closely. It was a female, and gravid. Pregnant. Kait could tell by the tumorous swelling of its abdomen.

But this was no surprise. Adult female thieves were always gravid. They were one of the creatures—there were many—that carried their eggs around with them for as long as they needed to, until they found a host. They could delay the implantation almost indefinitely.

Kait straightened. She wanted to do nothing more than to twist her fingers and pop the thief's head off.

But she knew that would be the most dangerous thing to do. A beheaded thief could live for days or even weeks in that condition, until it starved to death. And all that time, it would use specialized heat receptors on its abdomen to seek out warm-blooded prey. Prey that included humans, vaccinated or not.

Clare Shapiro's theory was that by beheading an individual thief, or severely wounding it, you severed it from the hive mind. Without the guidance of the mind, the warning to stay away from vaccinated humans, its only goal was to kill you or to lay its egg in your flesh. In the colony's early years, two vaccinated Fugians—both children—had been killed and one adult, Emily Russo, had been infected by wounded thieves.

The vaccine hadn't kept the dying thief from laying its egg, but it had stunted the growth of the larva and delayed its attempted emergence for days, maybe even weeks. And, at the very end, the emerging wasp had been so small and weak that it had died while hatching out.

Too weak to emerge successfully, yet strong enough to kill Emily during the process.

Of course, converting a thief to pulp with the bottom of your sandal took care of all potential risks. But instead, Kait reached into her pocket with her left hand and withdrew the small brown bottle she'd brought for this purpose. She popped the top off and, in one fluid move, dropped the wasp into the bottle.

She got the cap back on just as it leaped to escape. For a few seconds it battered itself against the glass, but then—as captive thieves always did—it seemed to give up, settling back to the bottom of the small space.

As Kait replaced the bottle in her pocket, three more thieves rose from somewhere nearby and flew off, heading south. In just a few moments, they were tiny dots against the sky; and then they were gone.

KAIT LIFTED HER right hand to her face and breathed in the thief odor that clung to her fingers. Then she raised her head, drew in a deeper breath of fresh salt air, and turned back toward the beach to go help load the ship.

Remembering, as she did, the last words Trey had spoken to her on that far-off day when they'd sat atop the wall and watched the elephants. The closest he'd ever come to describing what he saw inside his head, the curse the hive mind had bestowed on him.

Don't go.

Why not?

"Because if you stay here," he had finally said, "you'll stay—"

He'd paused, searching for the right word. She hadn't hurried him.

"Ignorant," he'd said. Then, always precise in his language, he'd grimaced and shaken his head. "No. *Innocent.*"

She'd stayed quiet and, just for a moment, his haunted gaze had met hers.

"Alive," he'd said.

THREE

MALCOLM HAD INTENDED to stay awake all through the last night in Refugia. He'd made his speech, and afterward he'd commandeered a comfortable seat with his back against a wall and made sure he had a ready supply of single malt at hand. He'd attracted a small group of friends and admirers, some of whom would be traveling with him the next day and others who would be staying back. He'd had no intention of going anywhere until it was time to head down to the *Trey Gilliard* and set off.

Then Shapiro had shown up, much later than he'd expected. No: In truth, he hadn't expected to see her at all. He'd never imagined she could tear herself away from her precious bugs and worms and pickled specimens. He'd thought someone might have to pry her fingers off the doorjamb and drag her away when the time came to depart.

But in that deadest moment of the forest night, when

even the hyraxes and bushbabies had given up and gone to bed, and the first birds hadn't started testing out their dawn chorus, there she was, leaning against the wall beside him. He hadn't seen her approach, which was surprising. She wasn't exactly quick on her feet.

Sitting on the ground, some looking up from where they were sprawled, Malcolm's friends all seemed a little wide-eyed at seeing her. As if they were seeing an apparition.

And not a friendly ghost, either. More like a poltergeist.

Malcolm looked up at her. "Shapiro," he said.

"Granger."

"Done saying good-bye to your near and dear?"

But she didn't reply. She just put her hand out, and after a moment, he took it and let her pull him to his feet.

No one said a word as they walked away.

AFTER A WHILE, in the rumpled bed of the cabin they shared, Shapiro turned to look at him. The sheen of her sweat, reflecting the banked light of the oil lamp hanging on the wall, was like a pale bioluminescence outlining the sharp planes of her face.

"I saw Kait before," she said.

He shrugged. "Night like this, you trip over everybody."

"I don't care about everybody," she said.

Or anybody, Malcolm thought. *Excepting me, possibly.*

"I'm talking about Kait. Did you tell her?"

Now Malcolm was silent.

She grimaced. "What, are you hoping we sink before we get there?"

Still he didn't speak.

"Malcolm, just don't wait too long."

After a moment he nodded. And, though she was still frowning, she didn't push any further, just rolled over onto her back and looked up at the ceiling. With her scowl, her spiky gray hair, sharp jaw, and beaky nose, she resembled nothing so much as some powerful sooth-sayer out of a storybook.

Malcolm knew she was most likely right. He needed to be honest with Kait.

Just . . . not yet.

THEY HADN'T SPOKEN again that night. As he'd watched her, she'd gazed up at the ceiling, her eyes following a small pale gecko that pursued the moths drawn to the lantern light. Then, almost imperceptibly, she'd fallen asleep.

A few minutes later, Malcolm had followed. And that was a big mistake, because the dreams came.

As they always did.

THE DREAMS OF what he'd seen those early days, those early months, as he headed out in his Piper—the little plane he'd flown all over Africa, and brought to Refugia just days before the Fall—to retrieve all those supplies that the planners had neglected to stock. Or had run out of time to gather. Food, seeds, medicines, clothing. Replacement solar panels to keep the power on a little longer.

Doing essential work, and at the same time—alone among the colonists—seeing the last convulsions of a dying race. The sole witness.

The sole witness and participant.

Malcolm never told anyone, not even Trey, or Mariama, or Shapiro, about everything he'd seen. Everything he'd killed.

Every*one* he'd killed.

On his forays, he always tried to lie low. But that didn't always work, and sometimes he was noticed.

And being noticed meant killing. Killing whoever got in his way as he sought the supplies that would keep Refugia alive.

Sometimes this was inevitable: Last-stage hosts in that violent paroxysm that preceded the birth of the thieves within them gave him no choice, and he killed them without a second thought.

But on his first flights, he'd sometimes encounter desperate survivors, possibly even uninfected. People, humans, who'd seen or heard his airplane approach and hoped it represented salvation.

If there were too many clustered below, he wouldn't land, and often enough he returned to Refugia empty-handed. But if he was already on the ground, and someone saw him, made to come up to him, it didn't matter what they looked like or what they said, or how they begged, or even how old they were.

He was good with a gun, and no one ever got close enough to harm him.

But there hadn't been that many left even at the start, and each time he ventured out there were fewer. On the last flights he took on the Piper before it was grounded forever, he saw no one.

But that didn't stop him from dreaming about what he'd done, what he'd had to do. And what might still be out there.

And it was still one of the reasons he'd built that fucking boat. To find out for sure, either way.

AND . . . CHLOE.

The other reason that Malcolm had built that fucking boat. The most important reason.

Chloe, who'd shared a villa with him a stone's throw from Shela Beach on Lamu Island just off the coast of Kenya. Chloe, whom he'd invited, pleaded with, *ordered* to come to Refugia, in those final unstable days and weeks when the Last World dangled for one final time over the precipice.

But Chloe had refused. She'd laughed at him, at his intensity, the look in his eyes. "Since when," she'd said, in that tone so much like his, "have a bunch of fucking bugs been able to get your pants in such a knot?"

Then, because she loved him, she softened. "This is my home," she'd said. "Whatever happens to the world, I'm not leaving."

He kept trying, but he knew from that moment it was useless. And up until the very end, she—like so many others—hadn't truly believed. Like so many others who'd known of its existence, she'd considered Refugia's residents little more than a doomsday cult, and the colony itself another Georgetown or Waco.

So eventually he gave up, and instead he brought her the vaccine, and insisted she start taking it and keep doing so after he left. As there were few thieves on Lamu—in the weeks leading up to the assault that overthrew the Last World, there seemed to be few thieves anywhere—she didn't take this seriously either, but it was a promise she could easily keep. Or promise to keep, at least.

He also brought cuttings of the vine that produced the vaccine and planted them in the shaded garden behind the villa. Neither the soil nor the weather was a close match for the plant's rain-forest home, but the vine was hardy, and it did seem to be growing well, and even producing flowers before it was time for him to leave.

Again Malcolm insisted, pleaded, this time that she tend to the plants. Make the vaccine. Keep herself safe, and others as well.

Chloe had laughed.

"Fuck it all," he said finally. "Tell me you will, or I'm never going to shut up."

She'd thrown her hands in the air in mock horror. "Heaven forbid," she'd said. "I will!"

CHLOE. TALL AND angular, with dark-blond hair and a strong jaw and fierce blue eyes, and freckles and an abrupt way of speaking that brooked no disagreement.

Chloe. Twenty-three years old the last time Malcolm had seen her. Twenty-three still, in his dreams.

Chloe. His daughter.

FOUR

KAIT STOOD ON the deck of the *Trey Gilliard*, looking back toward shore. The ship was ready to go—*she* was ready to go—but about half of the crew still lingered on the beach, unwilling to tear themselves away.

Half of the crew of twenty-eight. That meant almost exactly one in every ten residents of Refugia would soon be sailing over the horizon and out of reach. Kait didn't share the reluctance of those exchanging last words, last hugs, but she understood it.

Malcolm had told her that back during what they called the Age of Sail in the Last World, the eighteenth and nineteenth centuries, such partings were routine. Hundreds of ships like this one crisscrossed the oceans, some carrying goods, other seeking to explore—and exploit—unknown lands, still others seeking scientific knowledge.

And always some were left behind. It was hardest for

them, Kait thought. You stood onshore, waving good-bye, and you knew it would likely be years before you saw your friends, your family, again.

Years or never . . . and you had to live each day without ever being certain which it was. For all you knew, and it must have happened often enough in reality, the ship whose return you were awaiting had sunk a week out of port, with the loss of all hands.

Only when a certain amount of time had passed—how long was that? Two years? Five?—would the likely truth begin to sink in. But even then, you would have always wondered, and there must have been a few times at least when people returned years and years after they'd been given up for dead.

During the ten years that Kait had lived in the Last World, the idea of anyone's being out of touch for more than about an hour was the sheerest fantasy. (Her school friends with cell phones had hated to let ten minutes pass without saying, "I'm here!" to *somebody*.)

But now they were back in the past again, everyone, with the old rules in force. Back in force for good, Kait guessed, and soon enough there would be no one left who remembered that it had ever been any different.

It was a beautiful morning, the high blue sky above, a fresh breeze snapping at the canvas. A beautiful day to sail, and Kait felt like she'd been waiting forever. But if others wanted to delay a little longer, she guessed she could, too.

Still, she didn't have to watch. So she turned away, walked past Dylan Connell—the first mate—and a few other crew members, and headed belowdecks to her cabin.

* * *

KAIT THOUGHT THERE had been plenty of time for farewells
the night before.

Ceremonies and speeches and a party that had gone
on almost all night. Scheduled events and casual interac-
tions spreading everywhere but centered around the
main plaza, where someone had built a little wooden
stage for the proceedings.

Lots of speeches. Kait, at the periphery of the large
milling crowd, listened as the head of Refugia's elected
council, Steve Francis—an architect who had helped
design the colony—gave the official bon voyage. It was
dull enough to make Kait realize that not every old habit
had been left in the Last World.

She listened more carefully to Nick Albright, who on
the night the world fell had helped Malcolm fly the plane
carrying Trey, Kait, and others here. Nick's speech was
interesting, a detailed description reminding everyone
staying in Refugia how safe and secure they would be,
even with Malcolm and so many others gone.

Malcolm spoke next, commanding as always in his
shaggy-haired, hawklike way. Standing on the stage, a
glass of something in his hand, he made jokes, cursed
without caring who was listening, and in general acted
like a fierce-eyed prophet, as he always did.

He described their plans aboard the *Trey Gilliard*, the
time frames he envisioned, and where they hoped to drop
anchor to undertake their explorations on land. No one
in Refugia had a greater knowledge of the African

continent than he did, or had traveled across it more widely when such travel was possible.

Listening, Kait was beginning to understand that every speech had an agenda beyond the actual words being spoken. Malcolm's agenda, his true meaning, was simple: I'm smart. I'm strong. I know what I'm doing.

It may be years, but I will bring these people back home, safe.

The last to speak—and the only one Kait made sure to hear—was Mariama.

Mariama Honso, perhaps the single most important figure in Refugia's brief history. One of the colony's founders, before even Trey and Sheila knew it existed. The one who'd taught them that human survival depended on the vaccine—and also on gathering experts, from physicians and biochemists to architects and glassblowers, and bringing them to live close to the vaccine's source.

Mariama had voyaged across the world, risking her life and suffering months of imprisonment, in order to reach Trey and tell him of her plans. Thus she became the one person most responsible for Kait's own survival as well.

Nor had her role diminished after the Fall. Although never allowing herself to be elected to any official post, Mariama's strength and determination had helped carry Refugia through its early, hungry, disease-ridden years. She always had a purpose, even if it was just finding the next meal, and she always inspired others to persevere as well.

Most people had thought that Mariama would leap at the chance to head off on the *Trey Gilliard*, but she'd chosen to stay behind. To stay onshore and wave good-bye to the departing ship and many of the people she loved the most.

Her speech was short and characteristically blunt. No hidden agendas for her. Watching her, Kait marveled once again that this short, gray-haired woman could be so strong, wield so much power.

"It's going to be hard for us," she told the others who were going to be staying behind. "Harder than you all think."

She paused for a moment. "But we'll get through," she said. "We always have, and we will again."

Someone in the crowd shouted out, "Do you promise, Mom?"

Everyone laughed, but Mariama didn't smile.

"I promise," she said.

THE INSIDE OF the ship smelled like fresh-cut wood and shellac and oiled iron and human sweat, overlaid by whatever Esteban and Fiona, the ship's cooks, were preparing for the first meal on their voyage.

If they ever began voyaging.

Most of the crew would be sleeping in shifts in hammocks strung in one of two dormitories in the center of the ship, but a few had been given private cabins: Kait, Clare Shapiro, Fatou Konte, and Malcolm, the captain. Kait's place in the hierarchy had been determined, she thought, by her place in Refugia's history, not by anything she'd done.

Still, she was happy for the solitude provided by her

cabin near the bow. It measured seven-by-nine feet, with a single small porthole that right now looked west, onto the open sea. Escape.

Her bed was a mattress on a wooden platform that unfolded from the wall. The only other furniture was a single chair and a small dresser.

But all she needed now was privacy. Glancing over her shoulder, which was unnecessary, she reached into the deep pocket of her cotton jacket and pulled out the small bottle. Holding it up, she checked to make sure that the thief inside was still alive.

Of course it was. Still alive, patient, waiting. Waiting for its best chance to escape, once again to serve the hive mind, or—if things turned out differently—to jam its stinger into her.

Its stinger and ovipositor.

Kait replaced the bottle in her pocket, where the thief would remain safe until she needed it.

THERE'D BEEN ONLY two people she needed to say good-bye to. The first—and this was more a responsibility than a desire—was her brother, Jack. Her half brother, born here after the Fall.

She'd found him with his teenage friends late in the night, when alcohol and emotions had begun to rule the party. Jack was holding a cup whose contents smelled like palm wine. His face was flushed, his eyes red at the edges, his expression blurred.

He raised the cup, perhaps in a kind of salute, or perhaps to offer her some of the wine. Whatever the intention, when she shook her head, he rolled his eyes. His friends laughed.

Kait ignored that. It was late. They were all drunk, and she wasn't.

But that was the least of the disconnect between her and Jack. The greatest rift, on the other hand, had proven impossible to overcome: the fact that she'd seen and lived in the Last World, and he hadn't.

It was a wall that couldn't be scaled, the unalterable fact that some Fugians had known what it was like to live back then, while others—the natives—never would. Never see cars and airplanes and computers and, above all, *people*. A world with millions, billions of people in it, not merely a few hundred you knew too well.

A world full of possibilities instead of the same old certainties.

Kait would have traded her past for Jack's in an instant—the killing of her birth parents by thieves, the terrors she'd lived through as the Fall approached—but there was no point in telling him this. For Jack, and all those born here, the Last World represented a kind of heaven. Dreams of heaven always trumped reality.

Jack gave her a hug good-bye, which surprised her. But then he turned away and, without a word, went back to his friends and his drink, which did not.

Some gulfs really were unbridgeable.

ONE LAST GOOD-BYE. With Sheila, Trey's widow, Kait's adoptive mother. Another of Refugia's founders who'd chosen to stay behind.

The only good-bye that meant much to Kait but, in the end, it was only a little more meaningful than the one she'd exchanged with Jack. In the end, what could either of you say when one was sailing off the end of the world and the other was not?

You could mouth heartfelt platitudes, which was what Sheila murmured into Kait's ear as they embraced. "Your father would be so proud of you," she said. "Both your fathers."

Kait was quiet.

"I want you to come home," Sheila said next. Then she stiffened a little, as if the words had surprised her, and she was wondering if she'd said too much.

Kait tightened her grip but still did not speak.

She felt as much as heard Sheila's sigh, which unexpectedly turned into a laugh.

"But as long as you're out there," she said, sounding a little like Trey would have, "for God's sake, would you finally find whatever the hell it is you're looking for?"

Kait nodded. And then, surprising herself, she found that she was crying.

THE ANCHOR LIFTED. The wind filled the sails, and the ship began to move, slowly and creakily at first, as if stretching stiff muscles, then faster over the smooth swells. A single noddy tern dipped and wheeled above the wake.

Kait, back on deck, watched the crowd on the beach as the ship left them behind. Though Jack and his friends hadn't come, most other Fugians had.

Mariama, Sheila waving, Nick. At first she could

recognize their faces. Even when distance began to blur the details, she knew them by shape and posture.

As they receded into the distance, becoming patches of color against the white sand, all Kait could think was: There are so few of them.

About ten minutes later, the ship reached the forested headland that lay to Refugia's south and went around it, and the people left behind were lost to view. Several members of the *Trey Gilliard*'s crew watched until the last instant, and most of them were crying.

But Kait had long since turned away, and though her eyes were wet as well, her tears were of relief.

Finally, she would learn who else was out there.

Finally, she would be able to *see*.

FIVE

NINE HOURS LATER, Malcolm stood on the bow of the *Trey Gilliard*. So far the crew had handled everything smoothly, and the breeze filling the sails on the three square-rigged masts was allowing them to maintain a steady speed.

To the west, the afternoon sun shone out of a clear blue sky of a kind they rarely saw in the forest. Heavy towers of cloud hung over the land, a green-brown mass two miles to the east. Tropical Africa, the thick rain forests that lay to the south of Refugia.

As Malcolm watched, the clouds were lit by lightning, then again. "Glad to be here 'stead of there," he said to the man standing beside him.

"Yeah." Ross McKay smiled. "Glad to be anywhere new."

Malcolm shifted his gaze. A big pod of dolphins, dozens and dozens of them, had met the boat not twenty minutes after they'd set sail, and now, hours later, they were still everywhere in the calm blue waters, some riding the bow wave, others in the wake, and still others leaping out of the water on all sides, shedding shining droplets from their silver-gray bodies, adults and babies all effortlessly keeping up with the ship.

"Dolphins communicate," Ross said, turning his head for a moment to look at Malcolm. "They have language."

"Yeah," Malcolm said. "I know. And know what else?"

Ross shook his head.

"I think that for years now, dolphin old-timers, geezers, been passing down stories about these huge toys that would come rumbling through their oceans. These big floating things that would split the water and create these roller coasters for them to ride on."

Ross was smiling. "You think?"

"Yeah. I do. And I'll bet the young'uns would just shake their heads and roll their eyes, and when the geezers weren't around, they'd say, 'Bloody galahs! What are they goin' on about?'"

He paused to watch three dolphins crest the wake simultaneously. "And then it all turns out to be God's truth, the geezers were right all along, and now none of them are going to let us out of their sight."

Smiling, those pale eyes of his widening at the thought, Ross leaned against the railing to watch the show.

Malcolm found himself thinking of how Shapiro would have mocked his flight of fancy.

Which made him want to share it with her. And he knew where she'd be right now: She'd headed into the cabin that would serve as her onboard laboratory soon after departure and hadn't made an appearance since.

Another person who was happy to be here. Happy as she was capable of, at least.

"Hey," Malcolm said. "Back in a mo'. Don't let these guys take off."

Ross shook his head. "Oh, they aren't going anywhere!"

SHAPIRO *DID* **LOOK** happy. In this little cabin at the stern, the ship's combined laboratory and surgical suite, she seemed . . . relaxed. At ease. Free.

When Malcolm entered, she was bent over the one toy, the one treasure, she had allowed herself on this journey: the nineteenth-century Wenham binocular microscope that sat on the wooden table she was using as a desk. All polished brass and shining glass in the sunlight coming in through the cabin's sole porthole, it was the only relic from the Last World that she cared about.

"Dr. Maturin," Malcolm said.

Shapiro straightened and peered at him over her shoulder. "Captain Aubrey." Then, "Are you just going to stand there goggling at me? If so, I'm going back to work. I'm losing the light."

"Come up on deck," he said. "There's a sight to see."

"The dolphins?" She nodded toward the porthole. "I saw."

"Come up," he said again.

She opened her mouth, but before she could argue, someone was standing behind Malcolm in the doorway.

The short, compact figure of Dylan Connell, who was fifteen when the Last World ended but somehow had already become an expert sailor by then. He'd helped build the boat, and as its first officer, he was the only one permitted to interrupt Malcolm and Shapiro.

"Need you to see something up top," he said, not wasting any more words than he usually did.

Malcolm asked no questions. With Shapiro, curious now, accompanying them, he followed Connell back onto the deck. This time he didn't pay any attention to the dolphins, or even to a whale he glimpsed breaching with a gigantic splash in the calm water to the west.

Instead, he headed straight toward the small cluster of people gathered on the port side of the ship, just beyond the second mast. Ross and Kait and Fatou Konte, and a couple of others.

They were all looking toward shore, where the clouds, lifting and dispersing as they did most evenings over Refugia, were tinged orange and purple by the low-angled sunlight.

Malcolm didn't need to ask what they were looking at. He could see it for himself: a thick column of gray-black smoke rising from some hidden spot just inland.

Beside him, Shapiro said, "Huh."

Ross McKay said, "Wildfire? Lightning strike?"

Malcolm shook his head. "Don't think so."

"Agree." McKay was frowning. "You don't get many wildfires in humid forest, anyway."

"Unless people are clearing the land for agriculture," Shapiro said, "and set it."

Saying what everyone had been thinking.

People.

People made fires that looked like that.

"Do we go investigate?" Kait asked.

Everyone looked at Malcolm. Already the column of smoke was slipping behind them. The clouds over the forest were turning gray as the sun fell toward the horizon.

"How far have we come?" he asked Dylan. "About a hundred kilometers?"

"More or less," the first officer said.

"That's still Guinea-Bissau." After a moment, he shook his head. "There are reefs along here, treacherous as hell, and all our navigation charts are too fucking old. It's not worth the risk."

There was silence. Then Kait said, "One hundred kilometers is about sixty miles, isn't it?"

No one answered.

"Sixty miles south of Refugia," she said.

Already, the smoke was out of sight. It might never have existed. Yet Malcolm could tell that it had awoken the imaginations of the small group who'd seen it. Cast the world in a new light, filled it with new possibilities.

Malcolm's heart was pounding. He knew he was the one playing the galah now, acting like a fool. But all he could think right now was . . .

Maybe.

They were a journey around the African continent away, weeks—months—of sailing that could, and probably would, end in disaster long before he ever found out for sure. Most likely he would never learn the truth.

But, still . . . maybe. The column of smoke, the possibility that it signified the presence of a human colony, told him that maybe Chloe was still alive.

Call him a galah, but at that moment, Malcolm Granger was, for the first time in years, happy.

SIX

THE BREEDING CHAMBERS reeked of sweat and urine and shit and filthy mammal. They smelled like the cages in a zoo Jason had visited once when he was a child—not one of the big, antiseptic ones in places like the Bronx and San Diego, but a run-down, out-of-the-way menagerie in some little Southwestern town he'd driven through with his parents. The kind with bare cages containing things like a patchy lion or a morose, drooling bear or a pile of stinking rattlesnakes.

The odor of sweat and urine and shit and despair.

Of all the places in the slave camp, this was the one Jason hated the most. It was also where he spent the most time—in these endless, identical stone-walled chambers, lit only by small square glassless windows high on their outer walls and located deep within the heart of the limestone-and-coral fort.

One of his jobs was tending to the creatures

imprisoned here. The little, large-eyed antelopes, the sullen bat-eared foxes, the huge, squeaking mass of pouched rats.

And the primates most of all: black-and-white colobus monkeys, vervets, and baboons that were so beyond the point of hopelessness that their eyes were as dull as sewn-on buttons on an old doll.

And the humans, too. Those who had once been human. Never a huge number of them, but always some.

His responsibility, Jason's, all of them. Keeping some of them alive to breed, others to be parasitized, used as hosts for the thieves' young.

Jason didn't know how the mind decided which individuals deserved to live, which to die. But after twenty years in the camp, he was pretty certain that it knew exactly what it was doing. That it had a far clearer view of the world, of the hierarchy of life on earth, than the human species had ever possessed.

And him? He just had to keep the captives alive long enough for them to fulfill the thieves' purpose.

The pouched rats were easiest to care for. Give them grain, give them old meat, and they did fine. Or at least they did well enough to produce a population that numbered in the hundreds and occupied a whole row of chambers on the western edge of the fort.

The rats were easiest, but under his care, the population of antelopes, foxes, and other mammals had gradually expanded as well. And the primate population, too. Even among primates—all kinds of primates—the urge, the necessity, to breed never seemed to go away.

Every year more hosts, and more thieves.

*   *   *

SWEAT AND URINE and shit and despair and . . . thief.

That smell above all, though after all this time Jason barely noticed it. Though he couldn't help but notice the thieves themselves, the thousands that infested the breeding chambers.

Especially in the cool of night, when they came to these cramped, enclosed spaces to absorb the heat their captives radiated. Coating the rough stone walls and ceilings, sometimes crouched still, sometimes moving in a black-and-bloodred mass or flying—a sudden buzz of wings—to a new spot.

Jason hated coming here at any time of day. But it was worst when it was crowded with thieves. Not because he feared them or because they disgusted him. After twenty years never out of their sight, he was long past fear and disgust.

Except, perhaps, self-disgust.

No. Because the temptation nearly overcame him when they were closest at hand. The almost unstoppable urge to plunge his hand, his whole body, into the mass. To see how many he could mangle before they rose and stung him to death.

But deep down he knew they wouldn't kill him. After he crushed a few—an inconsequential few—the rest would clear away. And let him live, because he was too important. Too important a slave.

But others? Weaker individuals? Less useful ones? They could easily be singled out, killed—or, worse, implanted, impregnated—because of him. He'd seen it happen often enough.

That was Jason's biggest fear, really his only fear by now: that the thieves, his masters, would let him live but kill others in his name.

Kill *Chloe* in his name.

So he never gave in to temptation.

Or, at least, he hadn't yet.

IN THE LATE afternoons, Jason would go back to the chambers to retrieve the bodies of any animals that had died during emergence—or for any other reason—and carry them up to the oven.

The giant pouched rats didn't usually need his help. They just ate whoever had stopped breathing, and for whatever reason. They were so efficient that Jason rarely found more than a few scraps of oily fur left by the time he made his late-afternoon inspection.

With other species, he had to clean out any new corpses. The cells containing the monkeys, for example, and also those that held the human slaves.

Or, to be more accurate, the slaves that had once been human.

JASON WAS STILL human. He'd been thirty-four when the end came. He remembered what life had been like before though he wished he didn't. It was when he remembered most clearly that he most wanted to leap off one of the fort's parapets, or plunge into a mass of thieves and dare them to do to him what he could not do to himself.

He wasn't the only human. There were others in the slave camp, though fewer every year. Fewer of them, and more who had lost the humanity they'd once possessed.

But neither of these groups mattered, the human and the once human. They were both just transitional phases in the thieves' plan, the scattered remnants of the billions who'd existed before the end came. Two decades in, they were still essential for the tasks they'd been given, but soon enough—in a matter of years, not further decades—they'd be easily, effortlessly, replaced.

Replaced by those who had been born here. Born into slavery and thus knowing no other life.

A generation from now, none would remember, or need the drugs the thieves pumped into their systems to make them forget. And the new generation would be perfect, malleable, unquestioning.

At that point, Jason believed, the human race would be truly extinct, and all that would remain would be slaves cloaked in a mockery of the human form.

JASON NEVER WENT to the cells, the breeding chambers, alone. Sometimes he'd be with one of the born slaves, but more often a ridden one. Someone who had once been human—whom Jason might have known as a human— but who now did whatever its thief rider commanded.

Or, rather, never questioned the tasks it was given to do.

Jason had no idea what brew of drugs the riders poured into their subjects. He'd been a parasitologist back before the thieves took over, so his area of expertise hadn't been wasps and their toxins.

He did know that the thieves' ability to use chemicals to control the behavior of other species—to enslave them—was typical of wasps, and of the earth's creatures in general. Humans might have thought they'd invented slavery, but in truth they'd been way late to the game.

He remembered reading a journal article about a wasp that injected neurotoxins into the head of a cockroach. The roach was immediately enslaved, following the wasp back to its burrow and waiting patiently for the wasp to lay eggs inside it.

And toxins were just part of the equation. At the very end, just before Jason's own free life ended, he'd learned of a wasp that injected a virus along with an egg into its host. Some kind of beetle, it had been, though he couldn't remember what. Maybe a ladybug?

But that wasn't the important thing. What mattered was that wasps were strong and clever enough even to enslave viruses—themselves organisms able to ravage life on earth—and turn them to their own purposes. In this case, the virus, replicating inside the host's body, would transmit the wasp's commands. And the helpless beetle would abandon all its own natural behaviors to do nothing but guard the cocoon in which the newly emerged wasp would live.

Nor were mammals immune from enslavement. Every day, his own life proved it.

*   *   *

THIS AFTERNOON, HE'D come to the breeding chambers to retrieve the corpses of a pair of colobus monkeys. He was accompanied this time by a ridden slave, lost in whatever dreams filled the minds of these creatures. Its rider was perched on the back of its neck, the stinger sliding in and out of its flesh in some complex pattern Jason would never understand. The ridden slave, as always, oblivious to the insertion of the needle.

Jason had known this slave's name once, he thought.

As the surviving monkeys huddled in the back of their cell, he and the ridden slave picked up the stiffening bodies. Eyeless, of course, their thick black-and-white fur coarse and matted with blood, the swellings on their abdomens now as soft and flaccid as popped balloons.

As they carried the corpses up to the fort's main plaza, Jason could see some slaves heading back from the fields and pastures, others starting to prepare the simple evening meal. This was the most brilliant thing about the workings of the camp: how closely it resembled a colony that would have been run by, and occupied entirely by, humans. Food, shelter, procreation—all the same needs and desires addressed.

At first glance, this camp *could* have been a human colony. A colony of free humans.

Until you looked more closely, saw and smelled the thieves, noticed the riders.

Until you understood that even those who'd stayed human this long were here to serve the slavemakers.

* * *

THERE WAS NO need for iron bars or high walls here because there was no place to go, nowhere to run. The slavemakers saw all, knew everything, and always—in every case—pronounced sentence and administered punishment.

It had been years since anyone had tried to escape.

THE OVEN WAS located on the fort's roof, overlooking the ruins of the old city, the channel, and Manda Island across the way. Sometimes the coals were kept banked—never extinguished—but now they were burning fiercely. Otherwise, their heat would not be strong enough to consume the bones of the dead.

Beside him, the thief rider pulled its stinger out of the flesh of its slave's neck. It must have nicked a capillary, Jason noticed, because its usually shining white stinger was smeared with pink, and a tiny pearl of blood formed at the insertion point.

Then the rider rose into the air, hovering fifteen or so feet above them. At the beginning, Jason had wondered if separating a rider from its slave might let the slave become human again, but, of course, it hadn't.

Not that it mattered. Riders and ridden were never apart for very long. And if a rider was killed—something Jason had seen happen twice—then another soon took its place.

Once this rider was safely above, Jason dropped the dead colobus on the ground. Bending over, he picked up a few of the ragged cloths—someone's old T-shirt, what must once have been a festively dyed beach towel but was now just a smear of brown—that were piled on the reddish roof tiles around the oven and wrapped them around his palms.

Then, grabbing the oven's steel handle, he swung open the rusty metal hatch. Hot air flooded out, hitting Jason like a slap. He took an involuntary step back, and noticed—as he had before—that the ridden slave did as well. Whatever was going on behind that expressionless face, and regardless of its great tolerance for pain, it did still have nerve endings.

Just as the rider that had retreated out of the range of the wave of heat had nerve endings. It could definitely feel pain even if pain didn't stop it.

And even if its death didn't make a bit of difference to the hive.

The thick bed of coals popped and roared at the influx of oxygen. With a familiar motion, Jason slung the monkey's body onto the bed. The smells of burning hair and cooking meat immediately wafted out on the waves of heat. Flames rose and wreathed around the corpse, which twitched in the pyre as its muscles and tendons shriveled.

Stepping aside, Jason waited while the slave tossed its own burden onto the flames. Then, as quickly as he could, he closed the oven door and stepped away.

Turning his head, he looked out over the fort's stone ramparts, as he always did when he was up here. Looking for just the slightest possibility that his world wasn't the only world that existed. Hoping to see something—

just a sign—that his future, the planet's future, had more than one inevitable course to run.

Hoping for rescue. A squadron of Navy ships coming up the channel, shining steel blue in the afternoon sunlight, the roar of their engines splitting the air and sending the clouds of thieves spinning upward in a whirlwind of fear. An invading force of soldiers in full hazmat gear, safe from thief stingers and jaws, bearing weapons that would set the air aflame with gouts of liquid fire and turn the whirlwind into ash. And machine guns to tear apart the ridden slaves and the born ones where they stood, as they ran.

Or maybe drones. Jason remembered all the controversy over drones, over remote warfare, in those last years before the world ended. Now he dreamed of looking up to see a streak of light through the sky, like a shooting star in daylight but getting closer and larger with every passing instant. Then the shooting star, the missile, would slam into the fort, the impact and explosion reducing it and all it contained to rubble.

The born and ridden slaves would have no chance to take more than a single step. And the thieves would be unable to rise even into a whirlwind before being incinerated.

And if the humans who lived here, the still-human slaves, died in the assault as well, that would be all right. That would be fine. The kind of collateral damage not even worth thinking about.

And Jason? As the missile approached, Jason would do nothing more than throw his arms wide and wait for oblivion. Wait for it, and welcome it.

But when he scanned his surroundings, he saw only the same things he always saw: the corn and taro and soy fields and palm-oil plantations that fed the slaves, human and animal alike. And, as usual, Chloe supervising a group of born slaves working the fields.

Chloe, who, like Jason, had stayed human by proving herself useful from the very beginning. By planting the fields in the first place, by showing she knew how to cook for a crowd.

Chloe, with her long, lanky form—so skinny now—darkly tanned face and limbs, and mass of blond hair tied back in a ragged ponytail, was the reason Jason was still here. The reason, many times over, that he was still alive.

Chloe, his blessing and his curse.

As he was hers.

ON MOST DAYS, Jason and Chloe's paths barely crossed until night had fallen and the slaves were all heading to the sleeping quarters. These were chambers buried deep within the stone walls, separate from but not much different than the cells where the animals were kept—rectangular, stone-walled rooms, their dirt floors covered with dirty straw, a single small glassless window in one wall to let in dim moonlight and breaths of fresh air. Sometimes.

Twenty or thirty slaves slept in each chamber. Cramped, crowded, filthy, but nothing compared to the hundred or so who'd been forced into them during the great slave trade of the nineteenth century. When the slavers had been some approximation of human themselves.

As they did every night, even in pitch-blackness, Jason and Chloe found each other near the corner of the wall opposite the window. Their usual sleeping spot. But even if it hadn't been, they wouldn't have needed to be able to see to recognize each other's bodies, Jason's compact and muscular and Chloe's seeming made entirely of long bones and taut skin.

By now, Jason felt as if he knew the shape and texture of Chloe better than he knew anything else on earth.

Having located each other and, together, claimed their patch of straw, they lay in silence. Talking, casual conversation, wasn't a punishable offense, until suddenly it was. And there was no way of telling when a slave—or even a thief—might take unexpected offense at even a casual sentence or two. So it was better to stay silent.

Sometimes this wasn't possible. Sometimes you had to risk speaking just to remind yourself you were still human.

But this wasn't one of those nights. So Jason just held Chloe in his arms, listened to her breathe, and on this chilly night absorbed the warmth of her body while giving her his own.

While all above and around them, coating the walls and ceiling of the chamber—of every sleeping and breeding chamber—were countless thieves, the cold-blooded creatures drawn to the mammalian warmth just as Jason and Chloe were.

Thousands of thieves, just inches or feet away from

them. Eyes reflecting the starlight coming through the window, wings briefly buzzing as they shifted position. A moving carpet drawing as close to the human engines as they could.

And tonight, as on other cold nights, Jason awoke to find thieves crawling all over him. Dozens of them, the sharp ends of their legs pricking his skin, their arched bodies brushing against the hair on his arms, their odor filling his nostrils.

Their stingers just a few centimeters away from his flesh.

He could tell that Chloe was awake beside him. Lying still, as he was, waiting for the night to pass and day to return so the thieves would rise and depart.

A thief walked across Jason's cheek. He felt the movement of mandibles at the edge of his mouth, and understood that it was not biting him—nor kissing him—but drinking his saliva where it had pooled between his lips.

This, too, had happened before. There was nothing to be done about it. Thieves loved salt, or salt in conjunction with the other chemicals that humans—primates—produced.

Jason thought this was why they always feasted on the eyes of their victims. They craved the salt in primate tears.

SEVEN

The Green Lands

THE WOODCHUCK CREPT carefully from the shelter of the woods into the grassy field beyond. It moved with a strange, humpbacked motion, slow and awkward, and the way it blinked in the afternoon sunlight gave it a dazed expression. Mumbling at the tall midsummer grasses, it looked about as threatening—and as easy to kill—as a caterpillar.

But the boy knew this was all a lie. A subterfuge. A woodchuck could move fast enough when attacked, and those mumbling jaws would open to reveal sharp, yellowing teeth.

Jaws that were powerful enough and teeth sharp enough to deliver the sort of bite that could easily end the boy's life. Maybe not right away, but certainly as a little time passed. The boy had seen what a single bite could become, what it could do.

And anyway . . . anything that could live here, even

in the green lands, deserved respect. The boy had seen plenty of creatures that weren't strong enough to survive, and the bones of countless more that had already died.

So he didn't underestimate the creature shuffling through the grasses. He never underestimated his prey.

The woodchuck, perhaps ten feet from him, sat up on its haunches and looked around. Hidden in a thicket just inside the forest, the boy stood very still and kept his breath down to the slightest vibration in his chest.

The instant the animal went back down onto four legs, he flew out of the woods toward it. The sensation really was like flying, like he imagined leaping off the top of his aerie might feel.

The boy was fast and nearly silent as he flew across the grass. And even as the creature detected his approach and twisted around, jaws gaping, he was bringing his stone club down on its skull.

One blow was all it took, really. The woodchuck, its skull dented on one side, blood pouring from its snapping mouth, writhed and spun in the grass before him. He watched it for a few seconds, then raised the club again and ended it for good.

HE SAT ON a big rock to skin and clean the carcass. Properly cured, the hide with its thick, glossy fur would become part of the blanket he'd use when winter came.

And the meat? It would be tough and gamy, but by midsummer, the woodchuck—itself preparing for winter—had begun to add fat to its flesh. The boy would get many good meals from it.

He was so intent on wielding his metal blade to cut every scrap of meat from the ribs that he didn't notice the lion until it was perhaps far too close to him. Whether it had come after his meat or had chosen to try to end him right then, it might well have succeeded.

But it didn't. It just stood there, half-hidden by the reeds that ringed the weed-clogged pond beyond, and stared at him. Long and slender, it had eyes that were the golden brown of the grasses that grew wild in the untended fields in autumn. The twitch of its long tail reminded the boy of the movement of the grasses as well, when the wind blew out of the northwest, bringing a hint of winter with it.

It was the first lion he'd ever seen, and its beauty seemed to fill his head. For a long moment, he and this magnificent cat looked at each other, neither moving. Then the lion gave its head a shake—the boy could hear the sound of its ears whipping back and forth—turned, and disappeared into the reeds.

Leaving the boy alone again, his heart pounding at what he'd just witnessed. Thinking about the animal he now shared the green lands with, and what that meant.

THAT HAD BEEN three years ago.

After the first encounter, the lion had mostly stayed out of his way. They'd come upon each other a few times since, usually in the more densely forested areas, but only when it hadn't sensed his presence in time. It was inevitable that the two big predators' paths would cross since the land that was good for hunting was only a few square miles in size.

On those rare occasions, the cat was always the one to turn away, to give ground, to cede authority. Never instantly, though. Always there was the same moment's pause, the meeting of the eyes, the communication between them. *I'm not afraid of you.*

Not fear, but respect. And then the cat would leave the trail and quarter off through the woods, moving like a ghost, vanishing amid the sun-dappled leaves.

Mutual respect. Still . . . the boy always kept his stone club handy.

But the lion was no longer alone. By now, the population had grown from one to five. The big male that the boy had first encountered joined by a slighter, slimmer female. And then three cubs, which were now about two months old.

The boy stood in his aerie, just below the ruined stone castle, gazing down the slope to where the boulders tumbled into a murky pond—the place he'd been sitting when he first saw the lion, and now the female had chosen the same spot to raise her cubs. It made sense: The boulders made for a warren filled with hiding places.

On this warm day, all four, mother and cubs, were fully out in the open. The female was lying on her side, idly washing herself—the boy catching glimpses of her rough pink tongue—but mostly just soaking the sunlight into her tawny golden fur. Beside her, and sometimes on top of her, the three cubs wrestled and chased each other, or pounced and chewed on their mother's tail.

The boy, watching, felt something move inside him. For just an instant, the control he always maintained slipped, and something more jagged emerged.

For that instant, he felt like bringing the cubs to an end.

It would be easy. Nothing was easier than a baby. He'd done it a few times, young birds taken from their nests, unwary squirrels venturing to the ground for the first time, even baby rats one long, icy winter when life had been especially hard.

He could have used a stone, or his club, on the female lion. A blow to her skull, and she would be no threat. After that, his strong hands would be enough to take care of the cubs, which he knew were still helpless without their mother.

It had never sat right with him, ending the young of any creature. But now the urge came on him, stronger than it had ever been. Powerful enough that it made his body shake.

He closed his eyes, knowing that he was leaving himself vulnerable. Part of him was still standing there, sensing every drop of sweat running down his face and tickling the hair on his arms and legs.

If some predator—like the male lion—chose this moment to stalk and attack him, he might not be aware of it until too late. Because most of him was far away, far beyond the borders of the green lands he ruled. Far beyond the wounded lands that bordered his kingdom on all sides, the jumble of people-made rock and steel.

And of bones, at least at the beginning. So many bones that he knew had come from creatures shaped as he was. But in his memory, only bones remained, and he knew that soon enough they, too, would vanish, and all that would be left would be the stone and steel.

The wounded lands, the dead place where he'd had the accident. He'd fallen, perhaps, or maybe a piece of crumbling stone had fallen on him. He didn't remember. He only remembered that the accident had almost ended him, that he'd barely made it back here to safety. Everything else was gone.

And realizing as time passed that the accident had also taken away his past. Leaving him as he was, alone. Alone in this world.

Standing still, the boy reached out. As always, he had but a single purpose.

At the beginning, after the accident, when he'd learned what he could do, the game had been easy to play. They were everywhere. They had no idea who, or what, he was. And they were swept away like grains of sand under the force of a great wave.

These days, they were warier, but that didn't matter. He could still find them, he could still reach them, and still they drowned.

WHEN HE WAS done, he felt exhausted, as he always did. The sweat was cold as it dried on his body, and he shivered.

He wasn't hungry, but he knew he had to eat. He kept food caches all over the green lands now—he'd nearly starved making his way back after the accident—and his biggest stores were buried at the foot of the statue of the dog, where underground springs kept his supplies cold.

But he felt too worn out to walk that far. So instead

he turned and went up the slope to the castle ruins. He knew he had stored some smoked meat there.

But he'd taken only a few slow steps before something stopped him.

Another lion. But not in front of him. *Inside.*

Inside his head.

And not like the slender cats that lived here in the green lands. It was of a kind the boy had never seen before: much bigger, much stockier, with a great black ruff of fur outlining its massive head and flowing over its shoulders.

Something he had never seen here, or even imagined.

Something *placed* there. Shared with him.

But by whom?

The boy was taken apart, overwhelmed by a flood of emotions. Terror, excitement, others he could not name.

With all his strength, he reached out. Not knowing whether it was to end things or begin them.

EIGHT

AISHA ROSE LAY at the base of her muhutu tree, dazed, a lump rising painfully on the back of her head, a trickle of blood tracing down her cheek. Above, the sun glinted through the leaves, and a colony of weaverbirds went about its business. Aisha Rose watched a black-and-yellow male using strips of grass to construct its globular nest, which hung like an ornament on the end of a slender branch. A brownish female perched nearby, watching the nest's progress with bright black eyes.

"What I like best about weavers," Mama had said once, in the clear tone she used to state facts, "is that the males have to do all the work building the nest."

Her eyes had gleamed. This was how she smiled, with just the slightest upward curve of the lips, but . . . eyes that shone. "And you know what the female does if none of the nests meet with her approval?"

Aisha Rose, hearing Mama's voice loud inside her

head, winced. Her vision blurred, turning the birds above her into dancing patterns of yellow and black.

"What, Mama?" she asked.

"They destroy every nest and make the males start over from scratch."

Aisha Rose was thinking about this when she felt something drip onto her bare right leg, just below the knee. Something that started out warm but quickly cooled against her skin.

That was a new sensation for her, in a world, a life, with few unfamiliar experiences. And that was how, instead of thinking about weaverbirds, she raised her head to see what had caused it, and found herself staring into the pale eyes of the drooling hyena that was considering whether to start feeding on her.

Its bared teeth revealed long yellowish canines and a thick pink tongue. It breathed out, and she smelled its breath, the reek of rotting meat, as the rank exhalation wafted across her face. The hyena made a moaning sound in its throat, the sound echoed by another, a little farther off, then a third.

She'd seen hyenas before, of course, out on the grasslands below Mount Longonot and in the zebra-rich plains that fringed Hell's Gate. But none had ever come here, to the canyons she and Mama called home eight months a year. Aisha Rose had always thought that its narrow, red-rock walls and secret caves made it a protected spot, safe from the biggest predators.

Or safe enough, at least. That was one of the reasons that she and Mama migrated here every year from their other home in the compound in Naro Moru, where

Aisha Rose had been born. Why they followed the game into the Great Rift Valley and sought out the protection of these twisting passages. For safety as well as food.

Well. So much for that. You were a fool to think you were ever safe on the real earth.

Shifting her weight just a fraction, Aisha Rose saw the hyena, the alpha, tilt its head. Its gray pupils dilated as it took in the new information: This potential meal wasn't recently dead, like one of the lion or cheetah kills it frequently commandeered. This piece of meat was still alive.

Not that that mattered much. Alive, dead, hyenas took their food as they found it. If it needed killing first, they killed it.

"The locals always knew the truth," Mama had said, the first time they'd seen a hyena, at a distance, on the shore of Lake Naivasha. "But we Europeans, in our racist way, judged everyone—and everything—by appearances. We saw lions as noble and brave simply because of how they looked, so golden and wreathed in a royal ruff. Hyenas, on the other hand, were sniveling, subservient, untrustworthy. *Native*."

Mama had watched the hyena loping along. "Look at how it walks!" she'd said. "We called them crippled. Sneaky. Weak."

Then she'd smiled. "But here they are, the cripples, doing a whole lot better than we are."

Aisha Rose could see the other two now, the alpha's pack, closer, moving sideways toward her with that familiar hyena hobble. Yes, they did walk like their legs hurt.

"Don't believe it!" Mama had said. "Hyenas *are* sneaky, but they're also smart, opportunistic, and . . . *strong*. So strong. They can kill a lion in direct combat, and do. Back on the dreamed earth, the native people considered them among the most dangerous animals in Africa. We were easy prey."

Aisha Rose could have reached out and touched the alpha, it was so close to her. She knew that the only reason she was still alive, the only reason it hadn't yet attacked, was because she was unfamiliar. Because it didn't recognize her smell.

"It's amazing, isn't it?" Mama had said. "Once, so recently, there was barely a creature on earth—from one-celled organisms on up—that didn't know our smell, our sounds, our *presence*, almost as well as we did. You never saw that world, the dreamed earth, but we were everywhere. *Everywhere*. And now we're the outsiders, the aliens."

Aliens. Alien prey. Given the life span of hyenas and most other animals, it was likely that this alpha female had never encountered a human before. That was true of most wild animals although maybe there were still elephants alive that remembered the world as it had once been, the world that Aisha Rose herself had never known. Elephants and tortoises and parrots and other long-lived creatures that still possessed fading memories of the dreamed earth.

If any wild creature did remember that time, Mama had told Aisha Rose, it was with fear and disgust. "Just as I remember it," she'd added. "As a world of nightmares. I'm so glad to have lived to see this one. The real earth."

Aisha Rose had stayed silent. Even now, Mama didn't know about the stain. The spreading stain. She didn't need to know.

The alpha female opened its mouth wider and bent toward Aisha Rose, another string of warm saliva falling on her thigh.

Yet the hyena's gesture was strangely indecisive. Like a bow. It seemed almost . . . respectful. Polite.

Please pardon me while I kill you.

But polite or not, the result would be the same. Its first bite would pierce her skin and rupture her blood vessels and crush her bones. A hyena's first bite was usually the only one it needed.

But, finally, Aisha Rose's mind was clear. And even as she and the alpha had been staring at each other, even as she'd been thinking about Mama's words, her eyes had been taking in the surroundings. And her right hand had been creeping toward a stone she'd seen from the corner of her eye. A roundish stone, smooth, brown and yellow.

A little too large, a little too heavy, for a hunt, but perfect for her current purpose.

Inside her head, Mama was quiet. This was Aisha Rose's task alone.

With a speed and strength that surprised both the alpha and herself, she grasped the stone, reared up—getting her legs away from those dripping jaws—swung her arm, and bashed the stone against the hyena's brow, just a little above its eyes.

All the while letting loose with the loudest shout she could muster.

The blow didn't kill the beast. Aisha Rose hadn't

thought it would. Hyenas' skulls were thick, and she wasn't *that* strong.

She didn't want to kill it, anyway, not unless it gave her no choice. Aisha Rose didn't kill. Or at least she didn't kill indiscriminately.

The hyena's mouth closed with a click of teeth. It sat back on its misshapen haunches and, for an instant, its eyes went out of focus. Then they cleared, and Aisha Rose saw its body tense. At the same time, yowling, the other two came dancing in toward her.

Coming for her, but still sideways, with their heads partly averted even as they showed their teeth. Not the steady, headlong lope—somehow eating up the ground in their humpbacked way—they used when they moved in for the kill.

She'd hurt the alpha female, she could see that. But more importantly, she'd startled them, all of them. Even scared them. What was this seemingly dormant creature that suddenly sprang up and attacked? And what else was it capable of?

Aisha Rose knew the answer to that question: not much else. But it didn't matter. She had the advantage now. Before the dominant hyena could decide between attack and retreat, she made the decision for it. With another bellow—this one so loud that Aisha Rose knew her throat would hurt for days—she leaped at it, swinging the stone again.

This time it collided with the alpha's midsection, making a loud, hollow thump. The hyena staggered back two steps, and what came out of its mouth now was no terrifying howl or laugh, but an unmistakable whimper.

That was enough. She wasn't worth it. Game was plentiful in that season, and she'd seen at once that all three had the bulging bellies of the recently fed.

They'd approached her because normally that would have made no difference. Hyenas would eat until they could barely move, and sometimes kill even if they had no appetite at all.

But to have a nearly full stomach and confront an unfamiliar prey that fought back? No, thank you.

"Humans are the only creatures that kill because their feelings are hurt," Mama had said.

Aisha Rose watched the hyenas depart, glancing over their sloping shoulders as they left to make sure she wasn't in pursuit. Surprising herself again, she gave a hoarse laugh at their cowed expressions. Hearing the sound, the three hyenas hurried their stride until they reached the mouth of the little side canyon that Aisha Rose and Mama had made their home this year. Then, with one last backward glance, they passed out of sight.

Still smiling, Aisha Rose tossed the stone aside and stretched her arms out in front of her. She knew these hyenas would never return, and if something else came hunting for her? Well, with Mama's help, she would deal with it, too.

Then she reached back with her right hand and touched the lump on the back of her head, wincing. The hair around it was matted with drying blood, but the wound itself had nearly stopped bleeding, and she could feel a scab beginning to crust over it.

The pain took her mind away from her encounter with the hyenas, and in that instant she remembered what had happened to her. What had left her so vulnerable that, if she hadn't awoken when she did, she might have died in agony instead, or in unconsciousness, without ever realizing she'd been alive at all.

Or at least she remembered *some* of it. And, just like that, the joy drained out of her, and she felt cold.

No. Not cold. Afraid.

Afraid in a way she could never be, even facing hyenas or anything else the real earth could threaten her with.

Except this.

THIS WAS WHAT had happened:

As she often was during the heat of the day, she'd been up in her tree, in her perch above the weaverbird colony. Sitting with her back against the massive trunk and her legs dangling over the wooden sleeping platform nestled between the trunk and one of the tree's sturdiest branches.

Not that there weren't any threats up here—she'd seen her share of snakes and scorpions—but she was doubtless safer in the tree than even in the rockiest, most inaccessible corner of the caves and canyons.

So . . . she'd been sitting safely on her perch, watching the world go by (as Mama put it), when . . .

When she'd seen the picture of a lion. But not one of her lions . . . something slighter, sleeker even than a young lioness. Something else. Something she thought she remembered from a book she'd looked at long ago, one of the picture books Mama had brought with her from the dreamed earth. Back when they had books.

A lion that lived on the other side of the world.

But . . . no. This wasn't a memory from some long-vanished book, but an image in her mind. Something that had come from far away.

And she knew at once where it had come from, and who was seeing it.

One of the others. The hundreds—or even thousands, she could not tell—of others out there who were like her. The ones she saw as lights inside her head, shifting constellations, galaxies wheeling and blurring. Never still, never fixed in place, but always changing shape and number as new ones arrived and others departed.

Always there with her, inside her, an earth filled with people who'd shared Aisha Rose's fate. And others, dimming, dwindling lights, who'd shared Mama's.

And still others, the ones that grew stronger every year. The spreading stain.

But *this* one, the one who had witnessed the lion, this one was different from all the others. He—and Aisha Rose was sure it was a "he"—was the most powerful by far. The fiercest light.

And the only one she could see. No: see *through*. See through his eyes, sometimes, just for a moment, just as she could see through the *majizis'* eyes.

Without knowing it, he gave her glimpses of the world he inhabited. A place of forests and streams and grasslands. Of *snow*, something she'd seen only from a distance, a white gleam atop the enormous mountain—Mount Kenya—that looked down upon her and Mama's house in Naro Moru.

Forest and grasslands and snow and ruins that seemed

to go on to the horizon. Ruins of a city gradually subsiding into itself as the years passed.

She'd glimpsed these things early on, when she was
still learning about the lights, when she was still beginning to understand what they were and what she was.

But then she'd come to understand how strong he
was. The strongest of all of them, besides her. But she
was strong because she had Mama with her. From what
she could see, he was entirely alone, and always had
been—or, at least, had been for many years. Alone, and
damaged, and terrifying because of it.

Terrifying to her because he didn't understand his
own power. Because he didn't know what he could do
to her, even to Aisha Rose, and how effortlessly.

She didn't think he even knew she existed. But she'd
known. She'd understood the threat. And so she'd built
walls, erected barricades, to protect herself from him.
And she'd hidden herself . . . until today, when she'd let
the barricades slip and seen his lion.

And then, because she was lonely, because she forgot
her fear, she'd created the image of a beautiful black-
maned lion she'd seen a month earlier, out by the big
lake. Naivasha. Standing there, every bit a picture like
the ones in books. The King of the Beasts.

Sprawled on her platform to escape the heat of the
day, she'd opened herself and placed the image of her
lion where his had been. After all those years of hiding,
it was such a simple act, a step she'd taken in what must
have been a moment of madness.

His response had almost killed her. Three times. First
with its own force, a massive, paralyzing blow to her

head, an explosion inside her skull. Second because it had caused her to fall from her perch. And third, because the hyenas could easily have disposed of her before she ever awoke.

That was the breadth of his power: to kill her in an instant or to leave her vulnerable to the death that was always awaiting her—awaiting everyone—on the real earth.

But she hadn't died. He hadn't killed her. In her high-walled canyon, at the base of her tree, she was still alive.

But for how much longer, now that he knew she existed?

She shivered, but as much from the chill as from residual shock and fear. Drawing in a breath, she looked around. The sun had already dipped behind the western wall. The air had noticeably cooled. It would be full dusk inside the canyon within an hour, and dusk on the earth above little more than an hour later.

She was *so* late.

Without hesitating, she headed deeper into the canyon and half ran through its caves and narrow passageways. Twisting and turning as she went, toward the surface now, her momentum sometimes taking her half-way up the walls as she ran. A path so familiar that she knew from instinct where to place her feet.

Singing as she went because she always sang as she ran.

She made it in time. The sun was still high enough though the evening's first rays were already staining the mountain's spires a deeper red. Vultures soared around the cliffs, and swifts winged overhead in a whirling flock.

"You're late," Mama said. Mama, sitting in their spot, the place where they came every evening, so Aisha Rose could perform her recitation.

Their spot was a small, hidden plateau on the lip of the canyon that afforded a view of the giant lake below, the game-rich plains that spread outward from it and, beyond, the Great Rift Valley wall.

"I was beginning to wonder, Aisha Rose," Mama said, "if you'd forgotten."

Mama's real voice had become so different from the one that Aisha Rose heard inside her head. The loud, declarative tone that Mama had once possessed, but that had been stolen from her, along with her strength and endurance, and, in truth, her life. Soon enough.

That loud Mama had become part of the dream. The real Mama's voice was scratchy and weak, her sentences interrupted by the kind of breaths that whistled in her throat but barely seemed to reach her lungs. A voice to match the way she looked: gaunt, the skin so tight over her bones that you could almost see the skeleton beneath. Her hair, which had once been as thick as Aisha Rose's own, now dull and ragged.

Mama was dying. She'd been dying since before Aisha Rose was born, and for the same reason everyone else like her died. Her fate was inevitable and irreversible.

Aisha Rose had known this from the start. It might have been the first thing she'd ever known, as she began to understand what the lights in her mind meant, and as she watched Mama's light fade, day to day, year to year.

But her eyes, the same strange blue-violet as Aisha

Rose's own, were just as clear and sharp as they'd been when Aisha Rose was a little girl, fifteen and more years ago. And her manner, if not her voice, hadn't changed either.

"I'm sorry, Mama—"

"Don't waste any time." Mama sat back in the wooden chair that Aisha Rose had made for her. "No lollygagging or daydreaming. Just begin."

So Aisha Rose began. "My name is Aisha Rose Atkinson," she said, her voice hoarse. "I was born nineteen years, one month, and twenty-six days ago, six months and three days after the end of the dreamed earth."

"Concentrate." The single word like the crack of a whip.

Aisha Rose paused, took a deep breath, shook her head. For an instant she felt a spark of irritation flare under her breastbone. So what if she got something wrong? She was tired. And hungry. Her head hurt. So did her throat. What did her recitation matter anyway?

Then she closed her eyes for an instant and brought her mind back to the sharpness Mama required. She knew exactly why it mattered.

"I was born nineteen years, one month, and twenty-six days ago, six months and *four* days after the end of the dreamed earth," she said. "Today's date is June seventeenth—June *eighteenth*."

"Good," Mama said. "Please go on."

"My father's name was Erik Atkinson. He was born in Johannesburg, South Africa, and died at the end of the dreamed earth, so I never met him. But I know I have his build, his smile, and his love of nature."

And his tendency toward distraction. That was Mama's line as well.

Aisha Rose said, "My mother's name is Francesca Oliviera Atkinson. She was born in Port Elizabeth, South Africa, and was alone on the real earth when she gave birth to me."

"But after that I was never alone," Mama said, as she always did at this point.

"After that," Aisha Rose said, as *she* always did, "*neither* of us was ever alone."

She let those words hang in the air for a moment, then went on. "We lived only in Naro Moru, Kenya, until I was nine years, three months, and sixteen days old. Since then, we've come here, to Erik's Gorge in Hell's Gate, in the Great Rift Valley, for part of each year as well."

A wave of dizziness stopped her recitation for a moment. "We migrate," Mama prompted.

"We migrate," Aisha Rose went on, "like the wildebeest and the zebras and Africa's other living things."

But for how much longer? she wondered.

NEXT IT WAS time for her sums.

"Mama . . ."

A waiting silence.

Aisha Rose sighed, and did her sums. Her times tables. Division problems. All in her head, of course, or scratched onto a rock face with a sharp stone. They'd never had paper here, and it had been years since they'd had any even in the house in Naro Moru. Like so many other things, paper had receded into the dream.

*   *   *

NEXT CAME HER reading. But which book?

Aisha Rose thought about it. Before their books had been destroyed by the wet and the mold and the little red mites that loved eating damp paper, Mama had insisted that Aisha Rose memorize as many of them as she could.

In the end, before they were gone forever, she'd committed nine to memory. She couldn't begin to guess how often she'd recited all nine since.

They'd finished one—Gerald Durrell's *My Family and Other Animals*—just last night, and Aisha Rose always got to choose which one to read next.

She thought for a moment, then said, "*I Capture the Castle*, by Dodie Smith."

"Begin," Mama said.

Aisha Rose closed her eyes so she could see the words. "'I write this sitting in the kitchen sink,'" she began. "'That is, my feet are in it—'"

SHE RECITED THE words until the sun had long since sunk below the surrounding cliffs and the darkening sky was crisscrossed by the little bats that roosted in the caves riddling these mountains. Somewhere far off, on their way to someplace else, the hyenas yipped and yowled.

By the end, Aisha Rose's voice was so scratchy that it didn't even sound like her own. But Mama didn't care, and there was no one else to hear.

"Very good," Mama said. "Now . . ."

That meant: Finish up.

Aisha Rose drew in a deep breath. "My name is Aisha Rose Atkinson," she said, "and I am human."

"Good. Say it again."

"My name is Aisha Rose Atkinson . . ."

"Good. Again."

NINE

Lamu

THE LUCKIEST ONES had died first.

The ones who had perished in the fires that roared across the cities and the ones who had been stung to death or killed by the late-stage hosts while trying to fight back at the very beginning.

Next were those, hundreds of millions of them worldwide, Jason was sure, who had died more slowly . . . but still within days or weeks. From thirst or starvation, many of them, as they hid in locked bathrooms, windowless basements. Or so terrified of what lay outside that they committed suicide, with gas or knife or gun, rather than face it.

Next most fortunate were the hosts. Yes, they had moments of lucidity that were horrible to witness, moments when they realized what had been done to them, what was growing inside them. And in the last stages, when they ferociously attacked anyone and anything the hive mind perceived as a threat, sometimes you could see awareness of what they were being compelled to do. The desperation to die.

But that final stage lasted for only a couple of days. Then came the hatching, the emergence, and merciful death.

Yet even the hosts were luckier than Jason himself and the dwindling number of others who were aware. The ones who *knew*. Who maintained the capacity to comprehend what was being done to them and to remember how different things had been once.

Even if "once" was now so long ago that it seemed as surreal as something he'd read about once but never lived through.

But still not surreal enough. Not for Jason.

Not until he lost more of his memories, lost the sound of the three words that remained as vivid in his mind as if he'd heard them yesterday.

Just three words.

HE'D BEEN ATTENDING a conference in Nairobi on emerging diseases. A conference he'd decided he couldn't miss, even as the world seemed to be hurrying toward some dimly seen precipice.

He could still remember his justifications. To anyone who was a parasitologist, or an epidemiologist, or any kind of scientist or physician working where the monsters lurked on the fringes of human society, the world *always* seemed to be hurtling to the edge of a precipice. It was their job *not* to look away, not to think about something else.

They were the experts who knew you didn't skip a conference just because the world was facing another threat, especially an emerging one. SARS, Ebola, multidrug-resistant tuberculosis: You put your chin up and marched forward; because if you didn't, who would?

So Jason hadn't thought twice about going that fall. About being seven thousand miles from Boston, and leaving his wife, Gail, and their daughters, Ami and Esi, alone.

Ami and Esi, ten and eight years old. Forever ten and eight.

They'd trusted him. Even Gail had. Gail had believed him when he told her she shouldn't worry, he'd be back in ten days, that they'd barely even have a chance to miss him.

The actual future was simultaneously so imminent and so far beyond their imagining that they might as well have been farmers discussing soil conditions on the eve of the Great Flood.

So off Jason went, comfortable in business class on a flight from Logan Airport to Nairobi, sitting beside an epidemiologist, an older man whose name had long vanished from Jason's memory. One of the final flights ever—one of the final thousands, at least—but it felt no different than any other.

The meeting had been the usual as well, spread across the ballrooms and restaurants in the Nairobi Serena Hotel. Jason had participated in two panels and attended many more over the course of four days. That was, when he wasn't in the bar or the Mandhari Restaurant, or taking an afternoon trip to Nairobi National Park, the only place on earth where you could watch wild lions and giraffes in the shadow of newly sprouted city skyscrapers.

Two of the panels he'd attended had been about the thieves. That was where he'd learned about the virus that a wasp species used to enslave a beetle, and about the recent discovery of a previously unknown virus in the bloodstream of those primates the thieves had used as hosts. Including humans.

He'd seen images of human hosts looking vague-eyed, absent, not seeming to see the huge swellings the thief larvae inflicted on them. (This blindness, and more specifically the way the wasps' toxins seemed to steal the awareness from their mammalian hosts, providing the common name—*thief* in English—that seemed to have been adopted nearly worldwide during those final months.)

Dreaming hosts, and ones that were far from asleep. The speaker had shown a brief, shaky clip—which had caused a stir in the audience—of what he'd called "the soldier phase." A last-stage host in full attack posture, its teeth bared, face contorted, its eyes somehow both filled with madness and strangely expressionless.

All things Jason had seen up close countless times since, but at the time he hadn't paid much attention to the presentation. When all was said and done, the thieves weren't doing anything other insects, their toxins, and the microbes they carried hadn't done first.

Like trypanosomiasis, a disease caused by protozoa and administered through the bite of a tsetse fly, which also caused those afflicted to lapse into semiconsciousness—otherwise, why would it more usually be called sleeping sickness? And, in its final stages, the rabies virus caused similar behaviors as those shown by last-stage hosts, yet no one at the conference was hosting rabies panels, were they?

And anyway, the world was full of dangers, threats. Yes, the wasps were a new one, and highly hyped, but at the time of the conference they'd caused far less destruction and death than malaria, leishmaniasis, Ebola, or countless other less glamorous diseases.

So Jason drifted in and out, jet lag and the notes he was writing for his own presentations stealing his attention from the subject at hand. If he had understood that this was the last time he'd ever sit with brilliant people, people possessing a deep desire to gain knowledge, then use that knowledge to help others live longer and healthier, well . . . he would have valued it more.

But he hadn't understood. Instead, it all remained merely a bitter memory. Bitterer still because it took the place of other memories, ones he could have had if he'd stayed home.

Memories of his wife, of his daughters.

No. *No.* Even that was a lie. He wouldn't have had any memories at all. He would have died alongside them that first night. They would have died in his arms, Ami and Esi and Gail, and he in theirs.

BUT IT WASN'T just the conference. If it had been just the conference, he *would* have gotten home in time to die.

In fact, the conference ended, and most of the attendees did fly home. Jason, on the other hand, extended his trip for three days to visit Lamu, a place he'd visited before and whose crowded marketplaces and peaceful coral reefs he'd loved. A three-day extension, and a lifetime.

He'd spent his first day there diving, the reefs seeming a little more stressed and underpopulated than he'd last seen them, three years before. In a world contorted by climate change, he'd wondered if there'd be coral reefs at all in twenty years. Would reefs be something Ami and Esi knew only from old videos?

He'd chosen to sleep at a guesthouse beside a mosque, just a stone's throw from Lamu Fort. The next morning he'd woken with the muezzin's call to prayer and walked into the center of town—the bustling waterfront already crowded at dawn with dhows and donkeys and fishermen and taxi drivers—for an early breakfast.

For something else as well. Something that forever after, when he was being honest with himself, when he was hating himself most, he had to admit he hadn't even been looking forward to: a Skype session with the wife and kids.

He'd rather have slept a little later, and anyway, he'd be seeing them in just a couple more days. He never forgot that.

Still, they'd scheduled the session, taking into account the eight-hour time difference between the two continents. His destination, the Lamu Café, had good food and excellent coffee, while also being one of the only places on the island with Wi-Fi.

And, largely due to its expat chef, Chloe Granger, who'd browbeaten the absentee owner into agreeing, the café made a practice of opening extra early to supply coffee to people heading out on fishing, diving, or other adventures. Or even, on request, extra extra early to make sure that those needing Internet had access to the news headlines, the workings of the stock market, or the miracle that was Skype.

Jason remembered Chloe from his two previous visits to Lamu, to the café. Admittedly, she was hard to forget, with her height (equaling Jason's five feet ten inches), her lanky frame, all long tanned legs and arms, her crazy blond hair tied back behind a headband to keep it out of the food, and—above all—her loud Aussie voice and utterly fearless manner.

Anyone who spent more than fifteen minutes in the Lamu Café remembered Chloe Granger.

JASON HAD WALKED along the waterfront with the sun rising over the channel and Manda Island beyond. Despite the hour, all along the way, locals in kikois and hijabs and Western clothes approached him, touting tours and money exchange and various goods legal and illegal because even though he was dark-skinned like them, it was clear that he was a tourist, and therefore likely wealthy.

On the walk, he'd come across the only thief he'd noticed—seen or smelled—during his whole trip. Just one lurking half-inside its burrow in a sandy patch beside the road. It was facing away from him, huddled low, and Jason wondered if it was ill or injured.

He'd had a stray thought: Maybe the thieves, after their explosive spread, had encountered a pathogen—a virus, perhaps, or a parasite of their own—that might help control their population naturally. Such things happened sometimes, nature doing a better job of controlling pests than humans ever could.

That was the last time that Jason thought about the thieves this way: as a solvable problem. As "pests."

CHLOE BROUGHT HIM coffee as he booted up his laptop. Then, as Skype was loading, he glanced at the news headlines.

It was Election Day back home—and eight hours in the past—and it looked like the challenger had defeated the incumbent. A rare enough occurrence to be of interest, unless you were Jason, who'd forgotten to vote by absentee ballot and had no faith in either party to understand the threats to the world, much less address them.

He plugged in his earbuds as Skype's familiar electronic ringtone sounded in his ears. He accepted the video call, and there they were. A little blurry, a little pixilated, but there, alive, in real time. Seven thousand miles apart and yet together.

Gail stood in the background, smiling. The two girls were wearing pajamas—Ami's pink, Esi's navy blue (anything but pink for Esi)—because it was after eleven o'clock at night their time, way past their usual bedtime on a school night. Sleepiness made smudges under their eyes and slackened the muscles in their cheeks even as adrenaline brightened their faces and made them chatty.

Jason told them about a moray eel he'd seen on the reef, five feet long and green, with a big toothy grin. That made them wide-eyed for a moment, even quiet.

But they were anything but quiet during the rest of the conversation, vying as usual for his attention as they interrupted each other with stories about school and friends and Esi's lacrosse team and the play, *Annie*, that Ami was going to try out for the next day.

At a certain point, Jason noticed that Gail was gone from the screen. He didn't pay any attention, though, because he knew that soon enough she would shoo the girls off to bed, then he and she would get to talk.

But when she came back into view, looking down at her phone and then tapping the screen, his attention sharpened. When she looked up again, he could see that she seemed concerned about something.

"Let me talk to Dad," she said to the girls, and her tone of voice made Esi stop in the middle of a word, and the two of them make some room for her to sit between them, nearer to the screen.

"What is it?" Jason asked.

"I don't know." Gail frowned and glanced down at the phone again. Up close, she looked tired as well as worried. "My mother just called, which is weird enough at this time of night. But before I could answer, it went dead—and now the circuits are all busy."

Even then, *even then*, Jason had suspected nothing. Gail's mother lived in New York City, in Queens, and though problems with their cell-phone provider were rare, every so often they all got reminded that the technology did, after all, rely on satellites to allow communication from city to city—or even room to room.

Right then, unafraid, unsuspicious, Jason merely

thought, *Technology!* And opened his mouth to say something reassuring.

But at that moment, the Skype window went blank. Black. For an instant, he thought that the connection had been lost—a common enough occurrence—but then he heard Gail say, "What the hell?"

Then, even over the earbuds in his laptop, Jason heard another sound. One he would soon come to know better than any other and live with in his nightmares. But that first time he didn't even recognize it: a harsh, almost mechanical chittering. And, underneath it, the loud humming of wings.

Gail said, "Jason—"

But whatever she was going to say next, he never knew, because one of his daughters gasped, and the other, at the same time, in a voice so distorted by distance that he never knew which it was, cried out—

Cried out, "Daddy . . . help us."

No words after that. Only the sounds of mandibles, and wings, and wordless screams.

For a few seconds, until finally, blessedly, the connection was lost.

THE ATTACK CAME to Lamu about fifteen minutes later. Jason always remembered that. He knew it might have scientific significance—the fact that the thief assault did not begin at exactly the same moment everywhere.

Of course, destroying a civilization doesn't require perfect precision, and sometimes can take eons to accomplish. If the thieves unleashed their attacks over the course of a few hours, did it matter in the long run? It didn't.

Still . . . during all the quiet, endless, deadening years that lay ahead, Jason had more than enough time to think, to wonder. And one of the things he wondered about was this delay, and what it might say about the hive mind.

That maybe the mind wasn't something magical, simultaneously commanding each of the countless millions of thieves. Some impulse that traveled at the speed of light, or no speed at all because it was somehow everywhere at once.

No. Maybe it was a network, a set of impulses that moved with stunning—but *not* incomprehensible—speed. Fanning outward from wherever the first attack began, thief by thief. The speed of waves, but not of thought.

At the time, during those fifteen minutes, though, Jason spent no time pondering such mysteries. There was no room inside him for anything but terror.

First he tried to call back on Skype, with no success. The screen froze, so he shook his laptop, a mindless act of panic.

Next he tried his iPhone, but neither the phone nor iMessage connected.

Then, almost overwhelmed by his helplessness, he went to one of the sun-flooded doorways and looked out at the busy waterfront, the fishermen and taxi drivers and tour guides, the sun pouring down out of a deep blue morning sky, the water glittering, and no one aware of the disaster that was happening elsewhere in the world.

He sensed as much as saw Chloe Granger come over and stand beside him. She'd been watching him, seen his panic, and now she said, "Jase, what's going on?"

"I don't know," he said.

But then a shadow came from the west and obscured the sun, and Jason, coming back to himself, did know. He understood that the disaster that had swept over Gail and the girls had reached them, too.

He understood for the first time that it would reach everywhere.

Chloe, watching, understood as well. What was coming and what it meant.

At the time, Jason didn't understand how she'd figured it all out so fast. A little later, when they had the chance to talk, she told him about her father the airplane pilot, the colony he'd gone to join, and his warning to her, which she'd scoffed at and disregarded.

At the time, though, as she grabbed his arm and pulled him back into the restaurant, he'd marveled at her decisiveness. Even so, at first he resisted, for some reason wanting to see, *needing* to see. To see in order to believe, to understand what had happened to his family.

But then, as the cries of panic came through the open doors behind them, and above all the sound of the thieves, he allowed her to lead him through the kitchen and into the big windowless cold room where the perishables were kept.

The room where he and Chloe and a handful of others would spend the next three days, only emerging when they were desperate for freshwater, when the electricity had been off so long that the heat and airlessness were intolerable and the remaining food had begun to rot.

Jason had been sure they would all be killed as soon as they opened the door. But he was wrong. Though they stepped into a world transformed, they were left alive.

A life sentence. Ever after, Jason knew that he should have stepped forward and joined all the others who died in Lamu that day and across the world.

Instead—

Daddy . . . help us.

TEN

Kissama National Park, Angola

"LOOK AT THAT," Ross McKay said, his eyes alight in his pouchy face. "They're so beautiful."

Malcolm followed the direction of the biologist's gaze: Two dozen unkempt black crosses were circling against the high blue sky to the east, with more winging their way in from the horizon.

"Vultures," Malcolm said. He shook his head. "Should've figured you'd think *those* buggers were pretty."

Ross smiled and rocked on his feet but said nothing. This was more typical of him.

Malcolm squinted but couldn't make out what the vultures were soaring over. But he didn't need to know for sure; it was almost certainly a kill, and where there was a kill, there were usually predators.

"My experience, I find myself just below a bunch of those bastards, I'm not usually doing much admiring. Too busy looking over my shoulder for lions."

He was joking. Kind of. No, not really. Becoming a lion's next meal was a definite possibility here, on their first foray onto dry land since they'd embarked from Refugia. Malcolm had chosen to come ashore on the coast of what had once been Angola, and now they were exploring one of the country's national parks—Kissama.

He'd been here twice before. He'd been nearly everywhere in Africa before the Fall, sometimes without knowing exactly where he was placing his feet.

Without knowing—or caring. Piloting his little prop planes on scientific expeditions, hostage-rescue attempts, and humanitarian missions didn't usually require him to keep up-to-date on current borders. He left that to the diplomats, NGOs, and government officials who were the experts . . . and also, Malcolm believed, some of the main reasons why Africa had been so fucked up at the end of the Last World.

The agreed-upon borders had been so stupid—no, so psychotic—that it was a miracle the world hadn't ended earlier than it did. Hutu and Tutsi jammed into Rwanda and Burundi, and both forced to speak the national language of English? Animists, Christians, and Muslims struggling over French-speaking Senegal? The Ambundu, Bakongo, and Ovimbundu here in Angola, fighting for turf in a country where they'd all been taught to speak Portuguese? Madness.

Human madness. The land itself had never paid any attention to the divisions that its human "rulers" had imposed on it. Even in the worst of times, at the tail end of the Last World, weather, altitude, rainfall, and the timeless migration of enormous animal herds had dictated the continent's true borders. As they had long before humans had come to dominate the landscape . . . and, he thought, as it would long afterward.

That was one reason Malcolm had chosen to come ashore on this stretch of savanna: It would be a bellwether. The abundance and condition of its wildlife would give Ross, Clare Shapiro, and the others their first evidence of how the rest of the continent was recovering from its human occupation.

Just as importantly, after nearly three weeks on the ocean, the crew was desperate for shore leave. They needed to feel solid ground under their feet, breathe air that didn't smell like salt—or bilge—and get some distance from each other.

Malcolm had left only a small crew back on the *Trey Gilliard*—they'd get their shore leave soon—and those on land were already at work refilling the water tanks and restocking food supplies. Malcolm could see a group under Dylan Connell's command spreading out in search of fruit, nuts, tubers—whatever they could find to augment the meat that he and Ross McKay, the two best shots, had been enlisted to bring back.

Kait was sitting on a large rock off to the side. Part of her assignment was to record the journey's progress in words and drawings, and there she was, alone with her pencils and paper. As he watched, she lifted her head and looked at him. She smiled and raised her right hand in a wave, then looked back down at the pad.

As she did, he noticed her left hand go sneaking

down to pat the pocket of the long cotton jacket she always wore these days, as if making sure that something she'd put there hadn't fallen out.

Malcolm noticed it, wondered about it, and forgot it.

KISSAMA HAD ONCE been among the richest savanna ecosystems on the western side of the continent, teeming with plains game of all shape and sizes. But by the end of the Last World, wrecked by the human greed and bloodlust that had slaughtered nearly every animal bigger than a meerkat, it had become a ghost town.

Malcolm had seen this up close.

His first visit had been to rescue three ransomed hostages—aid workers from Belgium—in a battered old four-seater Cessna 172. (He didn't remember which side was holding them, or for what reason, and he'd never cared.) That was the time he saw the rotting corpses, animal and human both, that demonstrated the hellish toll that madmen with automatic weapons could take on those with no defense.

He'd survived the hostage transfer and even succeeded in getting the plane into the air. Then, not at all to his surprise, he'd been forced to perform some creative evasive maneuvers to avoid the shoulder-mounted missile that the rebels had fired to knock him and the battered hostages back out of the sky.

His second visit had been more interesting. It had been after the Angolan civil war had finally come to an end—its most recent end, at least. As part of a small caravan of aircraft leaving Johannesburg, Malcolm had

flown a cargo plane containing four South African elephants to the park. The rest of the caravan had contained
giraffes, ostriches, and other creatures that had been
virtually extirpated during the war.

At the time, Malcolm had been happy to help . . . to
be paid to help. But he hadn't held out much hope that
the wildlife transfer would work. Yes, the animals arrived
safely. Yes, there was abundant food and territory for
them to thrive.

But despite a fragile peace, there were still plenty of
madmen out there with AK-47s and a desire to see blood
flow. Malcolm had no doubt there would be another
civil war, and another, endlessly, in perpetuity, with the
animals he'd brought—or their progeny—caught in the
eternal crossfire.

Instead, the thieves had come, claiming the whole
world as their territory, their domain. And so much
human blood had flowed, rivers of it, torrents, that the
animals of Kissama had been given a new chance.

IT DIDN'T TAKE much surveying to see that, just as Refugia's
savannas had been repopulated, year after year, by animals that hadn't been seen there in generations, Kissama
was now showing a similar resurgence.

Back then, Malcolm never paid much attention to Africa's animals. He'd left that to the fanatics like Trey and the
scientists he ferried around from place to place. Let them
get bitten by flies and catch river blindness and sleeping
sickness because they needed to spot some little brown job
of a bird or some poisonous snake. He'd be in the bar.

But as he watched a giraffe family, two adults and a baby, head in their rocking-horse way from one grove of acacia trees to another, he could see the appeal. And that solitary bull elephant watching them? Maybe it was a descendant of the ones he'd brought here all those years ago.

Yet somehow, among all that, Ross McKay had chosen the vultures to remark upon. Malcolm looked back at the distant flock. Then, with a sigh, he said to Ross, "I know you're going to tell me anyway, so get on with it: What's so effing beautiful about those bastards?"

"Their mere smelly, ugly presence," McKay said.

He smiled, that strange, locked-in smile of his that never reached his pale eyes. "Because if *they've* come back," he went on, "then everything has."

McKay looked into Malcolm's face. "Come on," he said, as if everyone on earth should know as much about those ugly birds as he did, "don't you remember? Vultures were on the way out back then, and fast, in Asia and Africa. This chemical, diclofenac, that farmers would give to their livestock to treat fevers and pain from wounds but was deadly poison to vultures."

Malcolm shrugged. He might have read something about it once.

"Listen," Ross said. "The population of just one vulture species in India dropped from eighty million—eighty million!—to a few thousand in about five years. And things weren't a whole lot better among the species here in Africa. I can see you're thinking, 'So what?'"

Malcolm didn't deny it.

Ross's expression had grown more placid, his voice

slower. "This is what," he said. "Vultures are an end point for pathogens—they eat rotting meat and its bacteria, none of which seem to infect them. Nature's cleanup crew, evolving for millions of years to keep the rest of us healthy."

Malcolm nodded. "Okay. I get it. With no vultures around, the dead cows just rotted away. Germs everywhere."

"It would have been luckier if they'd just rotted," Ross said. "But of course that's not what happened. There's always a worse case."

A flock of small parrots flew overhead, screeching. Ross tilted his head. "Because there was so much carrion around, the population of feral dogs boomed," he said. "They didn't do much of a cleanup job, but all that extra protein sure did encourage them to breed."

He paused and gave a brief glance into Malcolm's face. "You see where this is going, don't you."

Malcolm said. "Yeah."

"There were eighteen million feral dogs in India by the end of the Last World."

"And how many people dying from rabies?"

"About forty thousand each year. Mostly children, of course."

In the silence that followed, Ross turned to watch the distant soaring vulture flock. "Yet there they are once again, in their abundance," he said. "Aren't they beautiful?"

A FEW MINUTES later, he said, "Speaking of dogs—what on earth is that?"

Malcolm followed the direction of Ross's gaze. Among a small pack of jackals waiting out the midday heat in the shade cast by an acacia were two that looked markedly different from the rest. They shared the general size and shape of their more typical pack mates. But their coats, instead of the usual tan and silver, were a mottled brown, and their tails, instead of hanging down, were whiplike and curled partway over their backs.

"Dogs that have joined the pack," Malcolm said. "Or—maybe hybrids?"

But Ross wasn't listening. He was staring at the strange animals, and after a moment an expression that looked like joy flickered across his face. "They look to me," he said, "like an evolving species."

"A what?"

"A species on the road to becoming a new one."

Malcolm just looked at him. Ross gestured with both hands. "It looks like mongrels from some nearby village interbred with jackals here. If that's true, soon enough there won't be a single purebred left."

He paused, then said, "That would mean we could be seeing a new species being born. And I'll bet it's far from the only one—not now."

"You're acting like you have bugs in your brain," Malcolm said. "Every schoolboy knows that species can't change so fast."

"That's a discarded theory," Ross said immediately. "The walls between species have been tumbling down for years. Especially near the end of the Last World. Come on, Malcolm, don't tell me you never heard about pizzly bears?"

Malcolm, for once at a loss for words, stared at him.

Ross gave a little smile. "Up in the Arctic, climate change was bringing grizzly bears and polar bears into contact, and they were breeding to form a new species. Pizzly bears."

He looked at Malcolm's expression and nodded. "And children and pets were being attacked in the eastern U.S. by coyotes. Did you hear about that? Only they weren't coyotes, they were half coyote, half timber wolf. An evolving species."

Malcolm said, "Are you telling me—"

But Ross raised a hand. "One moment."

Then, in a fluid motion, he unslung his rifle, went down on one knee, raised the rifle to his shoulder, sighted, and pulled the trigger.

One of the brown animals flew up in the air, its mouth opening wide in a soundless cry before it landed, rolled, and settled into an awkward, final pose. The others leaped and scattered at the sound of the shot, but they didn't move very far away. Even now they were milling about, looking down at their still companion more with curiosity than fear.

Innocent again. For a while, at least.

"Of course, for every newly evolving species that flourishes, countless others fail," Ross said in his mild way, heading across the grass toward the dead animal. "Let's take a closer look at that guy."

AS THEY HEADED back toward the shore a little later, their haul including a pair of little gazelles—gray duikers—Malcolm said, "How many?"

Ross had one of the duikers slung around his neck, his precious jackal-dog in his arms. "How many what?"

"How many evolving species are out there? Right now?"

Ross shrugged under his burden. "Who knows? Certainly dozens. Hundreds. New mammals and birds and invertebrates—so many new invertebrates! It's a big, empty world just waiting to be filled up. And that's what evolution does best—fills empty spaces."

His smile was nearly blissful. "Imagine the wonders that await us! I wish I could live long enough to see them all."

Malcolm looked at him.

"Be my fucking guest," he said.

WITHIN ABOUT TEN minutes, though, Ross's mood changed. Malcolm, and everyone else, had seen it happen countless times, and it always started the same way.

Ross's characteristic benevolent gaze would darken. His face, usually seeming on the verge of a smile, would cloud, and he'd start looking around with a narrow-eyed, suspicious expression, as if suddenly seeing the world for what it was. His chatty demeanor would drain away as well, and you could barely get a sentence out of him, much less one of his typical explications of some arcane scientific fact.

Having overtaken him, Ross's black moods could persist for days. Back in Refugia, he'd leave his beloved research hanging midproject and fail to join the evening conversations around the fire pit that he normally loved so much.

Sheila would visit him, bring him food, stay for conversation, or whatever passed for conversation when Ross was in this state. But she would never share much, if anything, of what they talked about.

Eventually, he would reappear at the dining hall, skinny, harrowed, pale, but seeming to have conquered his latest bout of whatever afflicted him. Ross didn't have an exact name for what it was—he'd never cared enough to learn whatever the latest jargon was for a black mood—but he was sure they'd used to have medications to speed up the process. Just not on this world.

Malcolm watched Ross's mood shift with sad familiarity but no ability to counteract it, wondering what, if anything, had spurred it. Then Ross spoke, and he understood.

"Notice what's missing here?" the mammalogist said.

Malcolm sighed.

Ross gazed across the savanna, watched by antelopes and gazelles newly wary of the men who made loud banging noises and brought the smell of blood to the grassland. "Primates," he said. "No baboons. No patas monkeys. No *Chlorocebus*."

Yes, Malcolm had noticed. Noticed, and expected to see what he'd in fact seen. Of course there were few—or no—monkeys, just as there were no humans here. This was the thieves' world now, primates were their preferred host, and the primates here hadn't had access to a vaccine.

"It's tainted," Ross said. "It's all tainted."

Malcolm gestured at the jackal-dog the scientist was carrying. "Well, doesn't that just leave room for all those evolving species you were going on about?"

But Ross wasn't listening. When he was in this mood, he never heard a word outside the confines of his own brain.

SOMEONE HAD DISCOVERED a thief colony a kilometer or so down the beach from the bay where the ship was moored. A far bigger colony than any they'd seen in at least fifteen years around Refugia, a spread of sandy mounds covering at least thirty square meters that must have contained hundreds of wasps.

Malcolm didn't have to be there to know what had happened when the vaccinated crew approached the colony. The wasps had risen in the twisting cloud, the whirlwind, that demonstrated their alarm, then fled down their burrows. By the time he reached the site, there were none to be seen.

But their bitter, acidic smell lingered, of course. Even now, even after so much time, it still had the power to turn Malcolm's stomach.

The thieves were nowhere in sight, but their hosts were, more than a dozen of them sleeping away the "dreaming days" phase of their inevitable doom. No primates—Malcolm guessed the last baboon or patas monkey had vanished from Kissama within a year or two of the wasps' arrival—but of course primates weren't the only mammals acceptable as hosts.

The ones here, assembled in a flat grassy area encircled by the thieves' mounds and surrounded by the bleached bones of earlier hosts, included a couple of hares and other small animals. But the group was mostly made up of a kind of large, ugly rat Malcolm had never seen before, bigger and bulkier than the brown rats that still plagued Refugia and successfully survived on the *Trey Gilliard*, despite all efforts to eradicate them.

Malcolm, Shapiro, and the twins, coming to stand beside him, took in the scene. There wasn't anything to say, so for once no one—not even Shapiro—said anything. Ross had been right: However beautiful Kissama was, however heartening the returning of its plains game, its predators, it was tainted. The earth was tainted, and would be as long as the thieves dominated it.

After a few moments, Malcolm broke the silence. "Let's load up," he said, "and get out of here."

But then he turned, saw what Ross was doing, and knew that departing wasn't on the agenda. Not yet, at least.

ROSS HAD LEFT the antelope and his scientific specimen somewhere. Now he was walking up toward them—and the thief colony—carrying an armload of grass. Incongruously, he'd switched the rifle slung over his back for a roll of fine-meshed mist netting, and in his arms he held a bundle of savanna grass, still half-green. His expression was at its blackest, a mixture of anger and determination.

Malcolm knew better than to try to get in the mammalogist's way. Not in this mood. He'd be wasting his breath.

Shapiro, eternally hopeful or just plain cussed, tried anyway. She never minded wasting her breath.

"Ross, it's useless," she said as he approached. "They'll just come back—"

But he just walked past her as if she hadn't said a word. As they watched, he went to the first mound, squatted beside it, and plugged the mouth of the hole with a twist of grass. Straightening, he went to the next one and began to repeat the process.

It was Brett and Darby Callahan who, after exchanging glances, stepped forward to help him. Ross didn't acknowledge their presence, but he let them take some of the grass. Soon all three of them were methodically plugging the openings into each mound.

"Shit," Malcolm said, and went to join them. Soon a dozen crew members were engaged in the same behavior, even Shapiro, muttering about what a useless waste of energy it all was.

Eventually, all of the openings were plugged. All but one, the colony's emergency escape hatch, which was set far from the rest, at the base of a tree fifty meters from the main colony. This was the thieves' last resort in case of attack, a huge expenditure of energy to excavate but part of every large colony.

Ross didn't plug this escape hole. Instead, he positioned the netting over it, hooking it over the tree's branches so it formed a kind of cage around the opening. Then he weighted the edges down with stones, checked the mesh for tears and weak spots, then turned away, his expression now expectant.

By now, everyone knew what his intentions were. So it was with a gesture of respect—and an understanding of his mental state—that Darby handed him a lit torch and let him do what came next.

Head down, but walking with a steady stride, Ross

moved among the thieves' mounds, lighting the plugs of grass in each hole. Because the grasses were still partly green, they didn't flare up and burn out, but smoldered and smoked. Exactly as Ross wanted.

He did not ignite every plug. There was no need to. All the burrows were connected underground. Fill one with enough smoke, and you filled them all.

When he was done, he walked back to the escape hole and checked the net one more time. Silently the rest of them gathered around him, and watched, and waited.

Waited ten minutes, maybe fifteen, before wisps of smoke began to come out of the hole, flickering gray tongues passing through the mesh and dispersing in the breeze. No one said a word, but Malcolm could sense a sharpening of attention run through the group. He felt it himself.

The first thief emerged—a frantic blur of crimson wings—about five minutes later, zooming up through the smoke to the apex of the net, where it clung to the mesh. This first one, then two more, then three, and, finally, a deluge.

Dozens, hundreds, until the inside of the net was a crawling, shifting mass of black bodies and green eyes and flickering wings. The deluge slackening, then ending with a few last wasps, nearly overcome, unable to do more than crawl from the mouth of the hole and collapse on the ground.

When it was certain that no thief could have survived in the burrows, Ross gathered an armload of dry grasses. Pulling up one corner of the net, he shoved it underneath. Malcolm thought it was a measure of the thieves' fear of vaccinated humans—or of their inability to change their behavior even in the face of disaster—that even now they gave Ross a wide berth.

Malcolm knew that he should step in. But mist nets, perfect for catching bugs or bats but too fragile for fishing, were something they had an abundant supply of and little use for. So he let the inevitable unfold, even if it meant sacrificing something they should probably have kept.

Plus, by now he wanted the same thing that Ross did. Dead thieves. It had been a long time.

Ross lit the grass pile. This one flared up right away, yellow-orange flames licking upward to where the thieves were massed. And now the process was reversed: First one, then a few, then more and more, let go of the netting and fell into the flames. As their exoskeletons burned, they emitted a crackling sound, but soon every part of them had been turned to ash. The fire even consumed their smell.

By the time the flames shriveled the net, every last thief in the colony was dead.

BUT ROSS WASN'T done. From the start, Malcolm had known how this would end. So this time it was he who made the offering, holding out the knife he carried in his waistband.

Ross looked down at its three-inch blade, then raised his eyes and met Malcolm's gaze. He gave a little nod, his mood already seeming lighter.

Still without speaking, he turned and walked over to

the breeding area where the hares and other animals slumbered on. They provided no resistance at all as Ross knelt among them, slicing open first one's belly, then the next.

Kneeling amid their bleeding bodies as he carefully cut out one wriggling white thief larva after another, holding each up to the light and watching as it died.

This time no one helped. He wouldn't have wanted help.

Only when every host animal and every larva was dead did he stand again and face his silent audience, the knife dangling loosely from his hand. His pants and arms were soaked in blood, and he'd left smears across his right cheek.

He was smiling, himself again, as his eyes sought out Malcolm. "Permission to bathe before boarding, Captain," he said.

Malcolm looked at him for a long moment, then said, "Er . . . granted."

ELEVEN

Hell's Gate

ALL OF LIFE was a journey. A hejira.

That was one of the first things Aisha Rose learned from Mama: You were always on a journey.

Maybe that was why nothing in her life ever felt permanent to her. Never felt entirely *real*.

Especially for the past decade, when they'd followed the annual migration of the herds of game from their little house in the compound in Naro Moru—set in the foothills of Mount Kenya—to their canyon here in Hell's Gate. A round-trip that made everything else seem transient as well to Aisha Rose.

Everything except Mama. As long as the two of them were together, it didn't matter where they lived, or for how long.

Or at least that's what Aisha Rose had always believed. So, the night after the hyenas visited, when Mama said, "I want to go home," she was surprised by her reaction.

A piercing sense of loss not quite like anything she'd felt before. Loss and understanding, twinned.

"But, Mama—" she said.

But, Mama, it's the wrong season.

She bit back the words. A full moon had risen above the canyon, so she could see the smile on Mama's gaunt, ravaged face. But she would have seen it, seen it inside Mama, even if the night had been a moonless, velvety black.

"Darling," Mama said, something she called Aisha Rose only rarely, "it's time. You know it is."

Aisha Rose was silent, but she did know.

Time. Maybe past time.

AISHA ROSE HAD been expecting this, had known it was coming. So why did it still fill her eyes with tears?

She didn't know why, but it did. Yet she didn't make a sound, or move to brush the tears away. She just turned her head a little so the moonlight wouldn't make them glitter.

After a few moments, she heard the sound of a sigh. "Aisha Rose?"

"What, Mama?"

"I'd like to tell you about your father and me and the dreamed earth."

A story she'd heard a hundred times. A thousand.

"Yes, Mama," she said.

BEFORE THEY'D HAD Aisha Rose, Mama told her, she and Papa had traveled around the world. Every step a journey, and every journey an escape.

"We hated the dreamed earth," Mama told Aisha Rose. "All the noise, all the smoke, all the people looking into your eyes, your head, your life. All the *watching*."

Aisha Rose stayed silent.

"Everywhere we went, we were searching for something else. Some other alternative. Something . . . pure. That was *our* dream. To find a place where we could live away from all the crowds, all the noise." She paused. "The violence."

"Naro Moru?"

"Yes. Our little compound in Naro Moru." Mama laughed. "Well, not that it was *perfectly* pure. But we had our house, our patch of forest, the walls around it to keep people from watching, and your father's work nearby. It was as close to what we were searching for as the dreamed earth could offer."

Growing up, Aisha Rose had known every inch of those walls, that forest.

"So we stopped wandering, and stayed," Mama went on. "And then, about a year later, I learned I was going to have you. I was so excited!"

This was where Mama always skipped ahead. Skipped part of the story, in some ways the most important part. The part about Papa, and how Aisha Rose became what she was. The part that showed why she and Mama would be together forever.

The part that Mama didn't *want* to share with her but did anyway. Memories like broken glass, shards and fragments, sharp enough that they hurt Aisha Rose when she looked at them.

But she had no choice. She had to look. Look inside Mama and see what she'd seen.

MAMA AND PAPA had discovered that Aisha Rose was growing inside her just as the earth was about to awaken from the dream. Yet they didn't know the end was coming. Living behind the compound's walls, with no one watching them, they had forgotten how to be aware, alert. If they'd ever known.

They had no idea what the *majizi*, the thieves, were planning. And by the time they understood, the end was very near.

One day, Papa went out to work and didn't return.

Two days later, when Mama was almost frantic with worry, he came back. He wouldn't talk about what he'd seen, but his eyes were wild, and right away he went to the little room where he kept his guns.

You needed guns to keep yourself pure on the dreamed earth. That's what Papa and Mama had always believed. You needed guns, and you needed to know how to use them.

Papa took his guns and began to leave again. Mama tried to stop him, but he wouldn't let her.

I'll be back soon, he said. And then we'll be safe here. Then we'll wait it out, and afterward, we'll have everything to ourselves. The whole world.

Mama said, just us?

Just the two of us. A nation of two.

A nation of three, Mama said.

But Papa hadn't replied to that. He'd just taken his guns and left again.

And Mama, young and naïve, had believed him, and waited for him to return.

Things happened, that night and the next day. Things that Mama, alone, with no radio, no telephone, no computer, no Papa, could only guess at. She heard screams and explosions and other sounds she couldn't identify. She smelled smoke and saw the sky alight with flames.

It was all nearby, but still outside the walls of the compound. Outside the nation of Mama and Aisha Rose inside her.

Mama kept a gun close at hand, for four days and nights. But no one came, not the one or two friends they'd made in the area, or any strangers.

Until Papa came back on the fifth day.

Or . . . the thing that had once been Papa.

HERE'S WHAT AISHA Rose saw in Mama's memories.

Mama was outside, standing at the back of the house. The sun was low in the sky and hazy with smoke.

Papa came around the corner of the house, half-naked, blood spilling over his chin from his bitten tongue, dripping from his hands, and pouring from deep open gouges above the huge swelling on his belly. He was making a groaning, tearing sound in his throat.

He no longer had his guns, but that didn't matter. He was going to use his hands on Mama, and even though they were bruised and cut and bleeding, his hands were going to be enough.

Even like this, he seemed to know where he was. But did he know who he was? Who Mama was? Aisha Rose always wondered.

But it didn't really matter, whether he knew her or didn't. Papa went straight at her, taking these fast steps across the clearing to where she stood with her back against the wall of the house.

Mama had her gun, her own shotgun, yet she almost didn't raise it in time. She just stood there as Papa got closer and closer, bigger and bigger, and even when she did remember and raise the shotgun, she was too late. Papa was there, so close, reaching for her with his bloody hands.

And then he stopped. Stopped and stared, as if he'd seen something, sensed something, unexpected in her. He stood very still, staring into her face with his blood-rimmed eyes; and then—amazingly, astoundingly—he started to turn away.

And he would have left her alone. Aisha Rose knew this, because she knew how people like him acted, what rules they followed.

He would have left Mama alone because of what she had growing inside of her. Not Aisha Rose. The other thing.

But that didn't make any difference either, what he *would* have done, because as he turned away, the shotgun went off.

Aisha Rose could never tell, not even from Mama's memories, whether she had meant to fire or whether it had been an accident. But that didn't matter either, because on the real earth the gun did go off, its blast sending Papa backward and spraying his blood into the air.

That was the last Aisha Rose saw of Papa, the last thing that Mama's memories shared of him. Because the shotgun's butt jolted back and hit Mama in the stomach, driving all her breath from her body.

After that, the shards of Mama's memories were all about pain and fear. A different kind of fear. Panic, mind-wrenching terror that the blow from the gun might have hurt Aisha Rose.

When she could get her breath back, Mama ran inside. She left the shotgun on the ground, something she never normally would have done. But she was so afraid.

And more than afraid. *Awake.* Newly awake. As if by being struck, she had been woken from a deep sleep.

Mama never understood why, though Aisha Rose did. She did now, and had for a long time.

As Mama ran inside to the bathroom, she pulled off her blouse. And then she stood there, in front of the mirror, staring at her belly. Her belly, already round from Aisha Rose growing inside it, but with another swelling there too. A large one punctuated by a round black hole.

A swelling like the one that Papa had, only smaller.

As Mama looked, there came movement at the round hole. A flash of white. Mama's swollen belly quivered in a sudden spasm.

Then a tiny tide of grayish matter, thicker than water, with flecks of some darker substance in it, spilled out of the hole and dripped down toward Mama's belly button. It was followed by—

The surge of Mama's disgust threatened to overwhelm her. The first time she'd shared this memory, Aisha Rose had vomited.

The little flood of liquid from Mama's belly was followed by a white worm. No, not quite a worm: a waxy white creature with big black eyes, curved black mouthparts, and soft, half-developed legs. And it was not entirely white, not where the grayish liquid flowed from a rupture in its soft midsection.

The rupture caused by the impact from Mama's gun.

The creature wriggled through the hole, but even as it emerged, its movements were weakening, slowing. Only half of its three-inch-long body had appeared when its strength seemed to leave it. It drooped forward, hanging down like a scrap of lost flesh, its mouthparts wiggling feebly. After a moment, it stopped moving at all.

Again Mama's memories shattered. This time the shards were so small that Aisha Rose could never see any of what happened right afterward.

And Mama never shared any of it. "The only thing I remember," she said, and these were words spoken out loud, not memories Aisha Rose had stolen, "was that somehow you were unhurt. My baby girl. Untouched."

She heard that word many times. *Untouched*. And every time, Aisha Rose wondered if Mama had ever suspected the truth.

But Mama never asked, and she never told.

DID MAMA UNDERSTAND what the worm growing inside her had done?

That wasn't clear either. But whether she understood the cause or not, Mama knew what was taking place, and so did Aisha Rose.

So when Mama said, "I want to go home," they both knew what she was saying.

"We'll leave soon," Aisha Rose said.

She heard Mama give a little sound, a cough or a laugh. "I might need some help along the way," she said.

Again Aisha Rose's eyes filled with tears. This time she didn't bother to hide them. "I'm here, Mama," she said.

"I know you are, darling."

TWELVE

THEY LEFT TWO days later, and at first it wasn't so bad. "Just put one foot in front of the other," as Mama had always said about facing a challenging task, "and eventually you'll get there."

But it was a near thing. From the very first step, Mama moved slowly, so much more slowly than she once had. Still, the prospect of returning to Naro Moru seemed to give her new energy. Her eyes seemed to have a light in them they'd been lacking, and even what her ravaged face showed seemed to recall the strong—and headstrong—woman she'd been once.

Using a walking stick Aisha Rose had fashioned for her, she stumped along the switchbacked roads leading up and out of the Great Rift Valley. They even sang together, just as they had on all their previous journeys.

But that was only at the start. Before they'd even

reached the lip of the Rift, Mama needed to rest for hours in the heat of the day. They made real progress only in the chill of dawn and in the last few afternoon hours before the sun set over the valley's far wall. Aisha Rose could have kept going at night, under the light of the stars and a moon waxing toward full, but Mama had to rest. At night, the heaviness of Mama's sleep frightened Aisha Rose.

By then, Mama had stopped even attempting to sing. Nor did she seem to be aware of Aisha Rose's voice, or of any other sight or sound around them. All her attention, all her energy, was devoted to putting one foot in front of the other.

While everything else became Aisha Rose's responsibility. Finding food. Filling their skins with water whenever they found a clear brook or spring. Keeping Mama going for as long as possible before the heat became too great or the evening too dark.

Still, somehow, eventually, days later than they should have, they made it back to Naro Moru. To the compound with its stone walls and patch of forest and its little stream, and the house where Mama had witnessed the end of the dreamed earth and the birth of the real one, where Aisha Rose had been born.

And found not a house but a ruin. A pile of rubble receding into the dream, just as everything human-made eventually did. The past rainy season had been long and unrelenting, and at a certain point it had overwhelmed the house, which had been tottering even before they'd left for Hell's Gate. The tile roof had simply collapsed, bringing down the sodden wooden beams and leaving only crumbling exterior walls standing.

To Aisha Rose, it looked just like all the other ruined houses they'd passed along the way. Just another building subsiding into the earth. Who would have thought that their house, which had stood for so long, would be immune?

It seemed that Mama had. She looked at the house in silence, but there were tears glittering in her eyes, then on her cheeks. Aisha Rose came up beside her, and stood as still and strong as possible as Mama leaned on her. Frail, insubstantial Mama, little more than fragile bones covered by translucent skin.

It was late afternoon. Aisha Rose looked around, at the familiar forest patch, the rushing stream, the huge clouds billowing across the beautiful African sky, and felt tiny, and so lonely. As if Mama, standing right there, were gone already. Blowing away with the clouds.

"Darling?" Mama said, looking away and speaking in such a quiet voice that she might almost have been talking to herself.

Aisha Rose, unsure, waited.

"When I die," Mama went on, "I don't want to be buried. Please don't take the time to bury me."

Aisha Rose didn't say anything. It was one of their moments that she realized the connection went both ways. What the worm had done to Mama, and what together they had done to Aisha Rose. She knew she could see Mama's thoughts—her memories—sometimes, but she often forgot that sometimes Mama could see hers.

She didn't protest, didn't tell Mama not to worry,

didn't say that she was just tired, that she would be fine. On the real earth, you knew what death was and that it couldn't be denied. You saw it everywhere, so you didn't waste time pretending it couldn't happen to you.

Aisha Rose said, "What do you want, Mama?"

"I want to be close to the sky."

Aisha Rose was quiet.

Mama paused. She was looking east, toward Mount Kenya. Though, as almost always, the mountain was shrouded in cloud.

"I want to go there," she said.

THERE. AISHA ROSE knew where she meant: the rose farm.

Aisha Rose had heard about it all her life. Their friends' farm perched on the slopes of the hidden mountain. A place that Mama and Papa went to relax, to be happy, before the dream came to an end.

And now Mama intended it to be the last stop on her final hejira. Aisha Rose knew better than to argue, to tell her that it was a two-day journey even at full strength, to recommend returning instead to Hell's Gate, where the weather was warm and there was always water to drink and food to eat.

She saw Mama's expression and didn't say any of these things. Instead, she just nodded, and got to work making a bed for them with reeds she gathered from beside the stream, picking ripe mangoes from a tree that had survived the rainy season, and not thinking about the journey ahead and where it would end.

*   *   *

THE TREK FROM Hell's Gate had taken them mostly along empty roads half-reclaimed by the brush. Of course, there were occasional signs that people had once lived there—patches of ground along the roadside where huts and shacks had once stood, like long-abandoned graves. The wind blew scraps of rusty metal and plastic whose origins Aisha Rose couldn't even guess at.

But the part of their hejira that took them away from the compound and toward Mount Kenya was different, taking them through what had been a far more densely populated area. They walked along a road whose asphalt, though now shattered by sun and rain and split by wind-bent saplings and creeping vines, still reminded Aisha Rose of the snakelike highways she'd seen in pictures.

Only instead of the gleaming automobiles in the pictures, this road held the bubbled, half-melted, rusty remains of the vehicles that had stopped forever when the dream ended.

Mama told Aisha Rose about them, a part of the dreamed life she hadn't often mentioned before. Matatus were little buses you'd cram yourself into and pikipikis were motorcycles you'd ride on the back of. Both allowed you to just sit and get taken places with no effort at all, Mama said, as if the very idea was a miracle.

To Aisha Rose it was less a miracle than something beyond her imagination. You had to experience being taken places without walking to know what it meant, and she knew she never would.

* * *

AUTOMOBILES MELTING BACK into the earth. Shattered gray asphalt that had once been a highway. The graves of old houses. The last of everything.

And always vultures circling above.

Mama, leaning on Aisha Rose to rest, watched the vultures, and said, "Some people believe that they can guide you to the afterlife."

"Who can?" Aisha Rose said, pointing. *"Them?"*

"Yes." After a moment, Mama laughed. "Who knows if it's true? But I'd like to find out. So, darling, when it's time, I want you to let them take me."

Aisha Rose was quiet.

"Please, Aisha Rose."

"All right."

They went on.

AT FIRST, WHEN they left the desolate, wounded flatlands behind and began climbing into the lush green foothills, it didn't seem like the last stage of a journey. It felt like a blessing, a relief, even a thrilling escape.

And Mama seemed stronger as well, walking with a little more energy and purpose. Knowing that her destination lay close at hand.

They were following grassy trails made, Mama said, by animals. Large antelopes, she said, or even forest elephants or rhinos. "They make roads, just like we do," she said. "Like we did."

The trees and plants were much thicker and greener

than the ones in the forest patch in the compound back home. Bent, ancient-looking trees whose branches were hung heavy with spiky plants that seemed to live on air. Glossy shrubs with broad shiny leaves slick from the moisture, the clouds that wafted through turning everything a milky gray-green. Soft moss that sprang back under Aisha Rose's feet and made her want to lie down on it and sleep.

They didn't see any elephants, but smaller creatures were everywhere: bushy-haired squirrels and little gray-brown antelopes that dashed across the path in front of them, even a little golden cat with gemlike eyes that paused beside the path to stare at them as they rested. As Mama rested.

And the birds were like candy, like fruit. Big green ones that ran along tree branches like lizards and let loose with wild lunatic cries. ("Turacos," Mama declared, smiling.) Parrots that came screeching out of the mist and went screeching back into it. An eagle that rose above them and disappeared into the mist.

And vultures, too.

AT THE END of their second day of climbing, they reached a flatter, much more open stretch. Not quite level land, but a gentler slope that had been turned into terraces. These had once been fields here, split by a stream tumbling downhill.

Mama's face was alight with emotions that were so vivid, so naked, that they frightened Aisha Rose. "This is it," she said, breathless. "Their house is right up there on that knoll."

"Mama . . ." Aisha Rose said.

But Mama was already well ahead, and Aisha Rose's voice was carried away by the wind.

MORE OF THE house—the grandest Aisha Rose had ever seen—was intact than any other they'd passed along the way. It had been built of stone, great sheets of yellow-white stone quarried from somewhere on this enormous mountain, so even though the rain and the mist and wind had done their work, much of it still stood intact. The red-slate roof covered the interior walls, and now glassless windows showed where you could have sat inside, looking out over the fields and valleys.

To Aisha Rose, seeing a house so well preserved was a little miracle. She wanted at once to go inside and explore, to imagine what it would be like to live in such a palace.

Yet, looking at it, Mama radiated sadness. As they stood there, all the energy seemed to go out of her, and she turned her back on the house, sitting on the remnants of a low brick wall that had once bordered a stone patio.

"We used to have drinks here," she said, her voice small and breathless. "We'd watch Naomi and Rick's boys, and we would talk about—"

But then she stopped. After a few moments, Aisha Rose said, "Where are they?"

Mama looked at her. There were tears in her eyes.

"The roses," Aisha Rose said. "Didn't you say that's

what they grew here? I know what they look like. Where are they?"

Mama blinked. Her gaze shifted past Aisha Rose. "They had big greenhouses there," she said, pointing. "But they're gone."

Aisha Rose looked. Perhaps there were still a few signs that there had once been buildings there. Perhaps.

"Mama?" she said.

"Yes?" A breath.

"Was I named after the flowers here?"

She knew the answer, had heard it often. But she wanted to hear it one more time.

"Yes." Mama smiled at her, a ghost of the big smile of Aisha Rose's memory. "The purple-red ones that were my favorite."

THE REST OF the day was awful. Especially as midday turned to late afternoon and the sun dipped behind the huddled clouds, and the air grew very cold.

Even while resting, even while sitting still, Mama could barely breathe. "I'm fine," she said, but already Aisha Rose could feel her slipping away. Her light dimming.

She had no appetite, and she knew Mama didn't either, but she went out searching for food anyway. She didn't know what else to do.

But it was nearly useless. She threw stones at a couple of perched pigeons and a hawk, but she, too, was chilled and tired and a little dizzy from the altitude, and she succeeded only in chasing them away.

In the end, she found only some red berries growing wild. She gave them all to Mama, saying—lying—that she'd eaten some herself while gathering them. But Mama, slipping away, just smiled and thanked her and put the berries carefully down beside her.

THEY SPENT THE night inside the ruins of the house, sheltered a little from the wind and gusts of cold rain by the crumbling walls. Aisha Rose built a small fire from wood she gathered from an old tree fall, but it was damp, spitting and hissing and casting only a little heat.

In Aisha Rose's arms, Mama shivered her way through the long hours, only falling into a harrowed sleep as dawn approached. Aisha Rose, who hadn't slept at all, rose as soon as Mama was asleep, built up the fire as best she could, then went to explore the ruins. She was looking for something to eat, something that maybe she could tempt Mama with. Maybe some birds' eggs she could cook, or some meat she could catch.

Something to postpone what she knew was happening.

But she found no nests, no vulnerable baby animals. She could hear birdsong outside, and she knew that the forests surrounding the old house and fields were full of wildlife, but all of that meat might just as well have been part of the dream.

What Aisha Rose did find was a metal door she hadn't noticed the day before. It was set in a wall that was still standing in the center of the house, the area most protected from the elements, and though rusty and stiff on its hinges, it could still be opened.

Wondering where it led, Aisha Rose pulled on the edge until it swung open far enough to admit her slender, flexible body. The milky early-morning light spilled through the open door to reveal stone stairs leading down into complete darkness. Cool but surprisingly dry, musty air wafted up and past her.

Food, she thought. This is where they kept their food.

She went back, made sure that Mama was still asleep, and dipped the brushy end of a dry branch into the fire. When it was lit, she went back to the door and, carrying her torch, scrambled through.

Her heart pounding, she went slowly down the steps. The rain and wind had never reached here, and as she descended, her hopes soared that she would find a trove. A dry, sheltered place to sleep, and maybe piles of the boxes and cans like the ones Mama had once salvaged from Naro Moru. Food that had made the transit from the dreamed earth.

Aisha Rose had long since learned everything there was to know about disappointment, about not expecting your hopes to be fulfilled. That's what the real earth was about: teaching you that dreams were never realized. Teaching you that same lesson again and again.

But never in her life had she experienced a greater gulf between dream and reality as when she reached the bottom of the stairs, raised her small, flickering torch, and looked around the hidden room.

She could see that there *had* been food here once.

There were cans, dozens of cans scattered around, and boxes and bottles as well, just as she'd hoped.

But they were all empty, any food or drink they'd contained was gone. Gone, Aisha Rose was sure, within days or weeks of the end of the dreamed earth. All that was left in the room now were bare shelves, a corner blocked off for a long-dry toilet and sink, and a wide mattress on metal springs.

And, on top of the mattress, four bodies. Two larger ones, a man and a woman's, and two small ones.

Not skeletons in scattered pieces, disordered by animals and weather and time. Not grinning skulls melting into the soil, as Aisha Rose had seen so many times before. Bodies. Whole bodies, though shriveled and black inside their drooping clothes, the skin on their exposed faces and hands shrunken over the bones beneath.

Aisha Rose knew at once what had happened. What had led to this scene.

The day the dreamed earth came to an end, Mama's friends and their boys had hidden here. Safe from the *majizi* in this windowless room—or safer, at least, than they thought they would be anywhere else.

So they'd stayed here, making this room their whole world. Eating the food they'd been smart enough to store and . . . what?

And waiting. Waiting for a rescue that never came.

Perhaps they'd chosen to starve to death over risking what they feared lay outside. Or maybe something else had killed them—the air or their food. Or maybe they'd taken poison on purpose and *chosen* to die here.

But what did it matter? They belonged to the dream now.

AND, WHEN AISHA Rose returned to the guttering fire, she found that Mama had joined her friends. Her friends and Papa and all the countless others who died when the earth awoke.

The light had vanished from her eyes and from inside Aisha Rose's head as well.

AFTERWARD, AISHA ROSE barely remembered the rest of that day. She knew she carried Mama, insubstantial in her arms, up to a rocky outcropping that overlooked the farmhouse, the fields, and the valley below. She placed Mama there, on her back, looking up at the giant African sky. Then she went back down to the stone wall where Mama had spent her last afternoon and sat there, waiting.

Sitting in silence, not moving, not thinking, for hours. Until late afternoon, when the first of the vultures noticed Mama and came down to the rocks to see what she was.

Then Aisha Rose stood and walked away. Heading back down the mountain. Beginning the next stage of her hejira, the one she knew would soon bring her and Mama back together again.

THIRTEEN

EVERY NIGHT, JUST as the sun fell behind the horizon, beyond the great continent that lay between the slave camp and the Atlantic Ocean beyond, and beyond that North America and Jason's vanished home and murdered family, the thieves rose into the sky in a great cloud.

No, not a cloud: a whirlwind. An enormous dust devil ascending to form an ever-changing black silhouette against the orange or bloodred clouds. Spinning and twisting, seeming to form a single creature that was heart-stopping in its vastness, then suddenly splitting into its component parts, even more terrifying in its overwhelming abundance.

Jason had witnessed it, the whirlwind, for two decades now, and he still wondered what its cause or purpose might be. He had a vague memory that some other creatures possessed by the hive mind—flocking birds, schooling fish—engaged in similar daily rituals, but not why. Perhaps it was an act of bonding, a way for each inconsequential individual ruled by the mind to come together, to act in concert, to refresh and renew their place as a component of the greater whole.

Or maybe it was something much simpler. Maybe the ritual always took place just before dusk so the wasps, which were largely diurnal, could expend unnecessary energy before settling in for the night. One last explosion of activity before they spun down to cluster in great carpets on the cell walls and the bodies of their slaves.

Maybe the whirlwind just helped them sleep better.

But Jason didn't think so. Even though he'd been trained as a scientist, and he knew that the explanation of the thieves' behavior—whatever it was—would likely be the simplest, most scientific one, the one that most closely followed Occam's razor. Find the most obvious explanation, and you'd almost always found the right one.

What the thieves did every night, he believed, was a declaration of strength. He believed that all over the world, thieves took these moments every day to proclaim their dominance over the planet and all that lived on it. They ascended in their great whirlwinds at sunset over slave camps, above the ever-dwindling population of humans and the mushrooming number of born slaves— the next step in hominid evolution—to celebrate their victory.

AND EVERY NIGHT Jason had paused in whatever job he was doing and watched the whirlwind, and felt a spark of the rage he'd felt at the beginning, when he'd first been enslaved, reignite. He'd stopped and watched so it *could* reignite, so he could be reminded that he still had the capacity to experience emotions, human emotions. That he could still become angry. That he still existed.

So every night the thieves ascended in the whirlwind that was their victory dance, and every night Jason watched and felt a surge of human rage that was soon drowned in helplessness. Hopelessness. Twenty years of this, and always the same.

Except . . . not tonight.

Tonight something was different.

CHLOE NOTICED IT, too. Jason, having just disposed of the stiffening corpse of a fox, was standing near the ovens, taking a moment to scan the horizon as he always did, when he saw her come up the stairs and walk across the roof toward him.

This was unusual—early on, they'd discovered that ridden slaves (and even, increasingly, other humans) would always keep them apart if they tried to meet during the day. It had taken a few beatings before the two of them learned that lesson, but since then, they'd rarely challenged it.

Jason would have put up with the beatings if it meant he got to spend more time with Chloe. Ten minutes—two minutes—of conversation could be enough to get him through another day, and if he had to risk his life to gain them, that was a chance he'd take a hundred times out of a hundred.

A risk he'd take for himself . . . but not for her.

And that was the slavemakers' strategy: They terrified you—and kept you in line—by threatening the people you cared most about. And not just with beatings.

Jason had known this about the thieves even before the world came apart. He'd read the literature. But he'd never quite believed it until he'd seen it here in the early days of the camp, when a man—a builder by trade who was helping Jason make the oven—ran away with his two children. He was brought back a day later with a rider, but left conscious, aware, for just long enough to see his children implanted with eggs before his eyes.

Children being least useful to the thieves as anything other than hosts. But most useful as a warning.

Even after all this time, Jason could recall the expression on the man's face. A warning that didn't dull with time.

SO WHAT WAS different about the whirlwind tonight? Why did something about it give him . . . a flicker of hope?

With just a glance at the ridden slave standing nearby—with its rider up in the cloud of thieves above, it was unmoored, still—Chloe came to stand beside him. Her eyes, always expressive, were narrowed, and her lips were pursed, deepening the furrows the sun and age had left on her face but making it clear that a mind and an imagination were at work.

It was amazing how much you came to treasure such simple things as imagination, creativity, even a sense of humor, in a world where they were going extinct.

"Look at them," she said, "their knickers all in a twist."

Jason took a quick glance around. Remarkably, no one seemed to be watching them. No one was coming to pull them apart, to punish them.

He turned to look up at the thieves above. He saw what she meant. The spinning cloud above their heads was tearing apart and re-forming more quickly than usual. Shreds and wisps would break away, then rejoin, but for just an instant, the integrity of the whole would be marred. Only in seeing these tiny flaws in the pattern was Jason reminded of the usual power of the hive mind, the way it could direct a thousand slaves, or a million, with effortless precision.

Even as they watched, the funnel cloud spun more tightly, the deep, almost choirlike humming made by the wings of countless thieves rising just a touch in pitch.

"I think—" Chloe began.

Then she stopped, making a sound that was either a cough or a laugh. Disbelief. Excitement.

A new possibility, one she'd never before considered.

"I do believe," she went on, "that they're nervous."

Jason looked away from the spinning mass, turning his gaze to the darkening channel. As dusk fell, everything to the east—water, sky, mangrove-lined Manda Island beyond, was one or another shade of gray.

Soon full darkness would fall, only the glimmering reflection of starlight revealing the channel's presence, but for now there was still enough light left for Jason to see that his long-dreamed-of rescue force was nowhere in sight. No armada of warships, no hazmat-wearing soldiers wielding flamethrowers. Nothing but the usual calm water, the day's last swallows and night's first bats flickering low over the water.

But . . . even so. Above them, the cloud tore apart, formed once again. The thieves' wings sang their uncharacteristic song. A song of unease, of—

Jason found himself crossing his arms over his chest, as if to keep the emotions he hadn't felt in so long from spilling out. "No. Not nervous," he said, and he knew she heard the exultant edge to his voice. "They're *afraid*."

Chloe was silent. Feeling her gaze on his face, he lowered his eyes and looked at her. Even in the gathering darkness, he could see that she looked far from exultant. Her expression held something different. He wasn't sure what it was.

"While they're not paying attention," she said, "let's go."

He knew at once what she meant. Chloe's defining characteristic: the gambler's mix, the quick calculation of the odds fueled by adrenaline and the irresistible urge to take the risk, the leap, the chance.

"Now," she said.

"GO WHERE?" JASON asked.

She looked disgusted at his lack of comprehension. "My villa."

Then he understood. But that didn't make it any better.

At the beginning, it had been such a tempting possibility that they'd risked beatings to grab every chance to discuss it. To find a way to escape across Lamu to the villa and gardens where Chloe had lived.

The gardens where she'd begun to grow the vine her father had brought her, the vine whose seeds and fruit could protect you from the thieves.

It had seemed like a fantasy to Jason. If such a vaccine had existed, he told her, he would have heard about it. But even though, scornful of her father's belief in the coming apocalypse, she'd never taken the pills he'd given her, she was unshakeable in her faith that they'd work.

But did it matter? No one ran away from the camp without being brought back, and no one was brought back without being punished for the act. Chloe's villa and its gardens might as well have been a thousand miles away instead of two or three, and even back then, Jason hadn't been willing to take the chance.

It had been years since he'd considered the possibility. Clearly, though, it had never left Chloe's mind. Now she was standing there, staring at him, as if itching to take off at the merest word.

"Chloe," Jason said, "there's no way it's still there, the vine."

Her shoulders went up in an angry shrug. "Why not?" she said. "It's a weed, Jase. It was already growing everywhere before—"

She stopped short, but Jason knew the rest of the sentence. *Before I went to the Lamu Café one day to open up early and never went home again.*

"And there's bound to be plenty more dirt for it to grow on now than there was back then," she said. "Cleaner air, too."

Jason was quiet. It still sounded like a fantasy to him.

"The vine will be there. The vaccine," she said. "Imagine, Jase—we'll be able to set ourselves free. All we need to do is go now, and we'll be untouchable."

Even this wasn't precisely true. Human slaves—or slaves in human form—might still pursue them. But, in truth, those ones didn't frighten Jason. They wouldn't be much harder to kill than squashing a single thief, and unlike the slavemakers, there weren't an infinite number of them.

"Jase," Chloe said, and her voice was more urgent, "let's *go*."

But even as she spoke, the whirlwind broke apart one last time, and the mass of thieves came streaming back down to earth. Whatever had frightened them had released its hold, and in that instant their behavior was back to what it had always been.

The rider reassumed its place on the ridden slave nearest to where they stood and inserted its stinger back into the slave's neck. Before Jason could take more than a few steps, he found himself falling to the ground under a deluge of blows, rolling into a ball and covering his face with his arms, as he'd done so often before while being beaten.

Not fighting back, no matter how much he wanted to.

Especially after hearing Chloe give an angry cry as her own arms were grabbed and twisted behind her. Jason got a glimpse of who was holding her, pulling her away from him, and saw that it was a human slave. A human man, yet acting no differently than a ridden one or a born slave would have.

Kenneth. That had been his name. *Kenny.*

Or that would have been his name if he'd still deserved to have one. To possess a human name, and therefore be considered human. But he'd given up that right when he'd become the thieves' enforcer. When he'd learned the same lesson that he and Chloe had, that by making yourself useful to the thieves, you could stay alive. Alive, unridden, uninfected.

But you had to be strong, and have a way to use your strength. At six-two and at least two hundred pounds, Kenny, who'd been a longshoreman in the vanished world, was extraordinarily strong. And, along with a handful of other men who'd quickly cottoned to his plan, willing to employ his strength to a different purpose.

More than willing, joyful. To become a joyful slave.

Jason felt his rage ignite once again, more fiercely than ever. Like the coals in the oven, that was an emotion whose embers might stay banked, but would never be extinguished. Yet still he restrained himself.

LATE THAT NIGHT, in the dank, stinking chamber where they slept, he and Chloe lay in each other's arms. Cradling each other carefully, aware of the new bruises they each sported, but not willing to forgo physical contact.

She didn't seem angry with him for having hesitated, and even though they didn't have the chance to talk about it, he thought she understood what he did: Their window of opportunity had been too small. They would have died trying to escape.

This time. But even now, the thieves' behavior was

subtly different. There were as many as ever in the chamber, taking advantage of their captives' body heat, but they seemed concentrated at the tops of the walls and the peak of the room's ceiling. As far from the slaves below as they could get.

Chloe shifted in his arms, bringing her lips close to his ears. "Still afraid," she murmured, just a breath, and he knew she was smiling.

"Yes," he said, as quietly.

Still afraid.

But of what?

FOURTEEN

AISHA ROSE STOOD in the ruined shantytown in Nairobi and thought, *Now I understand.*

Mama had shown her pictures of so many places on the dreamed earth, so many cities, but none of Nairobi. "I hated it there," she'd said in explanation. "So much dirt and noise and . . . anger. There were terrorist attacks, people shooting other people or blowing them up with bombs, and for what?"

She'd paused, and for a moment her eyes had become hazy. "I can hardly remember why."

Then she'd come back to the present. "And the shantytowns!" she'd said.

When she first heard that word—shantytowns—Aisha Rose liked the sound of it. It was cheerful: "Shanty!" But what would a shantytown look like? The pictures of big cities in books showed only giant skyscrapers, smooth roads like twisting snakes, and masses of people in colorful clothes flooding this way and that.

Aisha Rose was most fascinated by the people. The shirts they wore, the long dresses that flowed like waves around their legs. And their shoes, with toes so pointy and heels so tall that they made Aisha Rose laugh. Just imagine trying to outrun a cheetah in those, she thought. You couldn't even outrun a warthog.

And the people themselves! The men and women under the clothes. They were so strange and fascinating.

The strangest things was that their complexions, like their clothes, were all different colors, all different shades of brown and tan and pale white and almost yellow. If she hadn't seen the pictures, Aisha Rose would never have guessed that men and women on the dreamed earth came in so many different colors and shapes and sizes.

On this earth, the real one, Aisha Rose had only seen one person. One living person: Mama.

Until now.

SHE'D BEEN WALKING through the ruins for hours. She could see that it had once been mile upon mile of sad, hopeless houses and stores built from wooden planks and sheets of metal and hardened mud.

Aisha Rose tried to imagine what it must have been like back on the dreamed earth. During the dry season, with the sun assaulting the metal roofs. And during the long rains, when people's huts must have been washed away and every path became a sticky, stinking mess.

Today, she had to pick her way over a rubble of crumbled brick and the last fragments of rotten wood and the rusted metal sheets that she had to be careful not to cut herself on. ("You'll get lockjaw!" Mama had warned her.) And plastic, reduced to fragments and blown by the wind, accumulating in the spaces around the rubble piles. So much plastic that Aisha Rose wondered what people could possibly have needed with it all.

The shantytown was far bigger than she'd imagined, and empty. At least she didn't see many bones. After nearly twenty years, most of them had already returned to the earth. And if some were hidden away, under the crumpled metal or crumbled stone . . . well, she had no desire to go looking for them.

But they had lived here once, the humans. How many, though? How many had lived inside the vanished tumbledown shacks under the sheet-metal roofs? Aisha Rose couldn't even guess.

"Knock a hole in an ant mound," Mama had said. "A big hole. How many white ants will come spilling out?"

Aisha Rose had no idea. She'd knocked her share of holes in ant mounds, of course. Simply to watch the ants, with their naked white bodies and twitching black jaws, swarm out of the hole, looking for something to bite.

She knew it was a lot, though. Too many to count. And that was the point.

"As many white ants as there are in a mound, that's how many people lived in the shantytowns of Nairobi," Mama said. "And not just Nairobi. Many cities had them. Or slums. Miserable places to live. You'd be in this city with tall apartment buildings, expensive stores, fancy restaurants—"

"Like in the pictures," Aisha Rose said.

"Yes, just like that. But just a stone's throw away, people lived with no electricity, no working plumbing, rats in the walls."

Just like they'd had—and didn't have—since the end of the dreamed earth, Aisha Rose pointed out. In Naro Moru and in Hell's Gate, the only running water came from streams.

"That's true," Mama acknowledged. "But it was different then because you could see the way other people lived. You could see what they possessed, and know that you could never have it for yourself."

Aisha Rose could understand that. She had felt echoes of those feelings, that envy, that desire, just by looking at the pictures. What must it have been like to witness them for real, to be living close to the dream but not be part of it?

"People were sick at heart," Mama said. "No: sick in their souls."

"In the shantytowns?"

"Everywhere."

AISHA ROSE COULDN'T imagine what a Nairobi filled with an ant mound of people had sounded like. But the real Nairobi was quiet. When she held her breath, she could hear only the sound of the wind worrying the ruins, the whispery sound of the plastic, the distant call of a crow.

Oh . . . and the panting of the terrified creature

hiding behind a tall, tottering pile of rubble opposite the spot where she stood.

The creature she'd come all this way to find.

THE CREATURE: THE second human Aisha Rose had ever seen.

More accurately, had *almost* seen, because she'd caught only a quick blur of movement as she'd come around a towering pile of bricks and fractured glass and rotted wood. But she knew it was there, and not only because it couldn't control its panicky breathing.

She'd always known, before she'd even left Mama behind. It, or at least the dim light it had cast—a light like Mama's had been, not far from the end—was the reason she'd come to this sad, endless, lifeless place.

And now she was waiting, knowing how much of a shock her appearance here must be. Waiting for it to calm down, to show itself.

But the creature's breath was now coming in little gasps that sounded more like cries of anger.

Aisha Rose very rarely experienced fear, but she felt the hairs on her arms and back of her neck prickle. Her heart thudded against her rib cage.

The fear telling her to turn away. To leave. To retreat, and once out of sight, to run as fast as the sharp metal edges and piles of crumbled rock would let her.

To understand that this trip, this mission, had been misconceived from the start.

But she couldn't. After all this time, all this time alone, Aisha Rose had to do what she did next.

She had to see it. The thing that cast the light.

*   *   *

THE BOY STOOD at the foot of the colossal ruined bridge that had once spanned the churning river.

When he had last come here, years earlier, the bridge had still been intact. Now its ends still stood, one towering over him, rusted metal and chunks of stone, the other sprouting from the far shore. But in the middle the spans dipped toward and into the river's surge, forming sharp angles like the bent wings of an enormous, skeletal bird.

Back then, the boy had thought about crossing the bridge. But he hadn't. What would be the point? He could see the opposite shore, and it looked just like the one he stood on. The same wounded land, the same stone and steel, undoubtedly the same hulks of cars and bones and other bits and pieces of the past. He had no interest in those.

As far as the boy knew, the whole world was made up of wounded land. Whatever the world was, however big it was—and he had no idea—he thought it would all look the same. Except for his precious patch, the green lands.

So he'd turned his back on the bridge and retreated to his home. He had no need to go anywhere else. There was food and shelter, enough to live on, and as the years passed, he didn't even think about the world outside. Years without ever dreaming of returning, of seeing what lay beyond.

Until he learned about her. Until she revealed herself to him.

That had brought him back here, only to find that this route had been taken away from him. The river wasn't so wide here, but the other shore might as well have been as distant as the stars. He had no way to cross the swirling water.

And even if he'd been able to, what then? She could be anywhere. It had been a stupid idea, coming here.

The boy wasn't used to having stupid ideas, then wasting his time on them.

Being alone was dangerous.

No. He'd been alone his whole life and done just fine.

It was *knowing* you were alone that was dangerous.

AISHA ROSE TOOK a step forward, another. Then she opened her mouth and tried to speak, but her throat felt half-closed. She was suddenly afraid in a new way: afraid to make a sound.

Still, somehow she choked out the words. The beginning of her nightly ritual: "My name is—"

But that was as far as she got. At the sound of her voice, harsh in the silence of the dead city, the other, the creature, finally revealed itself to her.

Aisha Rose had thought she was ready. But when it came bursting out from behind the rubble, it was so much faster, so much more agile, than she expected. More like a sandgrouse or a guinea fowl flushed from the tall savanna grass than any mammal she'd seen. But, unlike those birds, it did not vault upward toward the skies, to safety, but came straight for her. Like a hunter, an ambush predator.

This must be what the prey animal sees, right at the last instant, Aisha Rose thought.

She had time to take a single step back. Then her heel caught on something, and she fell, barely getting her hands behind her to break the impact. She felt a jolt in her right shoulder, a muscle wrenching somewhere deep inside. And a hotter, more intense pain on her left palm, where something sharp had cut her.

In her fall, Aisha Rose had dropped her barricades, the walls that protected her. Overwhelmed by the creature's fear and anger, she lay there, stunned and infinitely vulnerable as it crouched beside her, its face in deep shadow. She could see only its wide-stretched eyes, yellow-white in a dark, wizened face that was still, barely, human.

Human but far beyond her reach. An open hole of a mouth containing crumbled yellow teeth. Hands like talons clutching at her.

Forcing herself into movement, she began to scramble away. But with a strange, disoriented spasm of its right arm, the creature hit her in the face, so hard that she went down flat again, bruising the back of her head. Sparks seemed to fly in front of her eyes, like the embers rising and spinning upward from a brush fire, and her thoughts became vague and disorganized.

The creature came for her again and, without thinking, her barricades still down, she did the only thing left to her to do. She reached out to it, just as she had done with the other one, the one who was like her, and just as she had done so often with Mama.

And saw inside it: a maelstrom. Nothing coherent. Just . . . a torrent of anger and fear and hatred.

The creature rocked back on its heels and gave a hoarse cry. And then it was on its feet. Running, crablike, but fast, so fast. As if to escape her intrusion. As if a little distance could protect it.

Then it was out of sight, its footsteps echoing, dwindling. But before it was beyond the range of her hearing, she heard it give a cry, its final one, an ascending shriek that again raised the hair on the back of her neck.

And, once again, she was alone in the abandoned city.

THE BOY STOOD still. He would never see her . . . but he could still bring her close. The walls she'd erected to keep him out would crumble in an instant.

But he might harm her. He knew that. He had to be so careful.

With ultimate caution, he reached out to her. And was shocked to find that her defenses were already down, exposing what she was feeling.

Fear. Not of him, but of something else.

And pain.

At first, he didn't know what was causing it, but he knew she was dangling on the edge, helpless against something that might be about to end her.

Then he could see the thing that was threatening her. And anything he could see he could end.

Shifting his attention in an instant, he ended its life. That thing that had been threatening her.

It was as easy as a thought.

* * *

AT FIRST THE realization of what he'd done, his gift to her, filled him with warmth. Perhaps she would recognize it and leave her barricades down. Show him another lion, or maybe even show him her face.

But minutes passed, and she did not acknowledge him. And then he saw her walls go up again, the ones meant to keep him out. His loneliness came flooding back over him, and along with it his anger.

He raised his hands to cover his face. Wishing she'd never known he was there. Wishing he'd never known she'd existed.

Wishing most of all that his mind would go back to what it had been. When all that occupied it was what he saw in front of him: the wounded lands, the green. The world he lived in.

Not this other, this other like him, this other who was out there somewhere, reaching out to him, hiding from him. Reminding him every moment that he was alone.

There was only one solution.

Realizing this, he felt his heart unknot. It would be so easy, ending her. As easy as it had been with the other thing, as easy as it was when he played his game.

It wouldn't take more than an instant.

THE BACK OF Aisha Rose's head hurt. Her shoulder, too. And the nasty cut on her hand, a broad slash across her palm filled with particles of stone and dirt, hurt worst of all.

Still, she thought she'd cut it on rock, not the metal edge of something. Which meant she probably wouldn't die of lockjaw.

Of course, as Mama had warned her often enough, she could die just as easily from infection. Infection was something Aisha Rose had seen in animals. The swellings, the smell when they burst, the maggots writhing in the dripping flesh.

"You need to find clean, running water to wash that out," Mama would have told her. "And make a paste of the sumeito plant and cover the cuts with it."

Mama had shown her this plant, the sumeito, a pretty flowering vine that had grown on the crumbling walls of the compound in Naro Moru. But Aisha Rose knew she wouldn't find it here, not in the shantytown or anywhere in this blasted city where—even after all these years—not much grew.

She knew she'd be able to find it outside the city. Clean water, too. If she got to them in time.

But before she could take more than a couple of steps, she stopped and stood still. Around her, inside her, the world suddenly seemed crystalline. Fragile.

And beyond the crystal clarity, a wave. A wave building, gathering force and power.

Aisha Rose waited. There was nowhere she could hide, nothing to do but wait, as the wave's strength grew. A darkness that obliterated the stars and constellations and towered over her. All she could do was stay still, stare up at it, and wait for it to sweep her away.

But then, just as it curled toward her, a gigantic hand coming to flatten her, to flick her away, the wave swept past her. In an instant, the city, the shantytown, went back to looking as they once had. And Aisha Rose was alone once again.

AISHA ROSE WATCHED the progress of the wave. Watched in amazement, in awe, marveling at its breadth and power.

And at that moment she began to understand the purpose of her hejira.

What it meant, and where it had to end.

HE'D STOPPED JUST in time.

He'd wanted to finish it. Wanted so badly to go back to what he'd once been. But at the last instant, he understood something: that even ending her wouldn't allow him to unremember her. No matter what, she would be there, inside him, all the rest of his life.

Anger and frustration rose in him then.

But at least he could still play the game. The game he'd been playing ever since he could remember.

Taking in a deep breath, he closed his eyes. Each time he played, he had to reach out farther, but that was never a problem. There was no place beyond his reach. No ruined bridge could stop him, no river, not when he traveled this way.

Soon enough, he found the nearest one. *There*. There it was. And soon, just beyond it, more. So many more. More every year, despite him, despite the game.

And he was suddenly everywhere among them. Between them.

They knew it. They were aware. Alarmed.

Afraid.

He had felt their fear many times before. He knew how the game would end, how it always ended, and so did they.

Only this time, he wanted more.

So he did it differently. He didn't end them where they stood, where they flew. Instead, he summoned them. Called them to him.

Stood in his spot by the river and filled their mind, and the spaces between, with his command, until he knew that they were helpless to do anything but obey, to flow toward him in a vast tide.

That's what they always did, obey. Follow. It was what they'd been designed to do.

He stood still for hours, until just before the sun set over the wounded lands behind him. Until the air was filled with the sound of their wings, and he opened his eyes to witness the whirlwind above him. Swirling there like fog, some already pattering to the ground around him in exhaustion, the rest tied together, yoked to his command, unable to escape.

He could have ended them all this way, by doing nothing else but waiting a little while. But he was bored of waiting. So, with a single stroke, he disposed of the desperate whirlwind then and there.

As he walked home, their bodies crunched under his feet, and their odor rose and wreathed around him, as thick in his nostrils as smoke.

FIFTEEN

EVEN AFTER ALL these years, most Fugians still weren't very easy in Mariama's company. They tended to give her a wide berth, to end conversations abruptly, to discover something else they needed to do when they saw her coming. Though no one was outright rude, she could tell they thought her strange, unpredictable, and possibly even a little dangerous.

She wasn't offended. Because they were right: She *was* all those things. Strange and unpredictable. And more than a little dangerous.

It was who she was. Who she'd been since childhood, growing up here in the Casamance. The region in southern Senegal that had been the site of a decades-long insurgency against the government in far-off Dakar.

The insurgency had been about many things, but—like most such conflicts before the Fall—the focus had been religion. The Muslim north battling the Christian and animist south.

And, like most such low-simmering revolutions, there had been no real end to the struggle. It had gone on and on, until the thieves demonstrated the meaninglessness of such conflicts, solving them far more decisively than humans ever could.

So Mariama had been raised in a world where snipers could shoot you from a thousand yards away, killing you before you even knew you were a target. Where your after-school activities could include laying snares in the rain forest or clearing mines planted by the soldiers from the north. And (as if that wasn't enough) where, long before the rest of the world had any idea the thieves existed, you had to live side by side with them.

A mine had taken the life of her father Seydou's older brother. Thieves had killed two of her young cousins. The insurgency itself had claimed several of her friends. And she'd witnessed more than her share of the deaths of people she would never know or care about.

Witnessed and caused.

If this all made her someone to be avoided if possible, so what? Her job in Refugia wasn't to make friends. It was to keep everyone, all those naïve, willful, idealistic people who'd gathered here to make a new world, alive long enough to see the world they hoped to create.

Idealism was a good thing, she supposed—though, in truth, she thought the greatest murderers in history had often been its greatest idealists—but it was useless if you perished in its pursuit. You needed someone around who was a realist. Someone who understood that survival required strength and the willingness to deal in death.

Was that a paradox? Maybe. Mariama didn't know.

Or care.

THE WILLINGNESS TO deal in death.

When Refugia was being built and populated during the final tumultuous months of the Last World, this had been its creators' greatest failing: neglecting to recruit a sufficient number of soldiers. Inviting so many architects and doctors and farmers but hardly anyone equipped to protect them.

Only a handful of Fugians were good with weapons. And even fewer—Mariama, Malcolm, and a couple of others—had ever used them in real life.

That was an important distinction. With enough practice, anyone could become a good shot on the firing range, or master in-close knife work, even learn the methods of killing with their hands. But pulling the trigger or wielding the blade when your target was a living human was something else entirely.

Though not to Mariama, and everyone in Refugia knew it. To her, they were all the same thing.

Strange? Dangerous?

Sure. You were who you needed to be, and did what you had to do, to keep your people safe.

MARIAMA DID HAVE close friends in Refugia, mostly those who'd witnessed the Fall with her. Or in the past she'd had them. But by now Trey was dead, and Malcolm had gone off on his great foolhardy voyage, taking Kait with him. That pretty much left only Sheila, and Sheila, as one of the colony's few remaining doctors, was almost always busy. (People didn't die from disease in Refugia too often these days—not, at least, compared to the early years—but they still got sick a lot.)

So Mariama was on her own most of the time. Which was fine, because she had plenty to do.

Plenty: making sure Refugia's walls—which she and Malcolm had insisted on building—weren't falling prey to the destruction that the rain forest's humidity and countless termites wreaked on all wood. Checking on the watch she kept stationed day and night in the towers at the corner of each wall. Making sure the wooden hides she'd built in several forest trees, and that the caches of food and weapons she'd left in each one, remained in good shape.

And patrolling a large area around the colony, a perimeter only she could see, much less care about.

"What are you looking for?" Sheila asked, one of the few times she'd joined Mariama on one of her restless treks through the forest.

Mariama could have come up with an answer. It would have been easy to say, for instance, that she wanted to locate and destroy any new colonies the thieves were attempting to establish. Because they did still try, every so often.

But instead she just shrugged off the question and waited for Sheila to ask the right one.

Which Sheila eventually did, one day as they stood

on the beach. The two of them were standing side by side, staring out at the distant stripe of horizon, as if expecting to see the familiar shape of the *Trey Gilliard* reappear there at any moment. Even though they both knew that would not happen for months or years, if ever.

"Mariama," Sheila said, "what are you afraid of?"

That was the right question.

Though Mariama herself was at a loss to answer it.

SIXTEEN

"COME INSIDE," CLARE Shapiro called from the open hatch.

Kait barely turned her head in response. Huddled against the cold, walking the deck alone, she'd been watching the ocean world swirling all around her, a mesmerizing kaleidoscope of silver foam and surging blue-green waves and deep blue skies and dark, long-winged birds. Birds everywhere, albatrosses and storm petrels and ones she didn't recognize, hovering just over the churning water or wheeling above the *Trey Gilliard* as it plowed through the waves.

The ship at the southernmost point of its journey, going around Cape Horn before turning north and heading up the east coast of Africa.

Not that land was anywhere in view. A three-day storm had driven the ship far to the south, easing only about twelve hours ago so they could get back on course. That was why Kait was out on deck, despite the cold—it had been either that or go insane from claustrophobia in her tiny cabin.

Claustrophobia and anticipation of what she knew she had to do. No, not anticipation: fear. After all this time, she discovered something she hadn't expected: She was afraid.

But as long as she stayed on deck, she didn't have to think about it. She hardly had to think at all.

SEASICKNESS HAD BEEN a problem from day one of their journey, something Malcolm and Dylan Connell had anticipated with a crew made up entirely of landlubbers. Even many of those who had thrived during the journey's early days succumbed during the storm. Some were so wretched that they were no help at all at a time when the old phrase "all hands on deck" finally regained its original meaning.

It turned out, though, that Kait was immune to seasickness. So for three days and nights, as the ship rose on one towering wave after another and came sliding down into the troughs with an impact that seemed to foretell a final, fatal splitting into pieces—a disaster that somehow Malcolm averted, time and again—she and just a few others were everywhere. Doing everything.

Doing whatever Malcolm commanded them to do ("You effing whackas!"), whether it was lashing down supplies, raising and lowering the sails in accordance with his almost mystical understanding of the wind and the waves, even going out in the middle of the night to help repair a spar that had splintered, as a cold, violet-blue fire sprouted from the masts overhead.

But now, at last, the seas had begun to settle. A little. Enough that the ship, accompanied by its coterie of seabirds, could ride the long swells and start making up the miles it had gone off course.

And enough time for Kait to think about what she had to do, and to be afraid.

EVERY DAY, SEVERAL times a day, she checked. And every time she was sure she'd waited too long, that her fear— her cowardice—had kept her from taking the step she'd been planning for years. Ever since she learned what had happened to Trey.

And every day she found that it was still possible. Was that relief or disappointment she felt? She didn't know.

"KAITLIN!"

This time Kait looked back. Shapiro was standing in the hatch, a tall, gaunt figure, arms akimbo. With her stiff posture and arrow-sharp bone structure, she reminded Kait of one of the albatrosses rising and swooping behind her.

Regardless of how much everyone suffered from Clare Shapiro's uncompromising tongue and dictatorial ways, they knew what they owed her. She too had proven unstoppable during the storm, and alongside Fatou Konte had ministered to those who hadn't been. The potion that resulted from their joint efforts—a mix of ginger, acacia, and decoctions from the bark and roots of the bakoro m'pegu, samenere, and other Senegalese trees—hadn't proven a panacea. But it had been effective enough to keep a skeleton crew at work.

"She sure as hell knows what she's doing," Kait had overheard someone say on leaving Shapiro and Fatou's laboratory/sick bay/dispensary. "Too bad she's such a witch."

"What was that last word?" someone else had asked.

Standing there in the hatchway, with her knotty shot-with-gray hair loose to her shoulders, Shapiro *did* look like a witch. Kait found herself smiling.

But the witch didn't notice. "Have something to show you," she said, and turned and walked away, certain that Kait would follow. Which Kait, of course, did, leaving the bright sunlight and the sliding waves and the darting birds behind.

Noticing as they went down a passage toward the sick bay/laboratory how steadily the older woman made her way. Almost as easily as Kait did. It was amazing what became normal if you lived with it for a while. That was the thing about humans, Kait thought: For better or worse, we're adaptable.

Shapiro walked through the door, letting it swing shut behind her. Kait, still smiling, caught it and went through as well. Then, crossing her arms, she said, "Okay, here I am. So?"

But it was foolish of her to speak to Shapiro yet. Kait had spent enough time hanging around the biochemist's lab to know the drill.

Whenever the scientist returned to her lair after being away, even for five minutes, she always ran through an inventory of her precious possessions. Making sure her antique microscope, her collection of slides, the racks holding the little bottles and tinted-glass mason jars containing the medicinal plants and other decoctions she and Fatou dispensed, were all where she'd left them.

And checking the sealed containers holding the living thieves she'd brought along as well, as if anyone would consider stealing *them*. The wasps were quiet, sitting still in the bottom of the jars, only their upright posture and the slightest movement of their heads in Kait's direction showing that they were alive.

Kait had always believed that Shapiro's laboratory was the last place a Fugian would come to steal anything, but she'd long since learned to be patient with the scientist's eccentricities.

Finally, Shapiro looked over at her. "So tell me what you see."

Kait didn't reply, just raised her eyebrows.

Shapiro frowned. "You've been here enough. What's different this time?"

So Kait looked around. At first glance, the cabin looked the same as always.

But inevitably, Kait's attention turned to the thieves. From what she'd seen before, once imprisoned, they just lived on, eating the bits of meat Shapiro dropped into their containers, mating if they were kept together. Never desperately beating themselves against the glass while attempting to escape. Accepting their fate while they waited to learn what would happen next.

But was something about these ones different? Unexpected? Kait thought . . . maybe so. But she couldn't tell what. Maybe something about their posture?

Seeking a closer look, she took a couple of steps toward the nearest jar, which contained two thieves. As she approached, the wasps tensed, their eyes focused on her. As usual.

But then, when her face was no more than three inches away, they leaped at her. Acting in concert, thumping against the glass so hard, Kait could feel the vibration of the impact in her chest.

The jar rattled in its wooden rack, and the thieves' extruded stingers left black smears of venom on the glass.

Startled, Kait took a quick step back into the middle of the room, lifting her hands in an automatic defensive gesture. Almost instantly, the two thieves fell back to the bottom of the jar. When they regained their feet, they again seemed calm. No, more than calm. Oblivious.

Kait turned to face Shapiro. "What was *that* about?"

Shapiro smiled. "You tell me."

Kait looked back at the thieves, unmoving in their prisons. "That behavior reminds me of the way they act after they've been decapitated," she said, half to herself. "Yet these ones are intact."

"Ah," Shapiro said. "But doesn't that depend on how you define 'intact'?"

As she pondered this question, Kait heard Malcolm shouting at someone ("Whacka!"), the squealing cries of the seabirds, and the never-ceasing sounds of the wooden ship itself, which was always creaking and groaning like a giant, living creature.

"Connection to the hive mind," she said at last. "That's the only thing that matters to them. It's what makes them whole."

"Ah," Shapiro said.

Kait looked again at the thieves in the jars, seeing them in a different way. They weren't calmly awaiting orders. Instead, they were looking for the opportunity to kill. To kill even those, like Kait, who'd been vaccinated, and then to die.

Which meant they'd been severed from the hive mind.

But how?

She met Shapiro's gaze. "What have you done to them?"

"But didn't you just say they're intact?" Shapiro widened her eyes. "I don't have the ability to perform laser surgery on bugs. Not for twenty years now."

She paused, her mouth pursing. Then she said, "I haven't done anything to them. So phrase your question differently."

Again Kait paused in thought, staring at the cabin floor, damp—as all the ship's wooden surfaces were—with what she thought of as salt sweat. Nothing was ever dry on a sea voyage, especially not after a storm.

A storm.

And then Kait understood.

Raising her gaze again to meet Shapiro's, she said, "Okay, I'll rephrase my question: What was *done* to them?"

The biochemist's eyes were bright. "You tell me, Kaitlin."

But Kait didn't answer, not directly. Instead, she asked another question. "How far did the storm blow us off course?"

Shapiro waited.

Kait rephrased again. "How far are we," she asked, "from shore?"

"Ah," Shapiro said.

THAT WAS IT.

After all this time, all her experiments, all her frustrations, circumstances had allowed Shapiro to make the most important discovery yet about the thieves: that distance could disconnect them from the hive mind.

If a healthy, intact individual, or even a few, were separated from the horde, they would behave like ones that had been decapitated, or whose heads had been severely damaged. Free of the prohibition that the vaccine caused in every thief still ruled by the hive mind, they would attack. Sacrifice themselves to kill, to breed.

"It makes all the sense in the world," Shapiro said. "I just wasn't smart enough to see it."

Kait waited for her to go on.

Shapiro tilted her head. "I mean, all their power? It's not magic. It was *never* magic."

Kait felt obscurely disappointed, even resentful. She found herself saying, "Then what was it?"

"It's always been a matter of broadcast and reception, and that has to depend on proximity." She turned her palms up. "Kait, there was always going to be a maximum distance beyond which the individuals couldn't stay in contact with the mind. Of course there was. We just never got far enough away to see it."

Shapiro, noting her expression, smiled. "Did you

know," she said, "that, right near the end of the Last World, neuroscientists demonstrated 'brain-to-brain' communication in humans five thousand miles apart?"

Kait blinked. "Brain-to-brain?"

"It's true, between India and France, for some reason. Neuroscientists and specialists in robotics did it, using an EEG on the sending side and TMS on the receiving, and, of course, the Internet in between."

Kait said, "Clare—"

Shapiro scowled. Then she wriggled her shoulders and took a deep breath. "Okay," she said more slowly. "A person in India would think something. If I remember right, something simple like the word *hello* in various languages. An EEG—an electroencephalogram, you know what those were, right?—would read that thought as changes in brain activity. Then a computer would translate it into the word and transmit it via the Internet to the receiver."

She paused, and after a few moments, Kait said, "Didn't they use EEG transmissions that way, like to help quadriplegics operate wheelchairs and robotic arms? They'd think a command, and the robot would obey?"

Shapiro nodded. "Sure. That was at much closer range, though. This was the first attempt at long-distance communication."

"And . . . ?"

"As I said, the Internet transmitted the signal to a receiver attached to the scalp of the person in France. From there it was sent directly to that person's brain by means of transcranial magnetic stimulation, via a device first designed to spur the activity of brain cells."

After a pause, Kait said, "Okay. I get that. But the recipient, the guy in France, what did he see? The word *hello* in front of his eyes, like on a screen?"

"No. Code, binary code. Flashes of light. But yes, in front of his eyes—or, rather, at the periphery of his vision."

"And it worked? He could decode it?"

Shapiro nodded. "Yes, about ninety percent of the time."

Kait took a while before she spoke again. Finally, she said, "So that's how you think the thieves do it. Electric pulses."

Shapiro nodded. "Basically. Each thief inputs a mass of signals, data, from those around it, then broadcasts it—and whatever it has to add—to all the other thieves in the vicinity. Who then do the same to others, who then do the same. All while inputting."

"And this happens instantaneously?"

Another nod. "Pretty much at the speed of thought, I'd guess."

Then Shapiro's mouth twisted. "Once we would have been able to test that." She shook her head. "I miss my toys."

"Still," Kait said, "it's a web of communication."

Shapiro smiled. "But not quite a worldwide web. The hive mind doesn't have fiber-optic cables or satellites to boost its signal."

She gestured at the quiescent thieves in the jars on the shelf. "Just take them far enough from the hive, and they're as isolated as an ant whose scent trail you've erased."

Kait took a step closer to the jars, but not close

enough to provoke the thieves. For a reason she didn't quite understand, she felt irritation flare in her chest.

"Okay," she said. "So now we know how they do it. Roughly, at least. Yay us. Now tell me: Have we learned anything useful?"

Behind her, Shapiro was silent.

"I mean, Clare," she went on, "what good is your insight—however . . . *insightful*—if we can't figure out a way to use it against the thieves?"

She swung around to look at the scientist, whose face had suddenly lost all its animation. For a moment Kait felt sorry for her. Poor woman, deprived of her toys, trapped in a world marching steadily back toward the Stone Age.

Finally, Shapiro stirred. "I don't know," she said, and she sounded unutterably weary.

But then, just like that, her eyes sparked, and she looked like herself again.

"But all insights, all data, are useful," she said. "Now it's my job to find out how."

NOT JUST YOUR *job.*

Kait stood in her cabin, feeling the ship scudding along on the long, unthreatening swells, a stiff wind blowing them back toward the coast. Soon enough, the thieves on board would be back in contact with the hive mind.

Her conversation with Shapiro had made her realize at last that she'd delayed her actions, her intentions, long enough. It was time.

Time to learn what Trey had learned. To see what he saw.

To understand the hive mind from within, and maybe be able to find a practical application in what Shapiro had just learned. To uncover a tool, a weapon, from what for now was merely knowledge.

Leaning against the wood frame of her bunk, she reached into her jacket pocket. By now, the feel of the little bottle buried there was as familiar to her as a set of keys might have been to someone in the Last World. Only this time, instead of just holding it in her hand, she withdrew it and looked at it.

From behind the tinted glass, the thief she'd captured on the beach stared up at her. It was very thin, with ragged wings and dull eyes. Kait hadn't fed it, and by now it was near the end of its long, slow starvation.

But its abdomen was still grossly swollen, and that was all that would matter. It would die soon, this gravid thief, but first it would fulfill its last mission.

Kait twisted the cap on the little bottle and pulled it off. Inside, the wasp's useless wings whirred. Its mandibles twitched. It knew she was there, knew what that meant.

Kait drew in a deep breath. She was so frightened, but she knew she wouldn't stop here. Not now.

With a sudden jerk of her hand, she dumped the thief out of the bottle and onto her bed. It fell on its back, far too weak to fly, and as it struggled to right itself, she reached down and grasped it behind its head with her thumb and forefinger.

Then, not allowing herself any second thoughts, she

sat down on her bunk, leaned against the wooden wall—feeling the vibration of the ship's beating heart—and, with her left hand, pulled up her shirt, exposing her belly.

The thief looked down at her bare skin, then up into her face. Its abdomen pulsed.

SEVENTEEN

THE THIEF STOPPED struggling. Kait thought that it guessed. It knew.

Severed from the hive mind, it had only one remaining mission.

She looked into those unreadable, multifaceted eyes. *All these years inside our heads,* she thought. *What have you learned about us?*

There was only one way for her to find out.

Kait took in a breath. She'd thought about this moment for years, wondering how she'd feel when she finally reached it. She'd be crying, she'd guessed. Crying from fear, or maybe from relief.

But it was through dry eyes that she spent a few moments looking at her own flesh, as if she had never seen it before. The slight curve of her stomach. The flat planes angling down toward her pelvis. The three small birthmarks arrayed to the right of her belly button like the stars in Orion's belt. The fine hairs that, as she watched, prickled with goose bumps.

Kait's shoulders were gripped by a deep, convulsive shudder that made her bones hurt. Then, swinging her left arm, she placed the thief on the curve of her exposed flesh, on top of the birthmarks.

It stood there, staring up at her. She could feel its legs against her sensitive skin, six discrete pinpricks.

For a second, maybe two, it did not move. Then its bulging abdomen arched. Its white stinger slid out from the end.

The stinger that was also its ovipositor.

WITH A MOTION so fast that it was a blur, it punched a hole in Kait's flesh.

This was the moment she had always feared. How would she be able to tell whether she was being killed or . . . impregnated?

And now, as agony swept through her, as if she were aflame, as if she were igniting and burning up from the inside out, she didn't know. But it didn't matter. Nothing mattered but the pain, the fire, spreading upward and outward. When it reached her chest, it would consume her heart. When it reached her brain, her mind, it would reduce it to nothing but black ash.

Somehow, she didn't smash the wasp that was torturing her. Somehow, she didn't scream or fall to the floor. Instead, she jammed her fist into her mouth, biting down so hard that she could taste her own salty blood. It was crucial that no one hear her.

The thief raised its abdomen. The stinger slid upward, out of her, leaving behind just the tiniest bubble of blood at the surface of her bone-pale belly.

But the pain did not stop, nor even lessen. Kait did not know how much longer she could survive it. Perhaps it was already too late. Maybe she was already dead.

Even in the fire of her agony, she thought about her parents. Her birth parents. Which of them had died first? Had her mother seen her father die? Had they seen the wasps that killed them? Had they watched the stingers enter their own flesh?

Kait closed her eyes. If there was anything else to see, it could happen without her bearing witness.

She didn't have to watch, but she couldn't stop herself from feeling the ovipositor reenter her. For a moment she felt only the sensation of the dagger inside, a jagged tearing of her flesh. A sharper, more tangible pain amid the flames that had now spread throughout her body.

But then her nerve endings, somehow still functioning, registered . . . something new: a cool liquid being injected into her. No, not cool, cold. Freezing.

The thief emptied itself and filled her. There was a pause, a moment of stasis, and then Kait felt the needle pull upward once more and withdraw. Leaving only ice behind.

Ice that spread outward from its reservoir beneath her skin. That extinguished the flames as it raced down her legs and up through her trunk and into her heart, which pumped it upward into her brain.

And, in an eyeblink, the pain was gone.

Kait sat up straighter in her chair. Opened her eyes

to see the thief topple sideways and fall to the floor. It lay on its back, legs twitching, ovipositor still extended. In just a few seconds, as Kait watched, its movements grew more feeble, and finally it folded its legs and stiffened in death, like any other wasp, any other insect.

Kait looked away from the dead wasp, looked inside herself instead. The ice had spread through her body, to the end of every vein, every capillary. She could feel her cold heart thudding against the cage of her ribs, battering to escape. She could feel the individual strands of her hair against the skin on the back of her neck. She could feel the hole in her belly, the excavation the thief had made, the tiny passageway that the larva would soon widen into its airhole.

The pain was gone, but what had taken its place? Deep inside her was a single pinprick. Not of light, of darkness. Deeper darkness.

The egg. Already changing, already transforming.

Even as she focused on it, Kait felt something else sweep upward all the way to her brain, her mind. She'd been expecting this, knowing it was coming, but even so, it nearly overwhelmed her.

The amnesic chemicals the thieves pumped into new hosts. The drugs that protected their young by making you forget what had just happened to you.

Sitting on her bunk, leaning against the ship's quivering wall, Kait found herself wondering why she was there. She knew who she was, remembered that just a few weeks ago she'd boarded a sailing ship and headed away from Refugia.

But everything after that was a blank. She looked

down at her fists, clenched in her lap, and could not remember why she'd bitten one, why it was bleeding.

And then she forgot to think about it at all.

ONLY . . . SHE WASN'T going to allow this to happen.

With a sudden, violent lurch, Kait slammed her fist against the wooden frame of the porthole. Then she was on her feet, standing in the middle of her cabin, staring around her, remembering.

With the pain's help, her memories returned. Amorphous, transient at first, but there. Present.

Somewhere deep in her mind, an image appeared. Or perhaps she created it. Her hands grabbing hold of something that was fleeing from her, and pulling it back in.

Holding on like her life depended on it, because it did.

Now she remembered catching the thief near the beach back home. Putting it in a bottle to keep till later. Placing the bottle in her pocket, where it had spent much of the *Trey Gilliard*'s journey.

And then retrieving it from her pocket. Here, just now. Spilling the dying thief out of its prison and placing it on her belly.

Watching—seeing—it penetrate her flesh with its dagger to deposit the egg. Feeling it repeat the motion the second time to ease her pain.

And to make her forget.

The forgetting. Even as she focused on what had happened, on her memories of the past hour, she felt them slipping from her grasp. Again she pulled, fighting against what felt like a tidal flow, the tide flooding away from her.

How did you fight a tide? It was so much easier to allow yourself to be carried away by it.

She was sweating, cold moisture against her skin. The tide started to carry her memory away, and again she pulled it back.

This was the battle she was going to have to face, again and again, countless times, as long as the larva was inside her. She'd known it was coming, known that this was the first—and ever after, greatest—risk she was going to have to face when she'd made the choice to—

To try to follow Trey. To see what he had seen.

Already she knew what had happened to him, all of it. The assault. The penetration. The pain, the agony, the icy balm.

Yet Trey himself had forgotten. Even he, as strong as anyone Kait had met in the Last World, had fallen victim to the forgetting. It had taken Sheila to figure out what was going on, to see the swelling and the airhole, and—almost too late—to cut the larva out of him.

The forgetting. A brilliant strategy, elegant in the way only nature could be. Necessary because primates were the thieves' preferred hosts, a rich meal and—more importantly—one that was likely to stay alive long enough for the adult thief to hatch out.

This was a crucial point. As the young thief grew inside them, host mammals always exhibited behavior that put their lives at risk: obliviousness to threats, a dormant period followed by unusual aggressiveness. So lay your egg in a rat or other small mammal in the wild, and both it and your larva were likely to get killed.

A primate made for a far better choice. Not that monkeys and apes were entirely exempt from danger. Leopards, an occasional eagle, a large snake, all might take one. And in the last decades before the Fall, a primate could also be a target for a bullet fired by a human hunting for bushmeat.

But leopards were rare, monkey-eating eagles and snakes rarer. And humans were comparatively recent arrivals in the thieves' historic home territory, providing both a new threat to the species and a new opportunity.

Yet even with all their advantages, primates didn't make perfect hosts. The problem was that they were too smart. An infected monkey's natural instinct, immediately after noticing the telltale swelling and circular airhole, would be to worry at it, dig at the hole, and eventually remove or destroy the larva.

By the time the larva grew so big it was impossible to miss, it would release a flood of toxins that would kill any host that tried to remove it. From what scientists in the Last World had observed in the wild, monkeys had learned to recognize this, to understand when it was too late to save an infected individual.

So the rest of the troop would turn their backs and abandon the host to its fate.

Yes, a brilliant evolutionary strategy.

As long as, in those early days when the larva was most vulnerable, before it possessed enough toxins to kill its host . . . the host forgot what had been done to it.

* * *

ONCE AGAIN, KAIT reined in her memories, pulled them back to her.

How many days was this battle going to continue? What chance did she have to succeed, to keep her awareness of what had happened to her—what she had *caused* to happen—against the rising tide of the drugs working their way deep into her brain?

Could she be stronger than Trey had been?

SHE WAS WAITING for something. She didn't know what. She only knew that until it happened, she wouldn't—couldn't—leave her cabin.

Going through what was already becoming her mantra—*I remember I remember I remember*—she waited as ten minutes passed. Fifteen.

Muffled, distant, the sounds of laughter from on deck reached her, more as vibration than sound. As remote from her as if everyone else still occupied the earth, but she was on some far-off planet. Waiting.

I remember.

And then it happened. She could feel it. A new violation, but something else, too.

An awakening. A . . . *remaking*. Kait herself being remade. Her flesh and her brain, her mind, being forged into something new.

Kait put her hand on her bare belly, and felt—at the same instant from within and without—the newly hatched larva move within her.

At the same time, her mind was remade as well. For the first time, she caught a glimpse of what Trey had seen. The things he had never told her.

Kait looked, and saw, and began to understand.

And despaired.

AISHA ROSE WENT very still. For a moment her vision blurred.

Or, rather, her outside vision faded. What she saw inside came clear.

So much time, years, had passed since the last time this happened, that at first she wasn't sure what she was seeing.

But then she focused, went back within, and understood. It was someone new. A new light that wasn't part of the spreading stain.

It was already dangerously close, and Aisha Rose still had too far to go. The distance, her weakness, and the creatures that now owned the real earth had left her short of where she needed to be.

Far from home. No: truly without a home for the first time.

But with a renewed goal, a mission she knew she could not abandon, as the new light called out to her.

There was just one problem.

EIGHTEEN

SHE COULDN'T BE sure, but Aisha Rose thought she might be dying.

Mama had told her that on the dreamed earth, people used that word all the time. "People would say it," she said, "even if they didn't mean it. Didn't come close to meaning it. 'I'm dying here,' they'd say, and no one would give it even a second thought."

Aisha Rose, days out of Nairobi, heading east across the savanna, realized that was another difference between the dreamed earth and the one she lived on and would die on. Back then, before the dream ended, you could say almost anything and mean something else, and everyone would understand anyway.

You could say you were starving, or chilled to the bone, or terrified, or dying, and mean that you hadn't eaten in a few hours, or you needed to put on a sweater, or that you were nervous about something, or that you were merely very bored. And no one would take you seriously. They'd know you were exaggerating, and that you likely had never been any of those things, not really. Nor had they.

But back then, it was to your advantage to say things you didn't really mean. On a huge and crowded earth, filled with floods of people like the ones in the pictures she and Mama looked at, you'd be invisible if you weren't noisy. No one would listen. You'd be drowned out.

But life was different now. If words themselves mattered at all—and Aisha Rose had begun to wonder if they did, even as she continued her nightly recitations—then they only mattered if they meant something. They only mattered if they were true.

THE TRUTH: AISHA Rose was chilled to the bone.

Huddled beneath a thorn tree that she was too weak to climb, she watched the sun descend toward the western horizon. Even the last trailing outskirts of Nairobi had dwindled and finally disappeared. Now all that was left was endless bush stretching in both directions. She was already starting to shiver.

These were the patterns of her days on the savanna. Midday here in the bush was so hot that the sweat slid off her body in sheets—except when she couldn't find enough to drink. Then her sweat would dry up, her tongue would swell in her mouth, the sun would twist her thoughts into disorganized fragments, and she would find herself losing minutes, even hours, as she staggered forward, one step at a time. Or, finally, retreated to the shade to rest and wait.

At first, when the heat began to ebb, when the sun began to lose its blistering strength, relief would almost overwhelm her. But it wouldn't last long, because she knew what the night would bring. In just a few hours, as soon as the chill began to seep—and then flood—into her, she would crawl under a blanket of leaves, a leafy fallen branch, or some vines.

It didn't help much, but it was better than nothing. Sometimes she had nothing.

Inevitably, the shivers would begin. Her teeth would click together, her skin erupt in a mass of goose bumps, and she'd shake so hard she thought that her translucent skin might split to reveal the bones planted so shallowly beneath.

Her whole body possessed by the cold, except for her left hand, the one she'd cut, which throbbed with heat. The palm was swollen and an angry red, and her forearm was beginning to get puffy, too. Within a few more days, she wouldn't be able to use the hand for anything.

Finally, dawn would arrive, the day would begin to warm, and she'd get back to her feet. Start her hejira east once again, every goal stripped away but that one.

But she was beginning to hear voices—not Mama's voice; Mama was silent—telling her she wouldn't make it. She would die days, miles, before she reached her destination.

Telling her that she could die here, or she could die there. Why fight to keep going?

But she didn't listen. She fought, and kept going, each day, as the sun rose and blasted her, and fell and tortured her.

* * *

AND AISHA ROSE was starving.

When had she last eaten? Yesterday? No, the day before. A green fruit plucked from a bush she did not recognize, fruit that had sat in her stomach like a stone. Some fat white grubs she'd found under a rock. And then some pink baby mice she'd dug out from their den and eaten raw, as their mother screamed at her from some nearby bushes. (The mother was too fast to catch, or Aisha Rose would have eaten her, too.)

Two days before that—or was it three?—she'd come upon the remains of a kill. She'd spotted it from miles away, of course, because of the vultures she'd seen circling above it and, as she drew closer, perched in the branches of nearby thorn trees.

And then, as she came even closer, moving as silently as she could through the dense bush that dotted this stretch of savanna, keeping upwind, the east wind always in her face, she could smell the kill as well. The rank odor of rotting meat.

The kill itself was shielded by the low bush, so Aisha Rose couldn't see what it was, or what predators might still be around, until she was so close that her heart was pounding from fear. The blood rushing through her veins made her more alert but also caused her feverish head to spin, her vision to cloud.

Finally, she reached the edge of a small clearing and could identify the kill: a zebra. It had undoubtedly been taken by lions, but by now the big cats had eaten their fill and abandoned it, leaving behind the pungent odor of their urine and the scattered remains of their prey.

The zebra's skeleton had been pulled into pieces. The bones were stained brown with old blood and yellow with gristle and scraps of meat that the lions had left behind. Here and there, strips of skin showed the black-and-white pattern.

Around the clearing, vultures tore at the remaining flesh and squabbled among themselves, hopping in their froglike way, twisting their long, bare necks like snakes, and hissing at each other. As they took notice of Aisha Rose's presence, they turned and stared at her, unafraid.

At the far edge of the clearing, a family of jackals stood in a patch of tall grass, also watching her. Eight in all, but four were unlike any Aisha Rose had seen before. Instead of typical long, fine silver-and-tan coats, theirs were shorter, coarser, and speckled with brown.

Sick with hunger, Aisha Rose leaned against a tree and thought. She couldn't be certain that the lions weren't still in the area, or that a pack of hyenas might not show up at any moment to feast on what remained.

Including Aisha Rose. This time.

And even if the big predators were far off, Aisha Rose wasn't even sure she could fend off the vultures and jackals. The only smart thing to do was turn and walk away. There were so many risks, and every one of them gave her this same message. Leave.

But she was so hungry. If she walked away from this kill, she might not reach the next one. If there was a next one within walking distance.

Still hesitating at the edge of the clearing, she looked

down at her own body. Her hips jutted out under her tunic and her legs didn't look that much different than a gazelle's.

She knew she had longer than a day, but how much longer?

So she took her knife out of the leather sheath on her right hip, drew in a deep breath to calm her pounding heart and steady her whirling head, and walked forward toward the kill.

A FEW OF the vultures took off from the ground, their heavy wings creating a breeze that blew the fetid air into her face. But the rest stayed where they were, opening their bloodstained beaks wide and hissing at her as she headed past them, to the zebra's vertebrae and ribs.

And she ate, pulling some of the soft flesh away from the ribs, breaking a smaller bone to suck out its marrow. Eating so quickly she thought she might choke but not caring.

She was so absorbed in her meal that she didn't see four of the jackals coming out of the tall grass toward her. At first quiet and then yipping and growling, showing their teeth, they were led by one of the strange doglike ones.

Aisha Rose stood as tall as she could. She shouted, though her voice emerged as a thin squawk. She waved her knife. She strode toward the jackals as if she didn't fear them even though she did. In all ways, she tried to make herself as large and threatening as possible.

It didn't work. None of it worked.

The jackals scattered at first, but soon enough—almost immediately—they started circling around her, keeping apart, waiting for the moment for one to come in and give her the bite that would start the bleeding. The first bite that might as well have been the last.

It wasn't really until that moment that Aisha Rose realized where she stood on the food chain.

On the totem pole, as Mama put it. Aisha Rose didn't know what a totem pole was, and had never asked, but she'd understood what Mama meant.

Lower than lions and hyenas, and jackals. Equal to vultures. Maybe.

She fled before the jackals had the chance to prove their superiority. When you were that low on the totem pole, you accepted the fact if you wanted to stay alive.

At least for another day or two.

THE NEXT MORNING, back near the thorn tree, she found two treasures.

The first was a patch of sumeito vines, growing amid a jumble of boulders in a sunny spot beside a patch of woodland. As Mama had told her to do, Aisha Rose made a paste of torn-up leaves and sap she bled from the stems. Then, tearing off a strip of the filthy shift she wore—the only cloth she had—she strapped the paste to the angry wound in her palm.

Almost immediately she started to feel better. Maybe that was all in her mind, but that didn't matter. As far as she was concerned, everything was in her mind.

The second treasure was a nest of ostrich eggs, its

enormous guardian—the male who guarded the nest—out of sight somewhere. Six giant eggs, newly laid, lying there on the bare ground.

She knew that the adult would return soon, and that when he did, he would defend the nest. She also knew that his large size and powerful legs meant he could easily kick her to death and well might.

So Aisha Rose Atkinson, furtive mammal, lurker, egg-thief, human, took one of the huge eggs and carried it off to safer ground. Where she cracked it open with a rock, just as she'd seen the white vultures do, and ate and ate until she was covered in dripping yolk and her stomach bulged against the shrunken skin of her belly.

Then, stronger, unafraid, she stood and set out once again.

NINETEEN

Kirindy Mitea, Madagascar

BY THIS POINT, Malcolm was in such a ferocious mood nearly all the time that no one but Ross McKay and Shapiro—and Dylan Connell, but only to get instructions—would go near him.

Even as he found himself cracking the whip, using words he'd picked up in a lifetime among people who didn't care what came out of their mouths, he felt regretful. Even a little ashamed.

But not quite enough to stop himself. You didn't spend two decades dreaming about something and be calm when you were just weeks away from finding out if your hopes were to be realized or dashed. Especially if you had to make a days-long stop on Madagascar. Not if you had a temper—and a tongue—like Malcolm's.

Fucking Madagascar. Pretty much the only country Malcolm *hadn't* visited during his old life, and thus a place he didn't give two . . . figs . . . about.

But there'd been no choice. Even if it had been feasible to sail directly from Refugia to Lamu, even if the *Trey Gilliard*'s crew wouldn't have put him on a waterlogged raft and sent him floating away, even if he wouldn't have deserved being treated like Captain Bligh . . . the ship, this expedition, had a goal. A purpose.

And the purpose wasn't to find Chloe. Not *just* to find Chloe.

They'd made three previous stops on the four-month journey. The one in Kissama, another in what had once been Namibia, and the third in eastern South Africa. Finding, in each case, abundant wildlife ranging from plains game to predators, big (lions) to small (mongooses).

Though virtually no primates anywhere. And *no* humans, or sign that any humans had been living there since the Fall.

Very few thieves, either—though there were always some, or at least the whiff of them—which had touched off a vociferous debate about how drastic the species' apparent population crash had been. It was the kind of argument that, having no possible resolution, could keep otherwise bored, shipbound scientists occupied for weeks, on and off.

Only count Malcolm out. He couldn't have cared less. He just wanted to *get on with it.*

Especially once they made it halfway up the east coast of Africa, making it feel like they were just a stone's throw from his destination. Madagascar? He could have flown from Antananarivo to Lamu in, what, six hours? He could have been there by tonight, if he still had his old Piper. If he still lived in a world with airplanes.

Fuck.

But here they were instead, at anchor, not going any-where, trekking instead around a godforsaken blasted patch of some island he'd never had the slightest desire to visit. A place so famous for its wildlife, its lemurs, that every square inch of it had been so exhaustively studied and analyzed and, in the way of the Last World, fought over, that even Trey Gilliard himself had had no use for it. One of the most famous wild places on earth, Mada-gascar, but to Trey—and therefore to Malcolm—it had been more like a zoo.

But not now. Not here. Not in this world. So here they were, and for at least two days.

Fuck.

WHILE MALCOLM FELT like a grumpy little kid, wanting to do nothing but kick rocks across the dusty ground (and there were plenty of rocks to choose from, and plenty of dust, too), the rest of the crew seemed to be fascinated by the bizarre environment of this dry and spiky corner of the island.

Everyone, but especially Ross McKay, who'd been anticipating this shore leave since the journey began. In truth, they'd stopped here for him because back in the Last World, Ross's specialty had been lemurs.

Those primitive primates, whose strange shapes, faces, and habits had made them familiar worldwide, had been found in only one place—Madagascar—so Ross had spent about half his adult life on the island. Including this part, Kirindy Mitea, a national park he'd helped establish.

It looked like Mars to Malcolm. Mars's rubbish tip. Plains of red and white sand, held together with the slightest fringe of coarse grass and bordered by the occasional bottle-shaped baobab tree and a forest of bare-branched, scrubby trees so spiky with thorns that it was a miracle anything would choose to live on them.

And, in truth, nothing much did seem to thrive there. Some little birds hopping among the thorns, a couple of dark hawks circling in the hot blue sky, a flock of flamingos they'd startled on the hike up from the beach. And one mammal flashing by: something with stripes and a bushy tail that was either a large squirrel or a small mongoose.

During the first few minutes of their exploration, Kait came walking up. Quiet and pale as ever, and wearing that big floppy shirt she always sported these days, but this time with a hunched, slow-moving lizard with googly eyes perched on her right shoulder.

Ross's smile looked like it might split his face. "Labord's chameleon!" he said in a tone of requited love. "Isn't it beautiful?"

Malcolm looked at the scaly, brownish green beast with the stubby horn that looked like a thumb protruding from its nose, and—for about the first time in forever—kept his mouth shut.

BUT AS ROSS wandered around the plains and forests, his beatific smile began to fade.

"They're gone," he said. Then again, "They're gone."

Malcolm, walking beside him, felt annoyance as a

tingling sensation in his fingers. He was ready to head to a more fertile part of the island, a place with more accessible supplies of freshwater and even some fruit and huntable game. Ready to head on, then move out entirely.

But Ross seemed so sad, so lost, that Malcolm kept his voice patient as he said, "What're gone?"

"The sifakas," Ross said.

Malcolm just looked at him. After a moment, Ross frowned, and said, in a tone of uncharacteristic impatience, "*Lemurs*, Malcolm."

His eyes shifted to the spiny forests beyond. "This place was full of them the last time I was here. Eight different species, including sifakas, red-tailed sportive lemurs, pale fork-marked lemurs, fat-tailed dwarf lemurs—"

Malcolm was quiet. Scientists had never thought of a stupid name they wouldn't give to some poor beast.

Ross's face was a mask of sorrow. "Them, too?"

A FEW MINUTES later, Darby Callahan came up to them. "Need to show you something."

Her face held little expression. But there was something about the movement of her eyes, a quick flicker from Malcolm's face to Ross's, then back again, that made Malcolm feel cold.

"Oh, no," Ross said, his voice little more than a breath.

A THIEF COLONY. The largest thief colony any of them had ever seen.

No. The largest *former* thief colony any of them had ever seen. Because it was empty, abandoned, and looked like it had been for months, if not years.

A ghost town. A ghost *city*, comprised of hundreds—maybe thousands—of windblown mounds and half-filled-in burrows spreading across the Mars-surface plain to the scraggly, unwelcoming forest beyond.

Lying amid the spiky grasses that outlined the mounds were bones. The weathered, bleached bones of uncountable mammals. Ribs and pelvises and femurs and tibias proportionately much longer than a monkey's or human's. Long finger and toe bones. And, scattered everywhere, strange sloping skulls with oddly foreshortened snouts and giant eyeholes.

So many different sizes. So many different species.

Even though he'd never seen a lemur skeleton before, Malcolm didn't have to ask to know what he was looking at.

He looked around and saw that everyone else knew as well. Everyone understood.

ROSS CRIED. HE cried silently, tears dripping down his round cheeks while everyone else looked away awkwardly. Humans being no better in the Next World at dealing with unexpected emotion than they had been in the Last.

Everyone looking away except, surprisingly, for Kait, who'd returned her chameleon to wherever she'd found it and put her arm around Ross's shoulders and led him away. Back toward the beach, the dinghies, and the waiting ship, with the others gradually following in their path.

Shapiro came up to stand beside Malcolm. Together, they watched the small, disconsolate group, so few and small against the tainted landscape, the sea, the sky.

"No human bones," Shapiro said.

Malcolm had noticed this, too. "It was a national park," he said. "Not many people around to start with."

"True." Shapiro turned to face him. "What's your theory? The thieves used up all the hosts, then died out themselves?"

Malcolm shook his head. "Nah, I think they're too fucking smart and well adapted for that."

"But they're all gone."

"Yeah. Long gone."

"So," she said, "where'd they go?"

TWENTY

THE SUN ROSE over the ocean, in an instant turning the eggshell blue sky a brilliant orange. The sudden vivid color caught the peaks of the gentle waves, more like ripples, that seemed to spread out toward the horizon, for a moment making them resemble lit candles.

She and Mama had used candles when they lived in the house in Naro Moru. Aisha Rose remembered it so clearly, that gentle flickering glow, so different from the garish electric lights she'd seen in the pictures.

The memory made her chest hurt.

She was wearing rags that could barely be called clothes anymore. She was filthy, smeared with mud and dried egg yolk and blood, her own and that of the animals whose meat she'd eaten along the way.

Filthy and stinking. The smell of rot. Rotting egg and rotting meat. And her, too.

Her fever hadn't returned—the sumeito salve had done that much—and the swelling had gone down.

But it hadn't gone away. It was just waiting, she knew that. Waiting for her to weaken, when it could once again run free.

She just hoped it would give her enough time.

IN THE MIDST of these thoughts, her stomach made a sound, a sudden high-pitched whine like the cry of a distant cat, and—amazingly—she laughed.

No matter how filthy you were, no matter how sad your thoughts, your body didn't care. When it was hungry, it demanded food.

And this truth, the fact that she was hungry, that she still had a body that needed sustenance, lifted Aisha Rose's spirits.

She knew that once she ate, she would have enough strength to navigate the final stretch before she reached her destination, now only a couple of days away up the coast.

Knowing what awaited her there, and yet here she was, still hungry.

So . . . what should she eat?

She looked around. Hanging high in the blue sky were three huge, spindly winged black birds, as angular and still as if a child had painted them there. Aisha Rose had never seen them in a book, so Mama couldn't tell her their names.

Down along the beach, white crabs shifted through sand just a little darker, browner, and less substantial than they were. Seeing her watching, one of them ducked into its burrow, the entrance a round hole in the sand that reminded Aisha Rose of one made by a *majizi*.

There were no *majizi* here. She knew where they were, where the stain grew and spread. But simply being reminded of them made her lose her appetite for the crabs, not that she would be quick enough to catch one anyway.

Stretching, she yawned, bending her neck back and noticing for the first time the big, round fruits with brown, shaggy outsides that hung perilously in the tree high above her.

No, not fruit. Nuts. Gigantic nuts.

Mama's voice: "Coconuts."

Then Aisha Rose remembered. She'd seen pictures of beaches with trees like this, slender palm trees with trunks like an elephant's, burdened with coconuts.

Coconut meat and milk were delicious, Mama had said, looking a little sad and thoughtful. There'd been no coconut palms at Hell's Gate or Naro Moru, so Aisha Rose had never gotten to find out for herself. Until now.

If she could get hold of one, that was. Looking up at the coconuts clustered under the palm fronds waving in the breeze—and then moving a few steps away while imagining what it would feel like if one fell on her head—she knew she'd never be able to shinny up the slippery trunk to retrieve one for herself. Perhaps when she was at full strength, but not now.

The other option, searching for one that had fallen, was easier. It took just about five minutes of walking along the fringe of the beach before she found one lying at the base of a tree. Its shaggy outer coat had been half torn off, revealing the green, shiny nut within.

Which, as Aisha Rose discovered while sitting cross-legged with the coconut in her lap, proved to be completely unbreakable.

After just a few moments clutching it between her knees and trying to find a way to open it with her right hand, a hopeless task, she retrieved her knife. With this she succeeded in cutting away the rest of the outer layer, but the green nut remained completely resistant.

When the very tip of the knife caught in the husk and bent, Aisha Rose's heart thudded. The last thing she could afford to lose was her knife, as far as she knew the only one remaining from the dream.

Returning it to the sheath, she stared down at the coconut. She was so hungry, but there had to be a better way.

Or maybe not. Aisha Rose lifted the coconut off her lap, propping it between her right hand and left wrist, and made to throw it away. As she hoisted it higher, though, she heard it make a gurgling sound. The sound of the milk rushing around inside the shell.

Taunting her. Aisha Rose's resolve hardened. If this thing, this nut, was going to challenge her, then she'd take on the challenge. She had no choice. It was what she did, who she was.

Aisha Rose Atkinson: not so high on the totem pole, certainly, but able to survive because she never stopped trying.

HER NEXT ATTEMPT involved a rock, a big, sharp-edged rock that—again, propping the coconut between her hand and undamaged wrist—she banged against it as hard as she could. But her weakness and wounded palm made both her strength and accuracy less than they once would have been, and she found herself growling with frustration as the rock bounced off again and again.

Now you can give up, part of her said.

But the rest, the bigger part, said no. Not yet.

So . . . what to try next? After a minute's thought, she had an idea.

Finding three more good-sized rocks, she arranged them beside the one she'd been using. Then, with all her strength, she hurled the coconut down on them . . . and stood there, stock-still, as the nut split into three pieces, two of them flying a few feet away and the third, the largest, settling amid the rocks.

Aisha Rose was lucky that the largest piece made up almost half of the nut, and that it had come to rest right-side up. Otherwise all, and not just some, of the precious gurgling liquid would have drained into the sand.

She squatted and grabbed the half before it, too, could tip over. Raising it to her mouth, she drank deeply of the milk, letting some of it run down her chin.

It was . . . a little sour. Kind of thin. To be honest, it wasn't entirely to Aisha Rose's taste. Nor was the meat.

But the feeling of triumph? Her victory over the coconut? That tasted sweet.

NOW THAT SHE was no longer ravenous, she knew it was time to start the next, the last, leg of her hejira.

Only . . . she still wasn't ready. Not quite. There was still one thing left for her to accomplish.

The time was drawing close when she'd need *him*, the one who frightened her so badly. But ever since that moment in Nairobi, when he'd almost swept her away, he'd removed himself from her. Turned away.

She'd reached out, but though she thought—guessed— that he knew she was there, was trying, he'd given no sign of acknowledging her, much less responded.

All through her trek across the savanna, she'd wondered how she was going to solve this and despaired at finding a solution.

But now she felt more hopeful. Oddly enough, it had been the coconut that gave her an idea . . . or, rather, her approach to the problem of opening the coconut.

She'd learned that sometimes it was better to stop being clever and to approach a challenge head-on. Sometimes you just had to bash it against a rock.

SHE'D NEVER SEEN the ocean except in pictures, much less swum in it. Mama had made sure she learned to swim in the big lake near Hell's Gate, but she knew this must be so different. Like something visiting from the dreamed earth.

Her heart pounding—from being in such an unfamiliar environment or from the decision she'd just made, or both—she headed down the beach. When a warm gentle wave covered her feet and then, retreating, pulled her gently toward the depths, despite her fears, she laughed out loud.

She'd seen pictures of coral reefs, and could see where this real one almost broke the surface of the water. Beyond the reef, the water was a darker, deeper blue, and the waves, stronger out there, sent spray up over the coral, where it caught the sun and glittered like a rainbow.

Aisha Rose drew a breath deep into her lungs, then coughed. The salt air was harsh, but she thought she could get used to it. She thought she could live here and be happy.

Or could have, in another life. In another dream.

She stood still for ten seconds more, then stripped off her rags, stepped forward until she was waist deep, and dove in.

Swimming a few strokes underwater with her eyes closed, she gloried in the warmth of the water against her skin. At first, her damaged hand stung and ached from the salt, but soon it grew numb. And the salt water, while making her eyes itch, also buoyed her, making even the hand with its awkward bindings seem lighter.

Aisha Rose felt . . . free. Rising to the surface, she took a breath and dove down toward the sandy bottom. A tiny blue-and-yellow fish stared at her, then burrowed out of sight, sending up a tiny white plume. Nearby, bleached shells shifted back and forth in the gentle surge from the waves rolling past above her head.

With a strong kick, she sent herself up for another lungful, then swam smoothly through the water toward the reef ahead. It was amazing to see, for once, something that was even more beautiful than the pictures had shown. Round corals like small cities, others with branches like a giant antelope's horns, still others soft, fans waving in the current that caressed her face.

And everywhere, fish. So many fish that she didn't know

where to look first. Big green-and-red ones that bit at the coral with sharp beaks—she could hear the scraping sound even through the water. Smaller bright yellow ones that were almost triangular in shape, with long, pointy noses like a shrew's, and others, striped yellow and blue, whose streaming fins reminded Aisha Rose of flags or clouds.

She had no idea what any of the fish were called, only that they put the colorful birds that had lived around Naro Moru and Hell's Gate to shame.

The ocean over the reef made its own sound, a roaring in her ears, but she had no idea what was creating the squeaks and moans and other noises. After spending her whole life thus far in a world where she knew every sound, what made it, and what it meant, this unfamiliarity thrilled her.

Coming to the surface again, she noticed that she had traveled farther from shore than she'd thought. She felt a spark of panic—she'd never been so far from solid ground—but it was soon extinguished. If getting back to shore were the biggest challenge she faced on the rest of her journey, she would be one lucky girl.

She spun in place. The sun, nearly directly overhead now, had turned the water around her into a sheet of silver. Perhaps ten strokes away, though, a gap between two stands of coral revealed the darker water she'd noticed from shore—a deeper, half-alluring, half-threatening shade of blue—and choppier surf stretching out toward the horizon.

Without giving herself time to reconsider, Aisha Rose swam out through the gap in the reef, and into the open water. Here she was tested, as the surf surging against the reef wall set up confusing currents, at one moment shoving her out toward the open ocean and at other times threatening to slam her against the sharp coral.

She swam toward the spot where the water changed color. Here the sunlight turned the swirling sand and fragments of shells below into white embers. Away from the protection of the reef, the fish here were larger and less gaudy. Silvery, bullet-shaped, heavy-jawed, with teeth as white and gleaming as jewels.

Here the sandy bottom below looked as far away as the valley floor from the rose farm. A shift in the current brought a sudden surge of colder water that at first, as if shy, merely brushed against her body, and then, as if more confident, enveloped her.

So suddenly that it shocked her, she found that she was floating high above the wall of a canyon. Festooned at its lip with waving purple and green fans, it descended almost vertically, growing dimmer and dimmer until the deepening blue water turned to black.

A black so vast and empty that Aisha Rose hung there, holding her breath until her lungs ached, just staring downward. Much colder water, rising from the canyon, engulfed her, and she shivered.

Illuminated by the last glimmerings of the sunlight— so brilliant above, so feeble below—something moved just within the range of her vision. Something huge and grayish white. A whale? A monster?

Maybe something ancient, from her book on long-extinct creatures, yet not extinct. Not extinct, just waiting for the world and the seas to become empty again, so it could reemerge.

Her book on ancient creatures had described such deep-sea monsters but had claimed they were all extinct. But looking down into the blackness below, Aisha Rose wondered how—even on the dreamed earth—people could have been so sure of themselves.

Had they really *known* what was extinct and what wasn't? Or had they merely been trying to make themselves feel better, more in control of an earth that, in the end, they had no control over at all?

Unexpectedly, on this day of surprises, Aisha Rose felt her body fill with a warmth that banished her goose bumps and chased away the chill. She lifted her head out into the sun for a breath, her body seeming to unfold at the long intake of air.

Finally, she understood something. Something important, even crucial:

The world was enormous, far bigger than she'd ever known from her own life or even from the pictures. And her place in it was tiny. Tinier than tiny. Mama's word: *infinitesimal*.

And if Aisha Rose's world was tiny, then so was theirs. The *majizis'* world, and with it the reach of their power. Even tinier than hers.

After all, she could visit the edges of this vast underwater universe, but the thieves, for all their strength and destructiveness, couldn't do even that. This place was forever beyond their reach, and so were the creatures that inhabited it.

Regardless of what they'd done to the dreamed earth, the thieves didn't own the world, not even the one up in the air, the sunlight.

It was time to give her new plan a try, and see if it worked. To find out if it was a beginning or an end.

A SMALL SEA turtle, brown-shelled and with bright black eyes, rose out of the canyon's depths. It appeared first as a blur, a shadow, then took shape as it headed toward the surface.

Aisha Rose, hanging there, watched it rise, saw it open its mouth, extend its scaly neck through the silvery surface not far from her, and take a gulp of air. Then it turned and plunged back down, pearly bubbles trailing behind it.

Aisha Rose lifted her head, drew in her own lungful of air, as much as she could hold. When she looked again, the turtle was far below her, its oval shell already glimmering gray and indistinct in the shadows. Soon it would be out of sight.

Kicking with all her strength, she chased after it, fighting the cold upwelling current that pushed against her like the palm of a vast, invisible hand, until she had reached the lip of the canyon, and the turtle was right in front of her.

Reaching out with her right hand, she grabbed the front of its shell. As it redoubled its kicking, she allowed it to carry her deeper into the darkness.

Turning her head, Aisha Rose looked up the way she'd come. She could see the silvery surface shifting in disorganized motions far above her, like some restless, unsettled creature.

Aisha Rose's lungs were starting to hurt. The urge

to open her mouth, to draw in one deep breath, was almost irresistible.

But . . . not yet.

First, she reached out to him. The only one who mattered. The only one stronger than she was.

He'd been ignoring her, avoiding her, for too long. That had to come to an end now, or else there would be no purpose to her going on with her hejira. It would be useless. She might as well breathe in the water now.

So she showed him who she was, and where she was, and what she was about to do.

And hoped he was watching.

THE BOY KNEW what it was like to be in grave danger. It had even happened to him though not often. Only once that he could remember, in truth: early on after his accident, when he was still weak and unsure of himself, and had awoken to find a pack of ragged, skinny dogs encircling him.

But he'd fought them off, killing two and sustaining no injuries. They'd been weak and hungry and, in the end, easily overcome. And that had been long ago, back when there were still dogs in the green lands.

Those had been the least of it, that lone threat and the more typical ones—hunger, cold, unexpected injury—he faced every day, every year. How much worse it had been for him when *she'd* been in danger. He'd felt so helpless, and helplessness terrified him.

But even that, knowing that someone, something out there might end her, wasn't as bad as this. Wasn't as bad as seeing what she was showing him right now.

Acceptance.

Surrender.

The embrace of death.

He had no idea what to do.

AND THEN HE did. But would it work?

He looked around, desperate, forgetting for a moment even where he was. Spotting the familiar landmarks: the castle above him, the tumbled boulders, the line of forest meeting the grassland.

And the little lake below. Too far?

Leaping from rock to rock, eating up the distance, he reached the lake's edge, sending the turtles toppling into the water from the logs and rocks where they'd been sunning themselves.

Much of the surface of the stagnant lake was covered in a fine layer of bright green weed. Taking two steps into the warm water, he bent over and skimmed some away with an open hand, leaving a patch of clear blue. The weed would quickly come flooding back, but for one brief instant the water reflected the blue sky above.

This instant his only chance. He wouldn't have time to try again.

He bent over the water until he could see his face in the surface, dark against the sky. At that moment, as gently as he could, he showed her who he was.

AISHA ROSE LET go of the sea turtle and drifted slowly upward.

She'd come here with a purpose in mind, but exactly what it was had grown as hazy as her vision. She wondered how much longer she would stay awake. She wondered what she would see when she slept.

But suddenly she saw a face, with skin much darker than hers, an old white scar running from the scalp across the forehead, and matted, curly black hair.

His face.

That was why she'd done this. To force him to acknowledge her. To risk unleashing his overwhelming power so he would reenter her life.

To be honest with herself: She'd never expected it to work.

But there he was. Everything about his appearance so surprising, so intriguing, and so . . . *curious* that Aisha opened her mouth involuntarily and breathed in a gulp of water. She felt the salt sear her throat and lungs, and knew she was about to cough.

She'd gotten what she wanted, but now it seemed like that wouldn't matter.

She expelled the seawater she'd taken in and, along with it, bubbles of precious air. Clamping her mouth shut, she watched them hurry upward, glimmering like tiny jellyfish, as if they, too, needed fresh oxygen and had little time to reach it.

Then, with some unexpected reservoir of strength, she kept herself from coughing, from drowning right where she was. Instead, she kicked as hard as she could, chasing the air bubbles toward the surface.

A race. More than that: a test.

Just another test in a life full of them.

* * *

MAMA HAD TOLD her about the afterlife when Aisha Rose was little.

They were walking along the road from Naro Moru back to their house. So early after the end of the dreamed earth, there was still food in cans, and Aisha remembered that they were taking some home that day. Corn and pumpkin and some kind of meat.

"On the dreamed earth," Mama had said, "some people believed, if you followed certain rules, certain precepts, you got rewarded with eternal life."

"Eternal . . . ?" Aisha Rose had asked.

Mama tilted her head and watched Aisha Rose's face. "You would live forever."

"Where?" Aisha Rose had gestured at the ruins spreading outward from them in all directions. *"Here?"*

Mama had laughed. "No one ever was quite sure where, I think," she'd said.

Suddenly, she'd looked distant, sad. "Amazing what people believed back then," she said.

Aisha Rose had looked around, trying to imagine. *Please don't let it be here,* she'd thought. *Please.*

The closest she'd ever come to a prayer.

I'M NOT GOING *to find out if there's an afterlife,* Aisha Rose thought now, surging toward the surface like a hawk in its killing dive. *Not here. Not yet.*

Yet only ten feet from the surface, the shifting silvery sheet so close, she couldn't keep her lungs empty any longer. She took a convulsive breath, a breath full of water that shocked her system and almost stopped her in place.

But only almost. If the ocean wanted to keep her, this was its last best chance, and it wasn't quite strong enough. Her arms flailed, her legs kicked more wildly, but still she rose. Less like a falcon than a hornbill or some other awkward creature, but she could see salvation, and it was close enough to touch.

Her head burst through the silver sheet and into the air. The sun was so warm on her face that it was as shocking as if it had been freezing cold.

Coughing and spitting, she spun around, expecting to see some toothy creature rearing out of the water at her. But there was nothing but the green-blue surface, the high blue sky with the sun burning in it, and a white bird diving into the water, emerging with a wriggling silver fish in its beak.

And a face. A young man's face.

Wanting to think, to remember, she swam the short distance through the gap in the reef and into the coral shallows. Then, floating on her back in the calm water, her heart rate returning to normal, she called the image back to her mind.

It *was* him. It had to be.

The first time, when she'd shown him the lion, it had just been a whim. A moment of loneliness leading her to a near-catastrophic decision.

But this time, she'd done it on purpose. She'd called out to him, and he'd answered.

She'd had no choice. She'd had to show him her face. Her true face.

Now she could go on.

THE BOY THOUGHT about what he'd just seen, about what he'd done. And, standing there in the little lake, alone, so consumed by loneliness that he thought it would tear him in two, he wept.

TWENTY-ONE

Manda Island, Kenya

"WHY ARE WE here?" Kait asked him.

They were standing beside one of the two enormous, swollen-trunked baobab trees that towered over the sixteenth-century ruins that Malcolm knew so well. The baobabs, perhaps five thousand years old, had probably not even registered the fall of the Last World, while the ruins of the Takwa settlement, built of pinkish gray coral, were perhaps only a little more weathered and crumbled than they'd been when he'd last seen them.

Malcolm felt something twist, wormlike, in his stomach at the question. It was time to tell her the truth, just as he'd told Trey, Mariama, and Shapiro.

About Chloe.

But he'd told the three of them years and years ago, and he found that he couldn't, not quite yet. As if speaking the words, revealing his hopes, would jinx them.

He knew he'd have to get over his superstitions. Everyone was going to learn about it sooner or later.

Still . . . he'd wait a little longer. So he merely said, "You know why."

His gesture took in some of the crew members out beyond the mangroves that fringed Manda Island, fishing from the two dinghies that had brought the rest of them ashore. Others were getting water from a deep, still-functioning well at the edge of the ruins or picking ripe cashews from a tree laden with them, while still others were hiking around in the low bush that covered the island just to stretch their legs before getting to work.

Ross McKay, who'd barely said a word since their stop on Madagascar, was standing off on the periphery. He was not even bothering to survey the wildlife here, not that there seemed to be much of it.

Malcolm looked over at Clare Shapiro, who was standing in the arched doorway of what had once been Takwa's great mosque. By the way her eyeglasses reflected the sunlight, he could see that her eyes were on him and Kait as well. But she was staying away because she knew what he had to do here, the news he had to give.

He shifted his gaze to Kait. She'd been leaning against the other baobab, but as he watched, she walked over to him, bearing a remote, unreadable expression.

Noting her careful, slightly awkward stride, Malcolm had a stray thought: *She's pregnant.*

But he dismissed it before it even took hold. As far as he knew—and everyone knew nearly everything in

Refugia—Kait hadn't had a boyfriend in . . . well, forever. Plus he'd heard her say many times that she would never bring a child into this world.

And even if she changed her mind about *that*, it wouldn't be just before a voyage she'd dreamed of for more than half her life.

Still—

"No," Kait said, coming up beside him. "That's not what I mean. Why are we *here*?"

Malcolm shrugged. "The crew was gonna string me up, I didn't give them some time ashore."

Her unblinking gaze held his.

He wriggled his shoulders. "Anyway, you know as well as I do, our next leg is going to be a fucking nightmare."

Their next leg being a voyage thousands of miles eastward to the vast island of New Guinea. A destination where some believed, on the basis of fragile, two-decades-old evidence, that a remnant of human society might have survived.

More hope than evidence, in truth. The valleys of New Guinea were so remote—and the mountains surrounding them so imposing—that many of the indigenous communities living there had remained undiscovered by the outside world until just decades before the Fall.

And then they'd proven uncompromisingly warlike. Papua New Guinea had been an Australian protectorate, and the western half of the island "owned" by Indonesia, but protected from what and owned how were good questions. All the Huli, Dani, Asmat, and others, with their ages-old rituals and countless generations of grudges, wanted was to be left alone to fight their own battles.

Battles against the elements, against each other, and, most of all, against outsiders. Human outsiders and, as the world teetered on the brink, thieves as well.

By invading even New Guinea, thieves had proven that there was no populated area they could not reach. But they'd also revealed their inability to thrive in cold, isolated highlands—and, most importantly, that they could be defeated when confronted head-on by a foe as willing to sacrifice its own as the hive mind was to sacrifice an individual thief.

Defeated once, at least. And maybe forever? Or at least for two decades?

That was where the hope came in. Trey's hope, fading as the years passed, as he himself did, that his brother, Kit—who'd retreated with his wife and daughters to Papua New Guinea just before the Fall—might still live.

Malcolm feeding Trey's hope, however forlorn and wishful. Using it as one spur to drive the building and outfitting of the ship even as his own hope lay here, six thousand miles closer to home.

He wondered if his own hope was any less forlorn than his dying friend's had been.

"Malcolm," Kait said. While his mind had been elsewhere, she'd been watching his face. "Please tell me what's going on."

He looked at her.

"You give yourself more credit for secret-keeping than you deserve," she said.

After a moment, he shook his head. Maybe she was right, and he'd always been more of an open book than he'd thought. Or maybe it was just that they were so close to his goal now that she could smell it on him.

Whatever the reason, it was time. Time to share with her and everyone else on board. It would be easier to start with her.

So, taking in a deep breath, he told her that he'd had a daughter. That she'd lived near here. And that he'd left her behind to go to Refugia.

"Remember the way it felt at the end?" he said. "When we were all so effing certain what the thieves were going to do, but they were lying low, so everyone else thought we were galah?"

He saw Kait nod. Of course she remembered.

"Well, Chloe was one of those 'everyone else.'"

Kait was looking him with an intent expression he couldn't figure out.

"So anyway," he said, after a moment, "when Trey called and told me to come help—help build Refugia—"

"You were in Kenya," she said. "I remember."

He nodded.

"Here. With Chloe."

"Yeah." He paused. "And here I was going to stay, even if it meant the Fall was going to take me with it. Until Trey called."

Kait's eyes were wide. "But he said you were enthusiastic about helping."

He just looked at her, and after a moment, she flushed.

"What was I going to say? Trey said the colony

needed me." He shrugged. "And where else were they going to find a pilot as good as me?"

There were still spots of color on her cheeks. "You must have known you'd never get back here."

"Not for years, if ever." He smiled at her. "I knew that, yeah."

"But Chloe refused to come with you."

He was no longer smiling. "She thought I was mad as a cut snake. Best I could do was get her to promise to grow the vine. Make her own vaccine."

Saying the words out loud filled Malcolm with an unexpected hopelessness. Now that they were so close to the destination, it all seemed worse than unlikely. For a moment, he closed his eyes, as if to keep his doubts hidden from this girl who seemed able to see into him.

But when he opened them again, he saw that Kait's face had turned an almost ghostly white. "What's wrong?" he said. Then, "You planning on fainting, let's wait till we get closer to the group, okay?"

But far from fainting, she was staring at him with an unnerving intensity. "Exactly where did Chloe live?" she asked. "Where did she plant the vines?"

Malcolm blinked at her tone, then pointed across the narrow channel past the moored ship and to the mainland, a white strip of beach and a row of ruined resort hotels. "Just a little north of there. In her garden in Lamu Old Town."

Kait put a hand over her mouth.

"Where we'll be going tomorrow morning," he said. "Some of us."

He wasn't sure what reaction he'd expected, but not the one he got. Kait reached over and grabbed his forearms, holding on so hard her hands felt like clamps. She was the one who looked as mad as a cut snake now.

"God, Malcolm," she said. *"No."*

YET SHE WOULDN'T tell him why. He asked, requested, demanded, in every way he could think of, but all she did was look at him through those dark eyes in that bone-white face and ask him to promise not to go. To stick with the original plan and head off for New Guinea.

"You don't get it, Kait," he said at last. "That was never the original plan. *This* was. And it's what we're doing."

Some of us.

She was silent.

"That's the other reason we stopped here," he said. "Not just so I could bash in your ears, but to get the lay of the land before we head across."

Not waiting for her to reply, he turned. Years earlier, one of the baobab's giant branches had cracked and bent to the ground. Now he pulled himself onto it and went up until he reached the first of the horizontal branches. Staying close to the bulbous trunk, he pulled himself up from one to the next, until he was standing above the ruins, the mangroves, and the island's smaller trees.

Never looking back, but knowing by her labored breathing that Kait was following. And it was she who saw it first, when they were standing on a thick limb perhaps forty feet off the ground. He heard her say his name, and when he finally turned his head he saw she was looking west over the channel.

He followed her gaze, seeing the frigatebirds soaring past at eye level, the afternoon thunderclouds building over the horizon, the ship's crew scattered below, the dark line of the mangrove forest that fringed Manda Island, the rusted, skeletal wreck of a freighter jutting out of the channel's turbid water, and—

And, to the north, rising above Lamu Island, a column of gray-black smoke rising a hundred feet into the air before being blown north by the wind.

Malcolm was silent. But his heart thudded in his chest.

"What's causing that?" Kait said. "A wildfire?"

Malcolm squinted against the angled sunlight, and said, "Looks like it's coming from Lamu Town, maybe even right at the fort." He shook his head. "Wouldn't be anything burnable there by now—never was much— and the fort itself's made of coral. No, that's no wildfire."

"It looks like the smoke we saw near Refugia," she said.

He'd had the same thought.

She was silent for a few moments. Then she said, in a changed tone, "Is that where your daughter lived? Near the fort?"

"Not far."

Kait's eyes were on the column of smoke. Her face was still very pale.

"It's a beacon," Kait said. "Calling us in."

Malcolm was quiet.

In a gesture that seemed unconscious, she reached a hand out toward him.

And spoke the words Trey had spoken to her so many years before.

"Please don't go," she said.

He was silent.

"Malcolm—"

ALL THIS TIME, all these years when the *Trey Gilliard* had been just a dream, then a skeleton, and finally a seaworthy ship. When the great voyage had been in the planning stage, lines on a map, the empty spaces emblazoned with the words, "Here Be Monsters." When the final preparations were being made.

All these years, and Malcolm had imagined what it would be like to tell Kait that she wouldn't be allowed onshore when they arrived at Lamu. When they went to seek the first human population beside their own.

She would yell, beg, even cry. Or perhaps she would burn with a cold rage, arguing coherently that dictates issued even by Trey Gilliard, her beloved father, should carry no weight now. That Trey was long gone, and regardless of what he'd seen—or guessed at—during his long, slow slide into death, he did not rule over her.

Kaitlin Finneran Gilliard, a survivor of the Last World and this one, was capable of making her own decisions.

Regardless of her reaction, Malcolm had known that he was going to have to overrule her. Lock her in her cabin. Tie her to the mast if he had to. He'd promised Trey, and that was a promise he intended to keep.

*　*　*

BUT IN THE end, back on the ground, when he told Kait that he, Ross, Shapiro, and a few others were going ashore to see what lay under the column of smoke—but that she would not—she merely nodded.

Said, "All right, Malcolm." And turned away.

As if she'd given up and could no longer even bear to look at him.

TWENTY-TWO

STILL AFRAID.

Or, rather: *Afraid again.*

Jason and Chloe stood on the roof of the fort and watched the thief swarm rise into the still, damp evening air. But not in the usual flight of dominance, of power, the one they'd taken nearly every single evening since establishing the slave camp.

No, this was the behavior they'd first demonstrated only weeks ago, and three times since, tonight most of all. Evidence of disturbance. Disquiet. Fear.

Once again, something was scaring them. And worse tonight than ever before.

Even as he watched, Jason still had trouble believing—comprehending—it. Often enough over the years, he'd witnessed individual thieves in the last moments before their deaths. He'd seen them trapped in the thick unyielding webs of the button spiders—Africa's version of the black widow—that infested the fort's shadowy nooks and rotted doorways. Snapped up by big, brown praying mantises, another insect that seemed to shrug off the thieves' venom. Held by a pouched rat that, in the madness of captivity or the agony of its last stage as a host, had made a sudden, suicidal grab with its agile claws.

In each case, the thief had died. In each case, Jason had thought it had known it was going to die, or at least had recognized the danger it was in. Even as the trapped wasps tried to escape, they showed nothing but determination and calculation and strength.

And then, at the last moment before falling, before the killing bite, a kind of acceptance. Watching, Jason had thought that was the moment they'd been abandoned by the hive mind. The mind cutting its losses, shifting its focus to the millions—billions?—of thieves with more useful information to impart.

But this was different. Again and again, the wasps' spinning cloud shredded and re-formed. The choirlike sound of their wings increased in volume and pitch, sometimes accompanied by a chattering sound Jason hadn't heard before. A sound of increased distress.

And as this all happened, the ridden and host slaves always seemed unmoored, cut off from their masters. Empty shells. No, empty packages of meat and bone, so vulnerable in their stillness that Jason thought he could kill all of them—or, at least, as many as he needed to— with only a single sharp machete.

And he knew where to find the machete, in a storeroom on the roof, not far from the ovens. Machetes and hoes and shovels and other farming tools that he and

Chloe and a few others had gathered during the first days of the slave camp's existence. When they realized how crucial it was to prove to the mind that they were worthy of being allowed to stay alive. And, so much more importantly, to remain human.

The lesson that Chloe had learned from her father: If you proved you had skills that would help keep the ones in power alive, they would do the same for you. That was why she'd begun organizing the terrified, shell-shocked, infinitely vulnerable human survivors not into a rebel force but a working community able to feed and clothe itself, and to serve its masters.

And Jason, an automaton, overcome with grief, had followed her lead. Proven his worth as a slave, having forfeited it forever as a human being.

STANDING NEARBY, THE ridden slave that had accompanied him to the roof stood still. Looking at it, Jason was possessed by an almost unstoppable desire to retrieve the machete and wield it.

Two decades' worth of stifled rage, expunged in just a few moments.

Again Chloe read his thoughts. She put a hand on his arm, and said merely, "Jase, no."

He knew. Everything they'd been planning would be destroyed if he allowed his rage to possess him. No matter how powerful his bloodlust—and it was almost overwhelming—he couldn't give in to it. Not now. Not today.

So he didn't. Somehow he didn't. Instead, he let his

analytic brain take over from his animal one. He found himself wondering for the first time how much effort the hive mind expended to control its slaves. And what kind of a threat would force it to abandon them.

He couldn't even guess. But he knew it must be something big. He even allowed himself to imagine it might be the assault force he'd dreamed of for so long.

But speculating about it made little sense. All that mattered was that the mind be distracted enough for long enough for him and Chloe to escape. To give them enough time to reach the vine, the vaccine—if it even still existed—and protect themselves at last from the thieves.

And if any slaves in human form, born, ridden, or willing, chose to pursue him . . . well, then he might finally get the chance to use that blade.

HE AND CHLOE stood on the roof and watched the wasps rise into the high blue sky. A moment later, a few, then more and more, hundreds, thousands, split off from the cloud and began to stream southward. Flying fast, but not in any kind of formation, just a ragged swarm heading over Lamu Town and out of sight.

Something new once again. A new level of distress. Beside him, he saw Chloe reach a decision. She put her hand on his arm. "The next time this happens," she said, barely above a whisper, "we'll go."

Jason nodded and opened his mouth to say something. But before he could speak, Kenny and two other human slaves, two other betrayers, came around from behind the ovens. Before Jason could even move, the two had grabbed

Chloe, one on each arm, and were pulling her away toward the steps. The steps that led down to the cells.

Shouting, spitting with rage, she fought them, but they were so much stronger than she was. Jason knew what was going to come next: One of the two slaves let go of her, but only to club her on the back of the neck with a fist. Jason saw her eyes roll up, and she went as limp as death.

Finally, Jason moved. But he'd taken only two steps before Kenny stood there in front of him. Jason saw a glint of humor in his eyes, even of joy, as he said, "So much for running off, huh?"

Jason tried to shove him out of the way. But Kenny, not wasting time in argument, hit him with a straight right to the chest. The punch so hard that at first Jason thought his heart had stopped. Before he even realized what had happened, he was lying on the ground, flat on his back, looking up at the sky.

Failing again. That was the only thing clear in his clouded mind: Once again, he was failing someone he loved.

He was never sure how much of what he saw next was a dream, and how much a reality. But lying there, breathless, no strength in his limbs, he watched the whirlwind of thieves pause in flight, then come plunging down toward him.

In his half dream, he saw himself covered in them, a thousand thieves stinging him in unison. Imagining the agony he'd so long awaited, and wondering how long it would last.

But the wasps weren't coming for him. As he watched, he saw the swarm fracture into small groups, then into individuals. They hurtled through open doorways, landed on the walls, and crawled into cracks in the crumbling mortar, sheltered under the fort's cornices and at the base of the walls.

In just a few seconds, every one of them had vanished from his sight. And so had all the slaves, save for Kenny.

Kenny was still there, standing beside the low coral wall that overlooked the channel. His arms were limp at his sides, and there was an expression of absolute amazement on his face.

Jason got to his knees, then, with the help of the wall, to his feet. He'd intended immediately to go after Chloe, but the expression on Kenny's face compelled him to follow his gaze.

And that's when Jason saw the sails in the middle of the channel, a whitish glimmer in the low-angled sunlight.

The sails. The ship.

Too far off for Jason to see anyone on board, to see any real detail. But he could see enough. It was like something out of the storybooks he'd read and dreamed over as a child: a wooden ship whose three tall masts were hung with canvas. A ship from the Age of Sail, battling an unhelpful wind, but still coming toward them.

Jason had scanned the channel nearly every day for twenty years to see a sight such as this. But now that his fantasies had become real, he realized it was all wrong. This was not the armada of his imagination. It was just one small vessel, sailing forward into a trap.

For the first time, Jason wished for a hive mind of his own, one that would allow him to project his thoughts to the captain, the crew. To tell them to turn around, to ride the wind and the current out of the channel and back to the open sea.

To abandon all hope of rescue and save themselves.

In his mind, his feeble, individual human mind, Jason shouted the warning.

But the ship came on anyway, and he could only watch.

AND THEN NOT even watch. As if waking from a dream himself, Kenny turned away from the sight, the apparition. For a moment it seemed like he'd forgotten Jason was there, but then he focused, and his wide-eyed gaze narrowed.

His hand grasped Jason's arm like a handcuff. "Come with me," he said. "Now."

Jason didn't move. "Where's Chloe?"

"Locked away safe."

"You going to do that to me, too?"

Kenny shook his head. "Why bother? You're not going anyplace without her."

Glancing again at the oncoming ship, visibly closer already, he yanked at Jason's arm, and said, "We need to get out of sight."

A tone in his voice that Jason didn't recognize at first. Then he did. It was fear. Kenny was afraid.

"You come," he said, "or I'll kill you right here and feed you to the oven."

Fear could have deadly consequences. Jason followed him down the stairs.

Down on the main plaza, the slaves were heading to the sleeping quarters. There were no thieves in sight. Soon, the fort would seem deserted to any outside eyes . . .

but for the smoke from the ovens, which undoubtedly had already caught the attention of the ship's crew.

They knew that there were people here, which meant they would come ashore and walk directly into an ambush.

Jason was no seer, but he could see the future with perfect clarity.

AS HE WAS herded into the sleeping chamber, he caught one more glimpse of the ship. It was much closer now though, in the last light, merely a brownish smear against the gray of the channel. Then the dusk fell and took it from his view.

TWENTY-THREE

AFTER ALL THOSE years where nothing had ever changed, where the deadliest threats—disease, hunger, even death by thief—had grown stale through familiarity, Ross McKay had begun to feel bulletproof.

Not immortal. Not quite. At fifty-four, Ross could feel the years sliding past, steady, inexorable. He was also well aware that the belief—so widespread in the Last World—that you were being cheated if you didn't make it to eighty-five or ninety had vanished. Gone the way of most other arrogant human assumptions, leaving him grateful to have lived as long as he already had.

And still . . . and yet. Whatever had sent the rest of the crew on the *Trey Gilliard*'s first voyage, Ross had volunteered largely to remind himself that the world contained marvels—and perils—beyond those that might kill you within walking distance of Refugia.

The expedition thus far had shown him a few. A very

few. The lions and other predators they'd encountered on their occasional explorations had been more a danger in theory than in reality. They'd been interested in these strange new visitors to their kingdoms but neither frightened nor especially threatening.

Plus, as humans had done for centuries, if not millennia, the *Trey Gilliard*'s explorers had brought superior weaponry with them. Enough to make sure that any lion considering making a meal of them would instead have thrashed and bled in the dirt.

So perhaps Ross *had* felt immortal. Once. Until he'd seen what the world truly looked like. The still-tainted world with its empty places, its piles of bones, its wreckage.

For him, the issue was no longer about immortality. It was: Having seen what he'd seen, having understood the truth at last, how badly did he want to die?

THEY'D MOORED IN the channel a few hundred yards off the ruins of Lamu Town the evening before, just as the sun was setting. The fort was seemingly deserted save for the thin thread of smoke still tracing upward in the last light.

What followed was a strange night, unlike any since the expedition had set off. Lots of quiet conversation, lots of questions with no answers, no small amount of fear. Some arguing that they should haul anchor and get out of there, but others determined to see what the empty fort actually contained.

Malcolm, his eyes a little wild in his gaunt face, put an end to the discussion. "At first light tomorrow, I'm heading over there," he said. "You want to come with me, that's fine, but I'll go alone if I have to."

"So why are they all so quiet?" someone asked. "Why hasn't anyone come down to the beach and shouted and jumped around?"

No one, not even Malcolm, had an answer to that. Or, rather, anything other than the obvious answer: Whoever was there wouldn't be welcoming them but setting a trap.

Aboard the *Resolution*, someone else pointed out, Captain Cook found himself treated almost as a god by some islanders he encountered and murdered in the Pacific shallows by others.

It was a long night.

IN THE END, five of them went: Shapiro, Malcolm, and the twins, Darby and Brett Callahan. And Ross. Five of them on the dew-slick deck, waiting to clamber down the ladder to the waiting dinghy.

Dylan Connell was staying behind, to helm the ship if it needed to depart in a hurry . . . even if that meant leaving behind those who were onshore. And Kait was staying put, too. Ross had expected her to raise a ruckus, but she'd accepted the decision without argument. She hadn't even attended the meeting in the darkened galley the night before.

Nearly the entire crew—only Kait was still missing— had assembled on deck in the milky morning light. Now they stood quietly, cold and glum as they watched the five volunteers gather.

All five of them armed, Ross with his Mossberg shotgun, Malcolm also with a shotgun, whose barrel he'd shortened, Shapiro with a .223 Bushmaster rifle, and—because the corrosive months at sea had left them short of firearms—the twins carrying knives.

Too much weaponry, or not enough? It was impossible to know.

Shapiro, following Ross's gaze and his train of thought, said, "Welcome us as we expect to be welcomed, or we'll kill you."

Malcolm didn't seem to be listening. Instead, he was standing by the rail, looking over the calm blue-gray water at the rocky shore, the decrepit ruins of the old wharves, the looming stone fort, which looked as bleak and lifeless in the morning light as it had the evening before.

Even the fire that had called to them the day before had died down or been damped since they'd dropped anchor. Overnight, they'd seen its red glow gradually dim, and now, instead of a column of gray smoke, only the slightest shimmer, heat waves rising in the chill morning air, revealed that there had ever been a fire there at all.

"Where the hell are you all hiding?" Malcolm said under his breath.

And why, Ross thought.

"And why?" Malcolm said.

BRETT CALLAHAN ROWED them in, under a sky that turned from pink to the palest blue as the shore drew closer.

The first boat in years to make this transit, the dinghy startled schools of flying fish, which skipped and soared for dozens of yards on flat black-and-red wings ahead of the bow before disappearing under the ripples again.

Ross spotted some dark shapes moving beneath the boat. Leaning over to look more closely, he saw they were bonito, at least four of them, each three or more feet long, shining blue and silver in the early light.

And all the while, the shore, and the dark fort just inland, drew closer, and still there was no sign of life. No bird, no animal, no human. No thief.

In the bow, Malcolm was whistling a tuneless song through his teeth. But Ross saw that his eyes were as unblinking, as intent as a hunting falcon's, that his left hand was already wrapped around the stock of his snubnosed shotgun, and the fingers of his right were always near the trigger.

THEY STEPPED ASHORE on what had once been a stone-and-steel wharf but was now a skeletal ruin of rusty metal spikes and chunks of crumbled concrete. Straight ahead, past what had once been small cement-block stores or offices, the fort stood like a gigantic, silent monolith marking . . . what?

Looking at the massive coral walls, up close a strange orange-brown, Ross found himself marveling at the time and hard labor that had been put into building this one enormous structure. And how many others like it were there across the world? So much wasted energy!

"Let's go," Malcolm said.

Ross, bringing his attention back, found he was having trouble catching his breath.

THEY WALKED UP past the waterfront ruins and into what had once been an open courtyard at the base of the fort. Even now, the twisted-trunked old trees that had bracketed the fort's entrance still stood, as sturdy as the fort itself amid the rubble.

"There was a market here," Malcolm said in a low voice. "People would sleep in the shade of those trees."

Then he shook his head and led the way toward the steps leading up into the fort. There were about twenty steps, discolored and, in places, broken into fragments, but still navigable with care and at a deliberate pace.

Here, Malcolm stopped. "These lead to the central plaza," he said. "I'll go first."

Shapiro made a sound deep in her throat, and Ross understood why. This was nobody's concept of an ideal approach, these crumbling stairs up to a plaza they wouldn't be able to see until they neared—or even reached—the top.

When no one else spoke, however, Malcolm did. "I know," he said. "They could roll a boulder on us and knock us down like bowling pins. But unless someone has a helicopter to drop us on the roof, there's no other choice."

No one spoke. Nor did they speak when, a moment later, the wind—which had been blowing at their backs—shifted, carrying down the steps the stink of thief.

* * *

PICKING THEIR WAY carefully around the sliding chunks of stone, they ascended, step by careful step. Above, a vulture, then more, rose above the fort's ramparts.

At the front, Malcolm alone seemed to know where to put his feet without even looking. His gaze was everywhere, seeming to see everything, and as they drew closer to the top, his expression grew even grimmer.

A step behind him, Shapiro looked . . . different than usual. There was a kind of joy in her. The scientist's joy in being on the verge of a fascinating new discovery. Or the fighter's joy at being at the onset of a battle.

Maybe those two things weren't so far apart.

Ross turned his head to glance at the twins. As always, those two narrow faces, with their nearly identical broad foreheads, deep-set eyes, and strong jaws, were expressionless. But they seemed nothing but resolute, determined, and the glint in Darby's eyes when she met his gaze showed something more: a reflection of Shapiro's joy.

After two decades in Refugia, she and her brother were finally in their element here, in the midst of the unknown.

Darby faced front again, leaving Ross all alone.

THEY WERE ABOUT halfway up when the whirlwind rose before them.

For the past twenty years, the presence or absence of thieves had merely been data. Information to be noted, recorded, but nothing more, and the data never showed great numbers.

The storm of wasps that rose around them was more than anyone in the party had seen since the end of the Last World. Thousands in twisting skeins, black and bloodred against the blue sky. Rising high in the air and pausing, hovering, all oriented to look down at the paltry group of humans clustered below them.

Looking up, squinting, Ross had one rational thought, *Where did they find enough hosts?*

But then that portion of his brain—the coolly scientific part—was unexpectedly overwhelmed by another, more primitive one. Ross looked up at the thieves, but for a moment all he could see were the lemur bones they'd seen back on Madagascar. The countless skulls scattered across the blasted plain.

In a sudden, seething, overwhelming anger, he swung his shotgun up and pulled the trigger. He saw the pellets tear a hole in the cloud of hovering thieves, but in an instant the hole was filled, an unstoppable tide in flood.

And then, a tsunami, the wasps came sweeping down and were among them. A great onrush of wings, the bitter odor everywhere, smears of flickering movement everywhere in the air before their eyes like a migraine's aura, the onset of blindness.

Ross fired the second meaningless barrel, tore apart the sweeping wave, watched it re-form.

By the time he refocused on the steps above, the humans had appeared. Or were they human? He couldn't tell. All he saw before they were upon him were their bodies, half-naked, scarred, and battered. But they moved so fast, like something out of a dream, like the savages in the adventure books he'd read as a child, when he'd dreamed of taking expeditions like this one.

Ross didn't even have the chance to pump new shells into his shotgun before the vanguard of the attacking force was upon him. But he knew he might not have done it, anyway.

He'd never killed a primate in his life.

IN HIS LAST moments, Ross McKay saw—

He saw last-stage hosts, their contorted faces lacking any remnant of humanity. Others, nearly as feral, who had thieves riding the backs of their necks. And still others who seemed to be human. Fully human.

He saw Malcolm, as always quicker and more decisive than the rest of them, let loose with blasts from both barrels of his shotgun, cutting two of the attackers nearly in half.

He saw Shapiro, ten feet away, aim more carefully and pick off two, then three others around Malcolm—two with riders, one without. But he knew—and he could tell she did, too—that it was hopeless. More attackers were already pouring down the stairs toward them.

Ross saw the twins move past him to enter the fight. Too late, and overmatched even before they began.

Or maybe it had always been too late, and the weaponry didn't matter.

He saw, bizarrely, a human, a man, one of *them*, come

leaping down the steps toward them. The man was carrying a . . . panga, a machete.

Even then, even in these last horrendous seconds, Ross found himself wondering who this man was.

But, as so often happened in science, he never got an answer to his question. For at that instant, a body slammed into his, sending him over backward. He glimpsed a face just inches from his own. And, beside it, the face of the thief attached to the man's neck.

As he fell, his attacker on top of him, Ross felt the back of his neck hit the sharp edge of one of the stone steps and heard as much as felt the crack of bone, his cervical spine fracturing.

This was a blessing, this injury. A blessing, because although Ross was witness to what happened next—for a little while longer—at least his body was free from pain.

TWENTY-FOUR

JASON STOOD AT the top of the fort's stone staircase, clutching the hilt of his machete in his right hand and watching events unfold. It was all happening exactly as he'd predicted, as if he'd imagined the worst case, the nightmare scenario, then made it happen. Like he was some malign god making his helpless subjects dance.

There *was* one unexpected thing, something he doubted even a trickster god would have thought up. The visitors were wearing regular clothes, not wasp-proof hazmat suits. Clothes that were neat and well cared for compared to the slaves' rags, but still merely regular shirts and pants.

And yet the strangers lived. All that exposed skin meant that they should have long since been stung to death. Gouged and eyeless. But they weren't. *Something*— some kind of invisible armor, a force field—was protecting them from the thieves.

But what? What was it?

Not that it mattered, not really. It wasn't going to do them any good in the end. Because their armor protected them only from thieves, not the slaves who were overwhelming them. More and more slaves were coming down the steps, and Jason saw among them the most ferocious and unstoppable of all: the last-stage hosts. Someone had opened their cells and set them free, and now they were leading the attack.

Despite their weapons and their bravery, the visitors stood no chance. They weren't even going to make it to the top of the stairs. Already one of them, a thickset middle-aged man, was mortally wounded with a broken neck, sprawled limply across the steps as a ridden slave tore at him.

That left just four, three in a tight knot, their backs against the stone banister. A woman in her sixties with wild gray hair and a fierce, fearless gaze, wielding a rifle. And, flanking her, two younger ones, a man and a woman, so similar in build and features that they must have been siblings. These two had come only with knives, and even though they each succeeded in killing a ridden slave—no easy task—Jason knew that they would soon be overwhelmed.

Even as he had that thought, Jason saw the older woman pause to reach into the pocket of her tunic for fresh ammunition. At this, the slaves surged forward again, and a ridden one grabbed the barrel of her rifle.

The barrel was so hot that Jason could hear the slave's skin sizzle. But of course that didn't matter. With a twist of its arms, it wrenched the gun away and threw it over the stone banister and out of sight.

The woman went for a knife she wore on her belt, but Jason knew that was a last, hopeless gesture.

A pair of shotgun blasts brought the slaves to a momentary halt and took Jason's gaze to the final member of the group, the shooter, a tall, lanky man with high cheekbones, fierce blue eyes, and a mop of gray-blond hair. A familiar face, even though Jason knew he'd never seen it before in life.

The arcs of blood that erupted as each shell from the man's gun found its target were impressive, but meant nothing. Two fewer slaves? Inconsequential.

Jason felt paralyzed by sorrow. No more than five minutes after the explorers' arrival, the great attack on the slave camp at Lamu Fort would be history. Soon enough, forgotten, with Jason left as the only witness to remember, or to care.

Except . . . that's not what happened. As a human slave—it was Kenny—struck the older man in the head with a rock, sending him to the ground, Jason recognized the man. He knew who it was.

The realization was like a door opening far too late, and Jason understood everything. Who these brave, foolhardy explorers were, and why, at long last, they'd come here.

Chloe, locked in the cells below, if she even still lived, would have laughed at him. "Jesus, Jase, took you long enough," she would have said. "I told you all about it. So where were you? Thinking about the sports scores?"

No. Jason had been listening to her. Only now, however, did he realize he'd never truly believed in it, in the vine or the vaccine. It had sounded like a fairy story to him, as surreal as a wooden sailing ship coming up the channel. And his and Chloe's planned flight nothing more than a suicide run.

But it *had* been true, her story. However worthless it was against the slaves, the vaccine actually existed and worked against the thieves. Even at the height of the battle, the wasps spinning and darting around showed every sign of agitation and distress, yet not a single one ever came within a foot of the visitors.

The vaccine existed. It worked. And that man being dragged toward the cells by two ridden slaves was Chloe's father.

And Jason, awake at last, knew that it was time—long past time—for him to stop being a mere witness, and finally, for the first time in decades, in forever, to *act*.

HE HURTLED DOWN the steps toward the clot of slaves surrounding the surviving humans. Thieves spun around his face, but he saw that the hive mind could not yet read his thoughts or his intentions. To the mind, he was still just another slave.

He swung his blade with all his strength, seeing it glint in the sun on the downstroke and reappear smeared with blood and fragments of shining white bone. A moment later, one slave's blood mingled with another's, then a third. The third was Kenny.

Each stroke severing the spinal column of its target, so one stroke was all he needed. Bodies, slave bodies, fell around him as he fought forward. Drenched in blood, gasping for air, his lungs and eyes burning, he cut through the wall of flesh toward the besieged visitors.

Every moment he expected a slave to wrench away his weapon, to turn on him. Or to feel the agony of a thief's stinger entering his body.

But he didn't, and then he was there. Standing in front of the older woman, meeting her fierce gaze with his own. Seeing her eyes widen and spark with something that looked like . . . curiosity.

He turned back to face the slaves, who had fallen back in the face of his unexpected assault. As he put his body between them and her, the woman, holding her own blood-smeared knife in her right hand, stepped forward and pressed her left side against him.

At first Jason didn't understand why. But then he did. *The force field,* he thought. The vaccine. However the hell it works, she's using it to protect me.

And, in fact, the thieves now gave him the same berth that they'd been giving the visitors. But already the slaves were regrouping, surging forward once again.

Jason raised his machete, but now the crowd was too close for him to take a proper swing. His next slash cut into the solid bone of a slave's shoulder, and when it twisted away it wrenched the blade's hilt out of his hand.

As the closest slaves reached for his throat, he heard from behind him, the sound of voices. Two voices together. The brother and sister, praying.

Jason closed his eyes. He didn't pray, but sent out his thoughts. If humans did share some connection, if there *was* some kind of hive mind in them as well, maybe Chloe could hear him.

I'm sorry.

I love you.

THE SLAVES' HANDS were already on him when he heard the sound of the thieves' wingbeats change. It rose in pitch and intensity, accompanied by the chattering sound he'd heard only a few times before.

The sounds of fear.

Jason opened his eyes. The two slaves before him, ridden ones, were standing so close that he was staring into their faces. Seeing not a trace of recognition there, even though Jason had lived beside them for years.

No recognition, but something else, something he'd never before seen in a ridden slave's face: confusion. As if their brains were filled with noise, with the meaningless whir of wings.

Jason saw their riders leave them then and fly upward. He tilted his head, his gaze following them. The two joining the many, the uncountable swarm.

About twenty feet over his head, the swarm had come together in a tight, churning knot, a kind of knotted vortex. It was astonishing—after all these years, he was seeing yet another new thief behavior.

And yet this behavior *was* familiar in some way.

It took him a moment to realize why. It was something he'd seen only once, on a dive off the Maldive Islands: a feeding frenzy involving bluefish, sharks, giant tuna, and finally even a whale, predators all drawn to that one spot by the prospect of feasting on a massive school of anchovies.

And the anchovies, in their terror and as a last hopeless defense against the ferocious assault, had drawn themselves into a spinning knot just like this one. The hive mind in extremis, with the survival of a few depending on the death of almost all.

A bait ball. That's what it was called.

The thieves had formed themselves into a bait ball.

They were acting like . . . *bait*.

AND THEN JASON saw why.

A girl, moving up the steps toward them. Moving with a loping, long-limbed stride like a cheetah's.

No. Not a girl. A young woman, perhaps twenty, tall but so slightly built and skinny that she could have passed for twelve. Dressed, if anything, even more raggedly than Jason was, and with a filthy wrap on her left hand that didn't conceal the infection spreading across her palm and up her forearm.

She was Caucasian, though darkly tanned, with tangled, unevenly cut blondish hair over a sharp-jawed face that seemed almost as expressionless as the slaves'. Expressionless except for her eyes, which Jason could see even from a distance were a strange, milky blue-violet. Her gaze was alive with interest as she approached.

And she was singing. Jason couldn't believe it. She was singing some wordless melody in a fine, strong alto.

Her gaze settled on Jason for a moment, and she fell

silent as she tilted her head and looked directly into his face. Next she scanned the motionless slaves, the ridden and born ones struck still and the human ones filled with sudden doubt and fear. Then, finally, she shifted her gaze to the spinning mass of thieves above.

Only then did she show any expression on her face, a tiny frown. But what was in her eyes was something else, something shockingly dark and predatory.

As if responding to the force of her gaze, the mass knotted together more tightly, spun more frenetically. The sound of the thieves' wings rose further in pitch, and the ball rose higher, as if seeking to escape, to flee, but unable to break free.

Without lowering her eyes, she stepped closer to Jason. He saw her mouth move, as if she were trying to speak to him, as if she were trying to find the right words to say.

Before she could, the first of the thieves began to fall from the sky. Plummeting helplessly, stunned or dead, just as they had in Jason's dream of rescue. Soon the stairs were carpeted in them, not even their mandibles twitching or their stingers seeking someone to take with them to the grave.

Jason heard the girl make a quiet sound, a tiny moan of ultimate exhaustion, of surrender. He looked just in time to see her fall to the ground among the thieves she had knocked from the sky.

TWENTY-FIVE

THE ATTACKERS CAME from the south, out of the forest. Mariama never discovered whether Rodrigo and Marie, the sentries on duty in the towers on the southwest and southeast corners, had seen anything, whether they'd had any warning at all.

Or maybe they'd been asleep. The predawn hours were hard for everyone, and the sentries had been nearing the end of their shift. The end of just another shift after countless hundreds during which absolutely nothing important had happened.

No one ever learned what had taken place in those last few moments, and how much Rodrigo and Marie might have prevented. All that mattered was that they died before they had the chance to ring the alarm.

The first wartime deaths in the Next World, as lacking in detail as countless millions that had preceded them in the Last.

* * *

THE ASSAULT ON Refugia came in three waves. The first was an advance force that climbed the towers and killed the sentries. The second followed almost immediately, as the southern and eastern walls were set afire, an act not designed to burn them down—the walls were too solid to go up in flames—but to spread billows of smoke and sow confusion and panic.

But not as much panic as the third wave provoked: the attackers that erupted from the tunnels connecting Refugia to the forest. The passageways designed to provide the colonists with secret escape routes in case of attack instead gave the invaders access to the very heart of the colony.

In retrospect, Mariama thought, perhaps this kind of attack had been inevitable. But only in retrospect, because in designing the tunnels she—all of them—had made a mistake both simple and profound. The kind that can't ever be repaired.

Mariama and Malcolm had built Refugia, with its high walls and its sentries, in anticipation of an attack by humans. In their imaginations, they'd visualized a disorganized horde of survivors who, upon discovering a colony that could feed and clothe itself—and protect itself against the thieves—would try to overwhelm it.

But neither of them had guessed that the attackers would be guided, directed, by the hive mind. The mind that saw everything and left the colony's inhabitants with few secrets to keep and nowhere to hide.

That was the part they'd missed. The part that ended the war for Refugia nearly as soon as it began.

* * *

MARIAMA EMERGED FROM sleep to find two men coming through the door of her cabin.

Two unfamiliar men.

For an instant, caught in transition between dreaming and waking, Mariama lay still. She heard her voice, still muzzy, say, "Who are you?"

Coming clearer, she saw that at least one of the two understood her words. But he did not respond. Nor did either of them hesitate as they took three strides across the floor to her.

Finally, almost too late, Mariama rolled away. As one of the two came across the bed—she could smell his rank breath, and the odor of thief as well—she twisted back around, and in her right hand she held a knife.

The M9 bayonet with the seven-inch blade that she had kept well sharpened, hanging from a hook in the wall beside her bed these twenty years.

By now she was fully awake, and she'd always been good with a knife. And she was still strong. As always, stronger than anyone—any man, any creature—ever seemed to expect.

The first attacker, dark-eyed and blank-faced, had his hands on her as she got her feet under her and pushed upward with all her strength. Her sudden movement knocked him off balance as she thrust upward with her right hand.

She felt the blade scrape against his rib before cutting through the flesh of his chest and into his heart.

Pulling the blade out, she felt his hands lose their strength, saw them drop, clenching and unclenching, to his sides. But even then, as his blood flooded out through the gaping wound she'd made, he stayed upright, allowing her to see the thief riding on the back of his neck.

Finally, he fell to the floor in a graceless collapse. As he went down, the thief rose and hovered at Mariama's eye level. She saw that it was struggling to fly, its wings damp with the man's blood. A moment later, after she'd snatched it out of the air and smashed it against the wall, it was dead as well.

If the other man had intended to attack, this would have been the moment. But he hesitated. And now, as she leaped off the bed, she saw a familiar expression on his face.

A human expression. Fear.

Before she could reach him, he'd turned and fled. Out of reach of her blade and her rage.

Leaving the door open behind him, which allowed Mariama to hear for the first time the shouts and screams echoing outside.

PULLING ON A T-shirt and cotton pants, she went out the door and ran through the earliest gray light of dawn to the edge of the plaza. There she stood still, half-hidden behind a bush, and witnessed the ruin of the colony she'd always considered her own responsibility.

Smoke billowed across the plaza, mixing with the rising morning mist and the twisting skeins of thieves. Figures ran here and there, some recognizable—people she knew, had known for the only part of her life that still seemed real—and others strangers.

Human strangers, some of them, and some not. Some being ridden by thieves, and others that Mariama saw—with a long-buried jolt of recognition—were last-stage hosts. Dozens overall, inexorable, unstoppable as they swarmed the plaza, entered the cabins, captured the Fugians who did not react as quickly as Mariama had.

Some of their captives were naked, the rest clad only in nightclothes. None seemed to be armed or in any condition to fight, and already some were cowering on the ground, awaiting imprisonment or death.

Some, but not all. As she watched, Nick Albright came around a corner and into the plaza. He was carrying a handgun, a semiautomatic .9mm SIG that Mariama had often seen him practicing with on the target range.

But even before he appeared, some of the last-stage hosts were moving in his direction. So, regardless of his gun's ability to spray its bullets around, he only managed to get off three shots—all at close range, none of which would have required target practice—before he was overwhelmed.

He gave a single hoarse shout as he went down under the onslaught.

Mariama felt a great anger rise up in her, a red anger that filled her skull. She wanted nothing more than to rush into the crowd of invaders, to take them all on, to spill as much of their blood as she could before she died.

But she knew she had to restrain herself. It would be a useless gesture to die for the other Fugians, as Nick had.

Maybe, by holding back now, she could save some of them.

Beginning with one.

She turned away from the carnage and began to run.

TWO ATTACKERS WERE dragging Sheila, still in her nightgown, from her isolated cabin. Two . . . humans, Mariama thought. Too alert and fast-moving to be last-stage hosts, and she could see no riders.

Two humans attacking her oldest, closest friend.

For just a few seconds more. Then they were merely two humans thrashing on the ground, blood spewing from their slashed throats.

Humans were easy.

SHEILA WAS STARING at the dying—dead—men. Mariama grabbed her by the arm and yanked her away.

For a moment Sheila, eyes and mouth both wide with terror, fought to escape Mariama's grasp. Then she seemed to come back to awareness, at least enough to stop struggling and draw in a big, ragged breath.

"Sheila," Mariama said, "*move.*"

Finally, Sheila came with her, and they headed away from the plaza and the cabins, away from the shouts and screams, which were already dwindling. The battle for Refugia—if it could even be called that—was coming to an end, half an hour after it had begun.

"Move where?" Sheila managed to say.

But Mariama, leading her forward, was silent. Either her instincts—or maybe they were just hopes—would prove correct, or they wouldn't. The two of them would live a little longer, or they'd die now.

In either case, there was no need for her to explain.

TWENTY-SIX

THE BOY STOOD atop his aerie in the pouring rain. The storm had come from the north, heralded by billowing dark clouds barely above ground level, that swept over the green lands and obscured the dark hulks of the ruined buildings marking the borders of his territory.

A cold rain, a harbinger of the changing seasons. A warning he had never ignored . . . until now.

He shivered. This was the kind of cold rain that got deep under his skin, the kind that blossomed into a thick weight in his chest that made it difficult for him to breathe. That filled his head with a quantity of green goo—semiliquid—that never seemed to run out no matter how much of it he expelled.

He thought of it as the green sickness. He'd come down with it a few times over the years, and it left him feeling so weak and shaky that it was hard to hunt, and it would sometimes last for days, even weeks, forcing him to rely on his stores.

It came most often in this season, especially when he was cold and wet. So normally he waited out rains like this one in one of his shelters.

But not this time. Not when he had more important things to think about, to accomplish.

And standing here in the cold rain wasn't the only thing he was doing differently. He'd also been neglecting many of his responsibilities, like gathering firewood, hunting, collecting fruits and nuts, smoking meat for winter stores.

And eating.

He'd always known that food came first. That his chances of surviving—the day, the month, the winter, each year—depended first and foremost on making sure he had plenty to eat. It was a simple, obvious conclusion.

And, equally obvious, it was most important to stock-pile food before winter fell, those long months when meat was scarce and crops nearly nonexistent. From the bees hastening from one late-season flower to the next with an urgency they never showed in midsummer, to the squirrels fattening themselves up as they built their winter nests high in the strongest oaks and maples, to the lions, the mother dragging one injured, struggling deer or raccoon after another back to the den for her cubs.

As part of that world, he'd always understood all this. But even so, now he spent hours every day, in every weather, at his game instead. His game. His work. His labor.

His *training*.

Training he'd neglected for far too long because he'd always believed he was already powerful enough. Until she'd shown herself to him, and he'd seen how truly vulnerable she was. That while he'd been measuring his life in years, hers might have only weeks, days, remaining.

That understanding, that series of revelations, had made his world flip on its head. All this time, he'd been learning the wrong lessons. He'd focused on the honeybees gathering nectar and pollen, the flocks of sparrows somehow feeling storms coming days in advance and feasting on seeds, the mother lion with her bloody prey, and missed the point.

He'd failed to see that the sole point of the bees' hectic foraging was to keep the queen and larvae alive. That the sparrows spent days, weeks, showing their babies how to find food, and that the mother lion, in bringing back an injured deer, had been training the cubs to hunt for themselves.

Training her cubs. The boy supposed that someone, his own mother, must have taught him to hunt as well. Trained him. Helped him stay alive until he could manage for himself.

Because he couldn't remember any of that, or her, he'd missed the point.

Training was all that mattered. And he was not yet powerful enough.

No: That wasn't true. He had the power.

It was something else he was lacking.

ONCE THE RAIN ended, the fog, chased by the wind, sometimes obscured the world from him—and him from the world—as it passed by.

But he didn't care what he saw and what he didn't, not here, not in his world. He was elsewhere, where he didn't need to use his eyes.

For hours he stood there, until the fog blew away and the sun broke through, drying his clothes—the mist rising from him like it did from the pond below—and warming his bones.

But he barely noticed. He was still far away, learning.

Learning how to reach out in new ways.

Preparing for the first time to take care of someone else.

His body might be wasting away, but the most important part of him—the only part he cared about—wasn't. That part was gaining strength.

TWENTY-SEVEN

THERE WAS COMPLETE silence.

No, this wasn't true. Jason could hear the cawing of crows fighting over something down by the old wharves. The whistle of the wind as it swept through the stone structures around them. Even the whispery sound of the dead thieves' insubstantial bodies tumbling along the stone plaza, driven by the gusty breeze.

No. Not dead.

Even as he glanced down, he saw one of the wasps' legs twitch. The tip of another's stinger, close to where the girl lay at his feet, much too close, gleamed white as it poked from a thief's abdomen.

Fighting off a sudden surge of panic, he bent over and hoisted her off the ground. She was so light, so insubstantial, all long skinny limbs and matted hair brushing against his face as he lifted her.

She was not dead, either. Still semiconscious, but

aware enough to link her arms around his neck and help him hold her as—expecting any instant the attack to resume—he looked around.

The frozen tableau was just beginning to shift again. The last-stage hosts had fallen to the ground, just as their masters had, but they, too, were still alive, making feeble, disorganized motions with their hands and feet.

Watching them, bile rising in his throat, Jason wished for a moment to be free of his burden. With his machete, he could free the camp of these monsters in just a minute or two.

The ridden slaves, five or six of them in view, though deprived of their riders, hadn't been affected so strongly. But stunned as well by whatever the girl had done, they were moving away, their normally expressionless faces showing something remarkable. Something that Jason never thought he'd see in one. Shock. Even pain.

And the human slaves—

The human slaves were running, saving themselves, like humans almost always did. Heading for the fort's catacombs. For where Chloe was, if she was still alive, and the breeding chambers, and her father, too.

Again, Jason was desperate to be free of the girl who clung to him. To fight his way into the catacombs or to die trying.

Instead, he turned to look at the leader. She was staring at the girl, but then she transferred the full intensity of her gaze to him. "What did you do?" she asked in a voice like wire.

He shook his head and answered her question with

his own. "The others," he said, and coughed. How long had it been since he'd talked out loud? Freely?

"From your ship," he went on. "Are they coming for you?"

She gave her head a fractional shake.

"Good." His gaze flickered over the awakening thieves. Soon enough, the ridden slaves, too, would be back under their control, and the hosts. The attack would resume, and this little pause would have had no meaning.

"Now go," he said.

In his arms, the girl gave a little moan. The sudden tension in her body showed that she was closer to consciousness.

"And take her with you," he said.

The male sibling stepped forward to take the girl from him. But the woman stopped him with a glance.

"That man," she asked Jason. "Is he dead?"

Jason's eyes sought out the torn-apart form of the stocky one who'd been killed at the onset of the battle.

The woman grimaced. "No. The other. The one they took."

Jason hesitated for a moment. He could read her thoughts. They were all prepared to die, these brave, foolhardy visitors, in the attempt to rescue the captive. *Malcolm.*

They would die, and Jason would, too, for no purpose at all. He wouldn't even have the satisfaction of taking more of the slaves with him before he did.

"I imagine he's dead by now."

For a moment her ferocious gaze clouded with what

he thought was grief. But then her chin lifted. "We have to be sure," she said.

"No, listen." He gestured at the tableau around them. At his feet, some of the thieves were back up on their legs. They moved with unfocused motions, like ones that had been beheaded, but they were coming back, and quickly.

"Either way, he's beyond your reach," he said. "Stay alive. Go. Now, or it won't matter."

The female sibling said, "Shapiro, look around. If we're going to move out, let's do it."

But the leader, Shapiro, was still staring at Jason. "How many of you are there?"

Of us. "Too many for you," he said. "And I'm the only one who won't try to kill you."

Shifting his grip on the girl, he looked down and saw she was awake and watching them with wide eyes. "Can you walk?" he asked her.

She nodded, then stretched her legs toward the ground. When he let go, she staggered a little on her feet. Placing her undamaged hand on his arm, she kept her balance.

"Take her with you," he said again to the woman. "Please."

Shapiro nodded, letting her gaze rest on the strange girl's face. But for one more moment she hesitated. "And you?"

Jason looked over his shoulder at the slaves gathering for a new attack. Waiting only for the hive mind to recover before they attacked again. Already, some were beginning to approach.

"Me?" he said, looking down at the thieves on the

ground nearby. They still weren't flying, but had regained enough mobility to move away, to seek a safe distance from the strangers' vaccine. Only his proximity was keeping him alive for now.

He'd expected them to run, to leave him behind, but now in an instant he saw another possible future . . . and the strategy that might make it happen. That could give him the chance to rescue Chloe.

"I'll be dead thirty seconds after you walk down the stairs," he said to Shapiro.

Without hesitating, she said, "Then you're coming with us."

He shook his head. "No. I'll stay."

Her gaze flicked over the mass of thieves covering the yellow-brown walls and stairs. A few of the wasps were already rising into the air—short, hesitant flights, but not for much longer. Two of the last-stage hosts were back on their knees.

"And die the minute we leave?" she asked.

"Yes."

"Then feel free to kill yourself," she said. She turned away from him and headed down the stairs, stepping past the body of her dead shipmate without a glance.

"But do it on your own time," she called back. "And not until you've answered every last one of my questions."

Jason had been counting on that.

He had no idea how much of the interchange the girl had taken in. But now she looked at him through those strange sea-glass eyes, took his hand in her undamaged one, and, with a tug that was much stronger than he'd expected, led him down the stairs. Staying close to him every step of the way, protecting him with her own force field, the siblings walking close behind.

Jason allowed himself to be led away from the fort, from Chloe.

Were she still alive, he knew she would want desperately for him to escape, to be free. As he would for her, she would willingly sacrifice her life for his.

But that wasn't Jason's plan at all. If this chapter of his story ended in death, as the last one did, this time he would not be only a witness.

And if one of them, and only one, would live, it wouldn't be him. Not this time.

TWENTY-EIGHT

Refugia

"HOW MANY DO you think?" Mariama asked. "I'm guessing . . . three. Four if I'm lucky."

Her eye to the rifle's telescopic sight, she was on her knees at the front of the hide, watching the activity in the plaza perhaps two hundred meters away. The hide, which she'd built years ago deep in the crook of a kapok branch and maintained ever since, and which gave a clear view over Refugia's southern wall.

Though Mariama hadn't built it for the view, but in case something very much like this happened someday.

"If everything breaks right, maybe five," she said. Then she paused, thinking. "I won't even have to worry too much about my aim. Not in this world."

Sheila, sitting behind her and in the corner of the platform, as far from the railing and the view as she could get, said, "Mariama?"

Mariama ignored her. "Just make them bleed and they'll die sooner or later. Sooner." She paused again. "Rather do it clean, though. Clean kills."

"Mariama." Sheila's tone was sharper. "Tell me what on earth you're talking about."

Finally, Mariama turned her head and returned her friend's gaze, Sheila's expression igniting a different kind of disbelief in her.

From what she could see, Sheila seemed to have spent the past twenty years actively forgetting every lesson the Fall had taught her. Even now, even in the face of all this evidence of human—and thief—nature, she seemed determined to hold on to at least some of her naïveté.

Mariama didn't have time for it. She had never possessed any illusions about the earth and its inhabitants, and she wasn't about to start now.

"You know exactly what I'm talking about." Mariama didn't bother to hide the edge to her tone. She gestured at the plaza below, where figures were moving around in the morning mist. "How many of them I can kill before they make it to cover."

Sheila, silent, looked away. Of course she'd known. For some reason, she'd just wanted to hear the words spoken out loud. Maybe she'd thought forcing Mariama to say them out loud would change her mind.

Well . . . no. It wouldn't.

Looking back over the railing, Mariama hefted the rifle in both hands. The Arctic Warfare, its manufacturer had called it, a name that had made her laugh when she'd first learned it. But she'd liked the feel of it, the power of its .308 bullets. After practicing with it out on the firing range, she knew she could hit a human-size target at six hundred meters, and what that direct hit would do.

That was the most important thing: that the Arctic Warfare, designed for use on the tundra, would do just as much damage here in the rain forest.

DOWN BELOW, THE invaders worked, bringing seasoned logs from the colony's wood supply and stacking them in the plaza.

As Mariama watched through the scope, two more came into view. They were already wearing stolen clothing, black pants made on one of Refugia's old sewing machines and colorful T-shirts hoarded from the Last World.

That made eight. Could she kill all eight before any escaped?

Probably not. Malcolm could have, if he hadn't chosen to sail away. The twins, too, probably, but they'd gone with Malcolm.

So many of Refugia's best fighters missing, leaving Mariama as good as alone. Why had anyone thought that was a good idea?

Because they'd gotten soft. Because they'd told themselves lies.

There was nothing to do about it. In getting Sheila to safety up in this hide, Mariama hadn't seen who else—if anyone—might have escaped. Even though she thought there must be dozens of others scattered around the forest, she had to assume the two of them were the only ones still free.

For about the hundredth time since they'd climbed the ladder up here, Mariama felt the familiar red anger flood through her. She wasn't a great shot. Good, but not good enough. She tended to get impatient, and her aim grew sloppy. Her skills were best up close, hand-to-hand, with different weapons.

Six would probably be her maximum.

"Listen," Sheila said. Mariama, focusing on the scene below, had nearly forgotten she was there, much less that they were in the middle of a conversation.

"They're still people, some of them," Sheila, the physician, the empathetic aid worker, said. "Still human."

Mariama laughed. She knew this would offend Sheila, but at that moment it didn't matter to her.

"And some of them aren't, not anymore," she said. "You saw that as well as I did."

Again, Mariama saw Nick Albright falling, heard his last shout.

"And anyway," she said, "who the hell cares if they're human or not?"

IN THE PLAZA, the eight invaders had finished stacking the firewood. Mariama had long since understood what its purpose was going to be.

At the far end of the hide, Sheila had been watching a thief crawling on a slender branch perhaps ten feet away. Though Mariama could only glimpse the thieves down in the plaza as sudden twists of grainy darkness amid the dispersing fog, she knew they were there, too. She could smell them, the reek of abundance.

She watched as Sheila looked away from the thief and down at the plaza. Then she sat forward and, head tilted, took in the scene below with sharper attention. After a few moments, her eyes widened, and she raised her hands in front of her as if trying to ward off something assaulting her.

A thought. A realization.

She swung around, and now her face was so white that Mariama thought she might faint.

"It's a pyre," Sheila said. "They're building a pyre."

Mariama was quiet.

Red spots rose in Sheila's cheeks. At that moment, something in her expression changed. Changed forever, Mariama thought.

Watching, she felt a mix of relief and sorrow. She'd always believed that the world *should* have room in it for people like Sheila: the empathetic ones, who valued sympathy and understanding as the highest attributes of humanity.

It should have, but it didn't.

Sheila's gesture with her arm was violent enough to startle the watching thief. It rose a few feet in the air before resuming its perch.

"Kill them," she said in a flat tone Mariama had never heard from her before.

Mariama shook her head. "Not yet."

Meaning, *There's still something I need to see.*

Again Sheila understood.

And covered her eyes with the palms of her hands.

* * *

ONE OF THE slaves went around the club building and returned carrying a lit torch. Moving quickly enough to convince Mariama that he was human, he applied the flame to several spots at the base of the stack of wood.

Soon Mariama could see flames licking around the smaller chunks and fragments. It would take a while to fully ignite, to become hot enough, but not that long. The wood had been well prepared.

Then all eight headed away and out of sight. But Mariama knew they would be back.

No more than a minute had passed when the first two reemerged, carrying a body between them. Looking through the rifle's sight, Mariama recognized who it was: Annette King, a teenager who'd been born in Refugia. Her face, a pale blur, stared up at the sky.

The two invaders tossed her on top of the pyre.

Seeing her, looking at that pale face, blank in death, and remembering the lively, sharp-witted young woman she'd been, Mariama understood something else. That though the majority of Refugia's dead were likely going to be made up of the usual casualties of a disaster—the old, the frail, the youngest, all those who couldn't move fast enough—they'd be far from the only ones.

They'd be joined by a less predictable cohort: the natives—those born here—as well as those who'd come when they were children. The ones who hadn't seen the Fall, the apocalypse. The ones who didn't grasp how important it was to run, who'd never learned that ten seconds might mean the difference between death and survival.

Thinking this over, Mariama must have made a sound, because Sheila, head down, hands pressed over her eyes, said, "Is it Jack?"

Mariama said, "No."

"You'll tell me when it is."

Mariama didn't reply.

Sheila said, "Mariama, you'll tell me."

"Yes."

The second body was another native, a boy named Michael who'd been one of Jack's friends. Mariama did not recognize the third, carried facedown, her clothes removed. She must have been one of the invaders.

The next, his gouged body nearly black with dried blood, was Nick Albright. Then a girl named Melanie Thomas, another Refugia native. Two others from among the invaders, and then three Fugians, including Spencer Browning, at eighty or so one of the colony's oldest citizens.

This courtly old man's desecrated corpse thrown, like all the others, with no care or delicacy atop the pile of sprawled, disorganized limbs and dead-eyed faces.

After that, the invaders did not return to the club. Instead they waited for the flames to spread, the pyre to grow hot enough.

So that was all.

No: not all. Seven Fugian deaths *here*, in this plaza, but already Mariama could see other columns of smoke rising over Refugia. Other pyres.

"They're done," she said. "No Jack."

Sheila dropped her hands and raised her head. Her tear-stained face looked wild, almost feral, wide eyes and mouth open so her teeth showed.

"You're sure?"

Mariama nodded.

But Sheila had also seen the smoke from the other pyres. Any glint of hope in her face was extinguished.

Then she blinked, seeming to regain focus. "They're just standing there," she said.

Mariama said, "Yes."

"So kill them."

Mariama lifted the rifle, placed the stand on the flat railing of the hide, and again bent over the telescopic sight. "This is going to be loud," she said. "You might want to cover—"

"All of them," Sheila said.

THE FIRST ONE in her sight had a thief rider.

Mariama had been sighting on the target's head, the close-cropped graying hair revealing a lice-bitten scalp. But now she shifted her aim, just a fraction, so when she pulled the trigger she knew that the bullet would blast apart the target's neck. Would kill the thief at the same time that it killed its slave.

The stock hammered against her shoulder, but she held the gun steady. Even as the sound of the shot echoed through the forest, she glimpsed a bloom of red, but already she was shifting to the next target. She noted that it was standing still, only its head turning toward where the first was falling to the ground. And then she pulled the trigger, and knew it was falling as well, even as she didn't bother to watch.

If she'd had time, Mariama would have laughed. The thieves could overthrow human civilization, enslave whoever was left, even destroy Refugia and all who lived there, but they didn't know and see all. These had never seen the effects of gunshots, so they didn't know how to react.

Not even the hive mind was all-powerful.

The next one, a female, smaller, slighter of build, had taken only one step away from the first two when the bullet's impact lifted her—it—half-off the ground. Mariama had missed the head shot on this one, but as it went down to the ground, writhing on its back, blood spouting from its chest, she knew that didn't matter.

Three.

For the first time Mariama took her eye from the sight and looked at the scene as a whole. She could see flurries of movement—people running, a skein of thieves—at the periphery of her vision, but paid no attention to them.

Refocusing, she saw that two of the invaders remaining in the plaza still seemed stunned by the unexpected assault. But the other three were running, heading away from the pyre, the pile of bodies, and their own dead, toward the shelter of the buildings beyond the plaza.

Three human slaves. Mariama sent a thought their way.

You guys left it too long.

But, though her need to hurry made her aim sloppy, her reflexes and the speed of the big bullets gave her the time she needed, barely. It took five shots, not the three it should have, but in the end, all three targets were lying on the ground.

All the humans. Two were still, their spreading blood outlining them in black, while the third, the fast one she'd missed twice, was on his knees just in the doorway of the club. He held the stump of his blown-away right arm pinned beneath his left in an attempt to keep the bright red arterial blood from draining away.

A futile attempt. Even as Mariama swung the rifle away, she saw him topple sideways.

Two cartridges remaining in the clip, two slaves remaining as well. Slow ones, though seeking refuge at last. One was being ridden. But the other, a female, was something else. She was no more than fifteen or sixteen, clearly far too young to have been born in the Last World. A native, like Jack Gilliard and the others here. A born slave.

Mariama brought each down with a single shot.

Then, finally, her ammunition clip empty, the gun hot in her hands, the smell of burned powder suffusing the air, Mariama lifted her head. She placed the rifle carefully at her feet, flexed her cramped fingers, rolled her shoulders, and took a deep breath.

Sheila was still staring at the scene below. Now only one of the targets, the human bleeding near the club door, was moving, and he only feebly. Other than that, the plaza was still except for the flames dancing in the pyre and the smoke swirling upward.

Finally, Sheila turned her head. Her face was pale, harrowed, but there were no tears in her eyes, no disgust or revulsion or horror in her expression.

"All eight," she said.

Mariama nodded.

"Not enough."

"No."

Sheila nodded. "But it's a start."

Finally, she had become part of the Next World. Finally, she understood.

A FEW MINUTES later, though, her mood changed. "You realize that we're doomed if we stay out here," she said. "You and me, and whoever else escaped."

Mariama, bent over the food stores in the cache, didn't bother to reply.

Sheila said, "If we have no access to the vaccine, our immunity will last about a week. Ten days at the outside."

Mariama was quiet. Yes, she knew this. All Fugians would.

"After that, we'll be completely vulnerable. They'll be able to kill us or—"

"Enslave us," Mariama said.

"Enslave us. Just like that."

"Yes."

Sheila said, "So what are you—*we*—going to do next?"

Mariama knew the answer to that question, the only answer, and thought Sheila did, too. But she chose not to reply directly.

Instead, she sighed and closed her eyes for a moment.

"I miss Malcolm," she said.

* * *

MALCOLM SAT IN the full darkness. He was alive. He knew he must be, because he could feel the rough coral wall against the back of his neck and head, hear the dripping of water from somewhere close by, and smell a mix of odors: wet limestone, his own sweat, animal smells.

He could sense against his skin an occasional waft of fresher air from the small square window high on the far wall. A beam of sunlight had been coming through it when he first awoke, but by now it had become part of the general pitch-darkness.

His head throbbed, and there was a crust of dried blood where he'd been struck.

But otherwise he seemed intact, and by now he was alert enough to guess where he was: the fort's slave quarters.

And he wasn't alone. He could smell animals and hear the rustlings and shufflings, the occasional squeak and yelp, that showed that other cells were occupied as well.

He wondered if any of the others had survived. Were some being kept in quarters like this one? Had they escaped? Or had they all died on the steps?

If not, if somehow they'd survived, would they come back for him?

If they didn't, how would he get out of here?

Fuck.

One thing was for sure. He wasn't going to just give up and start acting like a model prisoner, not for those bugs and their lackeys. He was going to get the hell out of this hole.

He'd start soon. As soon as his mind was a little clearer.

But for now . . .

He'd just rest a little first.

AS HE DRIFTED into sleep, Malcolm realized that he was scratching his belly. But it didn't occur to him to wonder why it itched, and by the time he awoke he'd forgotten he was even doing it at all.

TWENTY-NINE

THE BROTHER HAD rowed them back to the waiting ship. The short trip was carried out in silence, all of them lost in their own thoughts. Except, apparently, the strange, bright-eyed young woman sitting beside him on the boat, who seemed completely absorbed in staring into their faces, one after the other, when she wasn't watching the sky or the flying fish launching themselves into the air all around them.

And still singing her strange, wordless song. Singing almost the whole way back to the ship.

"Hey," Jason said, one of the times when she was quiet.

Even that single word felt strange. Everything about being here felt strange.

He tried again. "My name is Jason—"

But before he could go on, the leader, Shapiro, gray-faced with exhaustion, snapped a glance at him. "We'll talk when we're on board," she said.

And that was that.

* * *

IN THE LEE of the ship, before climbing the ladder up to the deck, they washed themselves off in the channel. The crew members went first, in their clothes, the dried blood washing off them into the calm water, little fish rising to pick at the flakes of blood.

They went in one at a time, leaving the others to keep an eye on the two newcomers. Which meant mostly on Jason, as if he was likely to commandeer the rowboat and take it . . . where, exactly?

Then it was the girl's turn. She was already the cleanest among them, having mostly avoided the bloodshed. But she went in anyway, stripping off her shift without any hesitation, then diving and wriggling in the water like a seal before climbing back on board and getting dressed again.

The wrap on her hand was soaked through, and the closer look he got of the infection beneath made Jason hope the ship had some medical miracle worker on board.

Finally, they let him wash, watching him closely the whole time. They'd already checked to make sure he wasn't carrying a worm around with him, but they still looked like they thought he might transform into a last-stage host at any moment and try to tear them apart with his bare hands.

Even so, as he scrubbed at himself, staining the calm water around him, he couldn't entirely blame them for their caution. Their fear. It would be hard to trust a grim-faced, filthy, half-naked man they'd just seen wielding a machete.

But then they brought him on board and—surrounded by wide-eyed crew members, many of them crying at the news they were hearing—immediately bound his hands in front of him. And though he still understood their reasoning, he felt a spark of anger flare inside him.

Then he quelled it. If his plan was going to succeed, if he was going to have a chance of seeing Chloe again, he was going to have to play the good soldier.

In contrast, his self-respect—and what these strange explorers thought of him—didn't matter at all.

A MAN JASON assumed was the ship doctor took the girl off somewhere. Then Shapiro led Jason into a large room set near the stern belowdecks, clearly the ship's mess. There she sat him behind a large rectangular wooden table and, without a word, left. The brother and sister— the man having acquired a handgun someplace—stood against the wall, watching him.

They didn't seem disposed to talk, so Jason just looked down at his scraped, scarred hands, slave blood still lodged under his fingernails, resting on the table in front of him. The rope they'd used to tie him was biting into his wrists.

When Shapiro returned, pale and grim, she was carrying a glass half-full of water. "I've set a watch," she said to his guards.

"Let us—" the brother said.

Shapiro shook her head. "It's taken care of."

You won't need a watch, Jason thought. *You've got*

your force field against the thieves, and the slaves aren't going to swim out here and attack you.

But he kept his mouth shut. He would have set a watch as well.

No. That wasn't true. If he'd been in charge, he would have given the order to sail away at once, putting a hundred miles between himself and the slave camp by morning.

And never looking back.

SITTING ACROSS THE table, Shapiro put the glass down near him.

Jason looked at it. It was a drinking glass. For some reason, this fact hit him harder than any of the surreal events of the past few hours.

These explorers had drinking glasses made of glass.

Made of glass . . . *after the overthrow.* Jason could tell this by its uneven surface, the bubbles trapped beneath its surface like bugs in ancient amber. There was no way this was a product from before—it would never have made it off the factory floor.

Here, though, on this world, it looked like a miracle to Jason. It meant that wherever the explorers came from, they had glassblowers.

He felt suddenly, unexpectedly dizzy, overwhelmed. Yes, this was the most surreal thing about this day: the bumpy, rippled glass, filled with drinking water, that sat at Jason's right elbow.

That there were still glassblowers on this earth.

* * *

SHAPIRO SAID, "ARE you protected in some way from the thieves?"

Jason shook his head.

"Then why didn't they sting you?"

He coughed, and said, "At first—at first I think they weren't expecting it. What I did."

His throat hurt. Reaching down, he picked up the glass between his hands and awkwardly drank some water. It was so clean that it tasted strange.

He put the glass back down. "And after that," he went on, "I think *you* protected me with your force field."

He grimaced. "I mean your vaccine."

In midnod, Shapiro froze. Her mouth opened, then closed again, and whatever color was left in her face drained away. Behind her, Jason's guards looked stunned as well.

"You know about our vaccine," Shapiro said finally.

He nodded.

"How?"

But he didn't answer her question. Instead, he said, "The man who was knocked down—not the one who died—was his name Granger?"

Shapiro didn't seem to be breathing. Her pupils were pinpoints in her gray eyes. When she spoke, it was with another question of her own. "Was Chloe there?" she said, her voice sounding a little breathless. "Oh God, did we—"

Jason was shaking his head. "No. Chloe wasn't in the battle," he said. "They locked her in the cells yesterday."

He drew in a breath. "I don't know if she's still alive, but I know you didn't kill her."

For a moment, the woman across from him seemed to waver in her chair. She raised her hands to her face and pressed her palms into her eyes. Then she dropped them back to the table. "What happened to her vines? To her vaccine?"

"She was imprisoned before she could reach them." He looked into Shapiro's eyes. *"Enslaved."*

"Do you know if they still exist?"

For a moment, Jason was going to tell Shapiro about their plans. His and Chloe's last-ditch race to see if the vines still existed, if the vaccine might work for them.

But he didn't. It was all too much.

Watching him with that inexorable gaze, Shapiro again opened her mouth to speak, then shook her head. "Shit," she said. "I have so many things to ask you."

"Most of the answers you can probably guess at," he said.

She nodded.

"And the rest don't matter. Not yet."

Not if we don't figure out a way to get Chloe and Malcolm back.

Another nod. She understood. Then she reached into the pocket of her shirt, pulled out something small, and put it on the table beside the glass. A rough-hewn grayish pill.

"Before we go any further," she said, "take this."

Looking away from her, he put the pill on his tongue. It had a bitter taste, almost like quinine, that remained in his mouth after he took a gulp of the pure water.

The vaccine. The protection, the weapon, that until that day Jason hadn't truly believed existed.

"**WHAT DID YOU** do with the girl?"

Shapiro grimaced. "The doctor is looking her over."

Then she turned and glanced back at the twins. "Darby, ask Fatou to bring her here as soon as he's done." She paused. "And then go and get some rest."

The woman nodded and went through the door, leaving her brother, with his pistol, still on guard.

Shapiro faced Jason again. They were both quiet for a few moments, perhaps with the same thoughts. The infection in the girl's hand was very serious. In the slave camp, at least, it would soon have killed her.

"We do still have antibiotics," Shapiro said, "along with a range of native medicines. But . . ."

Yes, *but* . . .

"Do you have the facilities onboard to amputate?" Jason asked.

And then almost laughed out loud. Laughed at the sounds he was making through a hole in his face. Words. *Facilities. Amputate.*

For a moment, he'd sounded like . . . the old Jason. The scientist. The free human.

Shapiro, not reading his mind now, merely nodded. "Fatou can do it, and I can, too, if I have to. Still . . ." She frowned.

Yes, *still.* They both knew that in this world, free or enslaved, you did what you could to keep people alive. You used whatever facilities—and skills—you had, and you poured all your knowledge and intelligence and effort into saving their lives.

And then, more often than not, they died anyway.

"At the very least, I'm sure she'll be able to tell us about herself, and what she did during the battle." Shapiro's eyes widened at the memory, and again Jason could see the glint of scientific curiosity in her expression.

She focused on him again. "But while we're waiting, why don't you start off."

Jason's mind had been wandering. Now he looked at her. "Start off with what?" he asked.

"Telling us about the girl."

He still didn't understand. "But how would *I* know?"

Now she just stared at him, bereft of speech. And then he understood at last, and laughed. Actually laughed.

"Shapiro," he said, "I don't know a thing about her. Not a single thing. The first time I ever saw her was today, when she showed up and saved our lives."

Shapiro said, "Then who the hell is she? And . . . *what* the hell is she?"

Not even noticing at once that, as she spoke, the door behind her was swinging open. The object of her astonishment walked in, eyes alive with interest and curiosity in that oddly still face, the doctor behind her.

It seemed the girl had heard Shapiro's question, and understood that it pertained to her. Standing before them, she seemed to quail for an instant. But then her chin lifted, and she faced them with the same calm fortitude she'd shown in battle.

"My name—" she began, speaking so loudly that her eyes widened.

She took a breath and tried again. "My name is Aisha Rose Atkinson," she said a little more quietly. But her voice was still strange, flat, with unexpected beats and emphases, as if months or years had passed since she'd last talked to anyone. As if she'd never done much talking.

She sounded, Jason thought, much as he might have if he hadn't had Chloe close by.

But she didn't hesitate. "I was born nineteen years, four months, and twenty-eight days ago, six months and four days after the end of the dreamed earth," she went on. "Today's date is September—"

For the first time she seemed to falter in her recitation. "September—"

Then her face crumpled. She closed her eyes and, just for an instant, swayed on her feet. The doctor, standing beside her, put a gentle hand on her right arm, and she steadied.

Still with her eyes closed, she spoke, only this time her tone was quieter still, more intimate, and filled with despair.

"I'm so sorry, Mama," she said. "But I simply don't remember."

THIRTY

"HEY, AISHA ROSE," Jason said. "My name is Jason Bett."

The girl focused on Jason, and immediately she seemed calmer.

He returned her frank gaze. The last time he'd seen her, Aisha Rose had been filthy and draped in rags. Now, transformed, she was wearing a long, flowing cotton dress, a pale blue with purple flowers on it. It must have been made before the overthrow, and Jason was astonished once again by the treasures the explorers had brought with them.

Aisha Rose's hair, which had appeared dingy and hopelessly tangled, turned out to be thick, luxuriant, and an unusual coppery blond. She—or someone else—had tied it back into a ponytail, revealing her high cheekbones, long jaw, and those glimmering eyes.

Jason saw a blush rise to her cheeks, and wondered how long it had been since she'd had anyone's eyes on her.

He smiled, and said, "You look great." And was rewarded with a smile—mostly in the eyes, though he thought her lips might have twitched upward, just a fraction—in return.

At the same time, he noticed that she'd been staring at his mouth as he spoke, and that now her own mouth was moving. As if she were testing out the words. Or tasting them.

He looked away from her face, down at her bare arms. Jason knew that the doctor must have tended carefully to her injuries, draining the worst of the abscesses and cleaning out the wounds. Fresh cloth wraps, whiter than anything Jason had seen in years, stretched from between her fingers up to the crook of her arm.

The cleanup must have been immensely painful, but the girl seemed as stoical and unaffected as ever . . . if you ignored the pallor in her face and the faint tracks that drying tears had left on her cheeks.

Keeping her gaze on him, she came around the table to his left, sat, and slid down the bench toward him. She didn't stop until their legs were touching, and he could smell the soap she'd used. And then she reached out with her right, uninjured hand and interlaced her fingers with his left.

As if she needed him, his presence, his hand in hers, for strength and support.

And the moment's awkwardness that she'd shown upon entering did seem to have disappeared, now that she was sitting beside him. She seemed entirely calm as she looked around the room, and said, "So where is she?"

Shapiro blinked. "Where is who?"

"The one who is like Mama . . . and me."

A silence followed this statement. Finally, Shapiro said, "Aisha Rose, believe me, there is no one on board who is *the least bit* like you."

Aisha Rose showed her irritation only in the tiny furrow that appeared between her eyes. She gave a tiny shrug, and said, "No, she will be here soon."

Then, letting her gaze swing across the room, she said, "You are all such different colors!"

Now Jason thought that a kind of joy resided behind her flat, stiff tone.

He saw Shapiro give a small nod. As if she were speaking to a little girl, she said, "Haven't you ever seen people of different colors before?"

Aisha Rose answered at once. "In books," she said. "When Mama and I lived in the compound, I mean. Books with pictures about life on the dreamed earth."

"The dreamed earth," Shapiro said.

The girl nodded. "Before the real earth awoke. Before it became real. Mama told me what it was like, and showed me, and we also had books."

She paused, scanning their faces once again. "You are some of the same colors as the pictures we look at," she said, "but not all."

Jason understood the meaning behind the girl's words. Some of it, anyway, and Shapiro seemed to as well. "You've never actually seen people those colors, though," she said. "For real, I mean."

Aisha Rose shook her head. "Of course not. It was always just me and Mama, until now."

At her unmodulated voice, her matter-of-fact tone,

Jason had a revelation about this strange young woman sitting at his side. He'd thought she'd slid next to him, sought physical contact, because she needed his support.

But now he realized that he'd gotten it wrong. She didn't need him; she'd brought all the strength she needed along with her. If anything, she was there to share her strength with Jason. To support him. To *give*, not to take.

Jason felt tears come to his eyes.

If Shapiro noticed any of this, she didn't seem to care. She had begun to stare at Aisha Rose with a strange, unsettling concentration.

"Aisha Rose," she said, and her voice sounded a little breathless and strained. Not with fear, or revulsion, or surprise, Jason thought. No: with certainty.

With comprehension.

Aisha Rose, all calmness, said, "Yes?"

"Tell me something. Is your Mama always with you?"

"Yes, of course."

"But you buried her."

For just an instant, Jason felt the hand tighten in his.

"No," Aisha Rose said after a brief hesitation.

Shapiro nodded, but she didn't look like someone who'd been caught heading in the wrong direction. She merely said, "Why not?"

Aisha Rose said, without hesitating, "Mama didn't want to be buried."

Now, for the first time, the doctor, Konte, spoke up. "Where was this?"

"At the rose farm." She saw the question on his face. "On Mount Kenya."

Jason turned his head to look at Aisha Rose beside him. She was staring down at the table, and as he watched, a tear ran down her nose and dripped off. But when she spoke again, her voice was still composed.

"Mama told me," she said, "that on the dreamed earth, people believed that vultures would help you . . . ascend." She raised her head. "To someplace better than the dream."

Shapiro nodded. "That's true. Some people believed that."

"And the vultures did come." Aisha Rose's eyes were on Shapiro, but as she spoke, she leaned against Jason. Her bare arm was cold against his.

"But I still talk with her," she went on. She lifted her bandaged hand and placed it gently against the side of her head. "Here," she said.

Shapiro nodded. "I know. But before that, before she ascended, was she . . . tired a lot?"

The girl nodded.

"Ill?"

Another nod. "Worse and worse. She didn't want me to know, but I saw anyway."

Jason noticed that, as she and Shapiro talked about Mama, Aisha Rose's speech had grown softer, more supple . . . but also more childlike.

"I knew it was the worm. What the worm did to her, before it died."

Shapiro was sitting very still. "And this was after Mama was carrying you, but before you were born?"

"Yes." Aisha Rose's eyes were hazy. "At the very end of the dream."

At that moment, Jason knew what Shapiro had been driving at and what it meant. What it meant about Aisha Rose.

His heart thudded in his chest. And, though he kept his motions calm, when he turned his eyes to look at the young woman sitting next to him, holding his hand, it was with a sense of wonder.

The same expression he saw in Shapiro's eyes.

"HOW DID THE worm die?" Shapiro asked. "Did someone take it out?"

Jason saw Aisha Rose's chin lift. "No. I told you. It just died."

"And you saw that happen?"

The girl's lips thinned in exasperation. "Mama showed me," she said.

Then she paused, and when she spoke again her voice was lower, and filled with apology and regret. "No," she said. "Mama didn't show me. She didn't want me to see, but I looked anyway."

Shapiro was quiet for a moment. Then she said, "And what else did you see when you looked?"

"The end of the dreamed earth," Aisha Rose said at once. Her voice was bleak.

"You looked because you weren't there. You hadn't been born yet."

This time the girl just gave a single nod.

Shapiro lifted her hands and put her palms over her eyes. Then, her eyes still hidden, she said, "Aisha Rose Atkinson, tell me. Please tell me. What else do you see?"

Aisha Rose tilted her head as she looked at the older woman sitting in such a strange position opposite her. Then she turned to look up at Jason.

"I see what *they* see," she said. "When I want to."

"The thieves," he said.

"Yes, the *majizi*." She gestured with her injured hand. "And I see . . . lights. The lights made by the other ones like me."

Suddenly, her breath was short, her cold hand tightening again in Jason's. Maybe the support *did* go both ways.

"And I see . . . *him*," she said. "The one who—"

But before she could finish her sentence, the door behind Konte opened, and a woman walked through. A tall, slender woman of perhaps thirty, wearing a baggy, blue-and-white shirt and black pants. She had high cheekbones, a strong jaw, and a face betraying so little expression that she could have passed for Aisha Rose's older sister.

The doctor said, "Kait?"

But Kait gave no sign of hearing him. She was focused on one thing only: Aisha Rose.

And Aisha Rose was gazing back at her with such an expression of joy that Jason wondered if somehow this *could* be her sister.

"Oh!" Aisha Rose said, a gasp as much as a word. "I was waiting for you!"

Yet Jason, struggling to his feet, felt no joy. He knew what this woman—this *thing*—was. After twenty years, he knew what he was looking at.

He just couldn't understand why it was being allowed to walk free.

* * *

BESIDE HIM, AISHA Rose let go of Jason's hand and also made to rise.

But she never had the chance. Kait's eyes had been as dull as her expression, but now they seemed to come into focus. Her gaze sharpened, and in an instant her face contorted. Baring her teeth, a guttural snarl coming from her throat, she leaped past Shapiro, sending the scientist tumbling to the floor, and threw herself across the table.

Even as Jason reached his feet, he knew exactly what was about to happen. He'd seen it so often before, and he knew that he would once again be too slow, too weak, to prevent it.

AS THE SLAVE'S hands went for her throat, Aisha Rose simply said, "No."

THIRTY-ONE

WHEN JASON WAS a child, one of his closest friends died in an airplane crash. Something went wrong with the rudder system, and when the jet hit the ground nose first it was traveling at more than six hundred miles per hour. The impact left only two things intact in a field full of scraps and fragments: the black boxes, with their recordings of the conversation between the captain and the other flight officers.

During the final moments, the crew knew that they were helpless to delay the end. Yet in the last half second before the plane shattered against the earth, one of the flight officers said a single word: "No."

No.

No, this isn't happening. I still have control of my fate. I'm not about to die.

But then he did.

* * *

TWICE IN THE slave camp, Jason had heard the word used in the same way. Once when the thieves were gathering to take revenge on the wife of a man who had run away, and once when three of the ridden ones were unleashed on a young woman for some reason that Jason had never been able to figure out.

No, the victims protested. And then they'd died anyway.

BUT AISHA ROSE wasn't any of those people. Jason had no idea who she was, or even precisely *what* she was, but he knew that she was no helpless victim trying to deny the inevitable.

"No," she said, as Kait's hands went around her throat. At the same instant that Jason, half-standing, realized that she'd let go of his hand, Aisha Rose put her palm against his chest and shoved him so hard he fell backward. His head banged against the wall, and, for a moment, his vision dimmed.

He heard the snarling cry cut off, then the thud of a body hitting a hard surface. When he refocused, he saw that it was Kait who was sprawled in graceless unconsciousness across the table, her hands still outstretched. Even as he took in the sight, she groaned and began to move.

He stepped closer to Aisha Rose, ready this time to help defend her in case of a renewed attack. Staring down at her semiconscious attacker, though, she seemed calm, unafraid, merely interested in what had just happened.

No: more than interested. She put her hands together and said, in a tone mixing excitement and affection, "We'll have so much to talk about afterward!"

Finally, far too late, both Shapiro and the doctor were reaching for the awakening Kait. Aisha Rose said, "You don't—" but still the doctor took hold of Kait's arms and, twisting them behind her, pulled her to her feet. Behind them, Brett Callahan had his handgun at the ready though Jason had no idea whom he might be thinking of shooting.

Kait herself still seemed only half-awake. Her head hung down, hair obscuring her face. If Jason himself had possessed a gun, he would not have hesitated to use it on her. Now that he was away from the camp, he knew only one thing for sure: When you saw someone in Kait's condition, you killed them. You killed them, or they killed you.

Yet Aisha Rose clearly didn't agree. He saw that she had a long scratch on her neck, a thread of blood tracing down her collarbone and beneath her dress, which she didn't seem to notice.

As if feeling his gaze, she looked over at him. "I'm sorry that I hit you," she said in her formal way. Jason wondered if those had been her mother's inflections as well. And maybe a trace of her accent: German, perhaps, or South African.

"You're forgiven," he said to her. "I mean, that's twice today you've rescued me, and the day isn't over yet."

She smiled at him, using her mouth a little as well as

her eyes. She was definitely learning. "Rescued you?" she said, turning back to peer at Kait. "No. You saw. I was the one she wanted."

He nodded. That was true, but it was also true that last-stage hosts were rarely picky in choosing their targets.

Aisha Rose started to go on, but before she could speak, Shapiro jumped in.

"I don't understand," she said, raising her hands. "Tell us what just happened."

Aisha Rose looked confused. Jason, the only one who understood where the miscommunication lay, touched her arm.

"Aisha Rose, love," he said. "They don't have any idea."

She stared at him and made a little sound like a gasp. "What?"

"Nothing else explains it."

"Explains what?" Shapiro said.

Aisha Rose, ignoring her, looked at Jason with wide eyes.

"You see, they have this vaccine," Jason said.

"Yes. Dr. Konte wanted me to take it." She rolled her eyes. "Silly."

"But that's the point," he told her. "It's been so long since they've seen it, they don't even recognize the signs anymore."

Finally, Shapiro got a word in. "What the hell," she said, "are you two talking about?"

Without replying, Aisha Rose came out from behind the table and walked up to Kait. With her injured hand, she lifted the hem of the semiconscious woman's shirt up above her waist, revealing exactly what he knew it would: the huge, bulbous swelling overlying Kait's belly, and the black airhole that punctured it like a gunshot wound.

"This," Aisha Rose said.

"IT'S ALMOST READY to hatch," Aisha Rose observed, letting go so the shirt could drape back down, "but it is very small and weak. Does your vaccine do that, too?"

Shapiro wasn't listening. For a long moment she just stared at Kait, first at her now-covered belly, then up at her face. Then her own face flushed, the red even reaching down her throat and upper chest above her shirt.

She took a step closer, and only then did Jason realize that Aisha Rose's attacker was fully awake now as well. He felt a sudden surge of panic, of renewed vulnerability. Yet Shapiro did not seem afraid, only furious. Enraged.

"You did this to yourself," she said to Kait, in a voice so venomous that it prickled the hair on Jason's scalp. "You fucking did it *on purpose.*"

And Kait nodded.

"So did you get your wish?" Shapiro leaned forward so their faces were just inches apart. "Do you see what Trey did?"

And then she slapped her across the face.

But wonders never ceased. The blow did not seem to anger Kait, provoke her. Instead, she lifted her head, and, through tear-filled eyes, looked at Aisha Rose, and said, "I can see you."

Aisha Rose smiled. "Yes. I know. And I can see you. A new light."

She closed her eyes for a moment. "A clear new light. It's been so long."

Kait said, "Can you help me?"

"Of course."

"How?" Shapiro, rounding on her, spat out the word. "By taking it out and watching her die?"

Aisha Rose gave a little frown. "Die?"

"You saw it," Shapiro said. "Hell, you *showed* it to us. You must know it's been days—*days*—since we could remove it without killing the host. Without killing Kait."

"Killing?" Aisha Rose said. "Kait? No."

No. That word again. The same word, but this time possessing a completely new meaning.

You have no idea what you're talking about.

Don't tell me what I can and cannot do.

THIRTY-TWO

"BUT CAN WE do it now?" Aisha Rose said. "I'm quite tired."

Then she looked past Kait at the doctor. "Dr. Konte," she said, "please let go of her arms." She smiled. "I'm perfectly safe."

Konte looked skeptical, but after a few seconds, he released his hold. Kait, standing in place, didn't even seem to notice. She looked merely exhausted and ill, not aggressive, not anything like a last-stage host. Even so, Jason still felt alarmed, alert, ready for another transformation and attack.

Not that there was much he'd be able to do about it, with his hands still bound. Maybe at least he'd get his body in between Kait and Aisha Rose next time.

As if reading his thoughts, Aisha Rose looked back at him, down at his wrists, which were streaked with blood from where the rope had bitten in. Her mouth turned down. "Do you think that's necessary?" she asked Shapiro.

Without waiting for a reply, she dipped down, a fluid, unexpected move, and reached with her right hand beneath the hem of her long dress. When she straightened again, she was holding a bone-handled knife with a curved, honed blade. An instant later, the rope was lying on the floor, and Jason's hands were free.

He rubbed his wrists, and said, "Thank you." But she'd already switched her attention again, this time to the doctor. Jason found himself marveling at the way, seemingly without effort, this young woman had assumed her place as the group's alpha, even over the domineering Shapiro.

"Excuse me, please," she was saying. "Dr. Konte. Do you have a—"

She struggled to find the word, her face betraying exasperation. Mama would not have approved of such a struggle, Jason thought, and Aisha Rose knew it.

Finally, she gave up. "A place where you cut people open?"

He nodded. "It's the same place where I took you, but, yes, we have the facilities."

"Good." Again the trace of exasperation. "So can we go there already?"

THEY WALKED SINGLE file down the slick, salt-stained passageway toward the ship's stern. It was deserted though Jason could hear voices from abovedeck and from behind one or two of the closed doors they passed. Subdued sounds, reminding him of the losses these explorers—these brave explorers—had experienced and were still absorbing.

The room they entered at the end of the passageway was a combined laboratory, examining room, and surgery. A single porthole of rippled glass provided a glimpse of blue sky and green water.

Jason took in the counters and shelves, the array of instruments and devices he never thought he'd see again in this world, including a beautiful, nineteenth-century microscope. And, on the top shelf of the interior wall to the right, three tightly sealed old gallon jars, each containing at least one thief. The wasps were standing just inside the glass, perfectly still except for the flicker of their wings, staring down.

Seeing them there, so unexpectedly, made Jason's stomach twist and his throat constrict. Somehow, and just barely, he kept himself from reaching up, pulling the containers down, and crushing the inhabitants.

He wondered if he'd ever again be able to look at a thief without feeling this sudden burst of rage. But he controlled it, turning to Shapiro as she entered the room.

He noticed the way her body relaxed. This was her real home, he thought. Even with its pet thieves.

He'd known plenty of people like Shapiro back in what she called the Last World, and now that his recall of that time was flooding back, he felt like part of him was reawakening.

He'd never much thought about the concept of repressed memories, but now he was realizing how much he'd forgotten about the world that had been taken from him. All those sights and tastes and smells. The sound of quiet conversation.

In this little room, with its shining steel examining table, its microscope, its forceps and scalpels, its glass beakers and stoppered jars and pristine slides, its smell of medicinal alcohol and machine oil—the odors of science and technology, of civilization—Jason felt suddenly overwhelmed. Nearly undone by a combination of joy and grief, freedom and vulnerability.

Human emotions.

He was human again.

He missed Chloe with a fierceness that he thought might stop his heart.

AISHA ROSE CAME and stood beside him. This time he was the one who reached for her, and after a moment he felt her strong, slender fingers intertwine with his once more.

She radiated warmth. Jason could see that her cheeks had a pink tinge, and among the room's other odors he could detect the sweet, musky one coming from her pores: the smell of sickness that he remembered so clearly from his own daughters when they'd been ill.

Across the room, Kait was on her back on the examining table, and the doctor was sterilizing both the surgical site and his scalpel and forceps with alcohol. She lay there, head turned, her eyes on Aisha Rose.

Aisha Rose smiled at her, still mostly in her eyes, but not all. "Rest now," she said.

Kait looked like she wanted to respond, but her eyelids were already fluttering.

"Just rest," Aisha Rose said. "We'll talk after."

And Kait closed her eyes.

"WHY DIDN'T THEY kill you?" Jason asked.

Aisha Rose's gaze had been fixed on Kait, but she spared an instant for a glance in his direction. She knew what he was talking about.

"Are they afraid of you?" he said.

He could see her thinking about it, as if she'd never had to answer that question before. Finally, she said, "No. It's not that." She frowned a little. "Not *only* that."

"Then what?"

Her brow furrowed. "They don't see me."

He made a noise in his throat. Her gaze flickered again to his face, and she frowned at the incomprehension she saw there.

"No," she said, trying again. "They don't see me as *different* from them. When they see me, they see themselves."

She paused, then said, with the first sign of urgency he'd heard in her voice. "Do you understand?"

"I'm trying to." He took a moment. "Until you focus on them, they think you're another part of the hive mind, just like them."

She thought about his words, then frowned. "No, you still don't understand," she said. "They don't *think* I'm part of them. I *am* part of them."

He could see that she was about to go on, but Konte, standing by the table, raised his hand. The scalpel shone.

"This is a very interesting conversation," he said, looking at Aisha Rose. "But I've administered the anesthetic, it doesn't last long, and we don't have much of it. So could I have some silence, please?"

For a moment, Aisha Rose looked almost chastened. Then she said, "Wait one moment."

Letting go of Jason, she stepped over to the table and laid her uninjured hand against Kait's cheek.

For some reason, this gesture seemed to disturb rather than reassure the doctor. He looked into Aisha Rose's face.

She smiled at him. "It will be fine."

"But how can you be sure?" he asked.

For an instant, the girl's eyes flashed at his tone, but when she replied she sounded as calm as always. "You were listening," she said. "I told you—all of you. I'm sure because I'm part of them. I *am* them. Don't any of you understand yet?"

No one said anything.

"Then can we please stop talking," she said, "and go ahead?"

THE PROCEDURE TOOK about thirty seconds.

With careful movements, and under Aisha Rose's watchful eye, the doctor made a small incision and, using a pair of forceps, removed the worm. Which, as they always did when removed prematurely, died almost at once . . .

. . . while Kait did not. It was as simple as that.

And as terrifying while it was happening. Even Jason, who had quickly come to have an almost mystical belief in Aisha Rose, found that he was holding his breath as Konte extracted the worm, which was, in fact, far smaller and thinner than a last-stage larva should have been.

But though Kait's face was gray, her sleep more like unconsciousness, Konte said that her vital signs were strong, and he had no doubt she'd awaken soon.

As he disinfected the wound, Shapiro dropped the worm into a jar and turned to Aisha Rose. "So how did you do that?"

Aisha Rose shrugged, as if it were something she did every day. "I told it to keep the poison inside itself, so it did," she said. "Mostly. Enough."

Shapiro gave her a look. "As useful to have around as a Swiss Army knife, you are."

Aisha Rose, polite as always even in the face of nonsense, said, "Thank you."

THREE OF THEM went back to the mess: Shapiro, Jason, and Aisha Rose. No guard necessary this time, Jason noticed. They'd passed some kind of a test.

"The thieves at the fort," he said to Aisha Rose when they were seated again.

She tilted her head. "Yes?"

"You made them . . . spin around."

She smiled at the memory.

"They were in a panic," he said. "Terrified."

"Yes." The light in her eyes glimmered. "They are made to do that."

"To *panic*?" Jason said, unable to keep the disbelief out of his voice.

"No. To receive. And then to react."

He was quiet.

She looked at him more closely, then turned her palms up. "That's what the mind does. That's *all* it does."

Still, he was silent.

Watching his face, she grimaced in frustration. "No," she said. "I'm using the wrong words again."

For a moment her eyes closed, and she mouthed two syllables. *Mama.*

Eyes narrowed, she looked across the table at Shapiro. "That's not what the mind does. It's what it *is*." Her eyes narrowed. "You all know this, don't you? You've lived among them for so long. It must be obvious to you."

"But it's not," Shapiro said, speaking the words as if she hated them. "Aisha Rose—we're not like you. You know that by now. We don't *see*."

Aisha Rose frowned a little. But when she spoke again, it was with more patience. "You know that the *majizi*— the thieves—communicate one to the next. Almost as fast as you can think."

Shapiro nodded.

Aisha Rose put her hands together on the table, the slender undamaged one and the one whose bandage made it look like an outsized paw. "I used to ask Mama what communication is," she went on. "What it means."

"It means—" Jason said. "It means understanding. And reacting."

"*Yes.*" Then, more quietly. "Yes. That's what the *majizi* do, what they're made to do. Hear. Understand. React."

She looked at his face. "And because they're created to hear," she said, "and because they're created to react, I can make them do what I want them to."

Her shoulders twitched in what looked to Jason like a shiver. "Not as well as *he* can, though. He is so much stronger than I am."

But Jason was still focused on the first part of what he'd said. "I get all that," he said. "I saw it every day. The thieves gather information, millions, billions of bits of information every second, and model their behavior on what they learn. I just don't understand how *you* make them do it."

But now, at last, it was Shapiro's turn. "Oh," she said, "that part's easy. Because of the worm inside Mama. Isn't that it, Aisha Rose? The worm inside Mama changed her, and it changed you, too."

Now Aisha Rose was silent, but after a moment, she gave a nod.

Shapiro turned to Jason. "You must have seen it all the time, the way thief venom can remodel its victims' brains."

He nodded. "Change their chemistry, even alter their DNA? Yes, I think so."

He paused. "The ridden slaves, the last-stage hosts, they're both part of the mind. They need it to function."

"And the others?"

"Which others? The born slaves? They don't even need to be injected with venom to know what their responsibilities are."

"See? Exactly. They're an evolving species."

For a moment, her gaze went cloudy. Then she shook

her head. "New species changing to fit an empty ecological niche, just as new species have always done."

She gestured at Aisha Rose, whose eyebrows rose. "And that's what you are. Another leap forward."

Aisha Rose tilted her head, thinking about it. Then she gave a little smile.

"Maybe," she said with a shrug. "Still low on the totem pole, though."

JASON WAS MORE interested in what was in front of him than any discussion of evolution. "Okay, you can see them," he said to Aisha Rose. "See what they see. I know that happens. But how did you make them spin?"

She made him wait while she yawned. Then she said, her voice a little thick, "Well, I told them to."

"But how did you get them to obey?"

He glanced back at Shapiro for help, but her expression didn't make him feel any smarter.

Nor did her words. "It's obvious," she said, reaching over and tapping him on the side of his head. "Aisha Rose's brain is louder."

Jason was quiet.

"Just because you can't see or hear her broadcasting doesn't mean she isn't," Shapiro went on. "Any more than the fact that we can't see in the infrared spectrum or hear radio waves in the air means they're imaginary."

He began to say something, but she didn't let him.

"Whether we can detect it or not, every bit of information sent back and forth between thieves is energy transmitted and received," she said. "Bigger brain means more energy transmitted and greater impact. It means that no one thief can control the others—they're all the same size—but Aisha Rose can."

She gave the decisive nod of someone who's solved a knotty problem. "She's so loud they have no choice but to obey."

Jason thought about this, retrieving a long-buried memory. "Right before the end," he said finally, "I remember reading about a guy who could find his car in a lot—make it beep—at a much greater distance if he held the remote next to his head when he pushed the button. Something about the ions in his brain fluid amplifying the signal."

Shapiro again gave her decisive nod. "There you go."

"But still," he said. "Big enough—loud enough—to kill?"

"I don't see why not." Shapiro shrugged. "There's no receiver, or receptor, that would be invulnerable to a powerful enough signal."

Jason saw her gaze turn inward. "I had an aunt who lived in Oklahoma," she said. "She hated spiders, which was too bad, because there sure were a lot of them around there. Once when I was visiting, a tarantula came into her kitchen, this big hairy thing scuttling across the floor."

She smiled at the memory. "Aunt Ida just screamed and screamed—and nobody could scream like her. And that spider stood up on the tips of its toes and . . . died. Just died. Went still and stiff and never moved again."

She looked at him. "That sound blew out its brain—whatever spiders have for a brain."

"I've never tried that," Aisha Rose said. "On spiders."

Shapiro looked at her. "Yes, only on thieves," she said.

Aisha Rose considered that idea.

"We already saw at the fort that you can stun them," Shapiro explained. "And if they can be stunned, they can be killed. That's how nature works. *Anything* can be killed."

Shapiro paused for a moment. When she spoke again, her voice was quiet, almost as if she were speaking to herself.

"But how is it, exactly," she said, "that you do it?"

Jason looked at Aisha Rose. He hadn't been sure she was listening, but at that instant she put both hands to her head in an almost violent gesture. Jason saw that the white bandage over her infected hand was stained a reddish yellow.

"I say *fear me*," she said. "And they do. But not as much as they fear *him*."

Right then something new entered her expression. Something strong, even ferocious. A kind of predatory joy.

"He and I, we are the parasites," Aisha Rose Atkinson said. "The parasites that prey on the hive mind."

IT WAS JASON who asked the questions. The only questions that mattered, he thought.

"What you did to the thieves," he said. "Would you be able to do it again?"

She looked directly into his face, and before she even

spoke, he knew what her answer would be. Then she sighed, and said, "I don't know."

"Then no matter what happens, you'll stay here," he said, "and be safe."

She didn't speak, just smiled at him and shook her head.

THIRTY-THREE

FINALLY, THEY REMEMBERED to bring some food. It was about time: Aisha Rose couldn't recall when she'd last eaten, and from the expression on Jason's face, he was as hungry as she was.

There was fish soup—two portions for her, four for him—and hard biscuits, which hurt her mouth, and pickled vegetables, which she stayed away from. Jason ate everything, sometimes looking at the food like he couldn't believe he wasn't imagining it.

But the two of them still weren't allowed out of the mess. Shapiro said she wanted them to rest. That didn't make much sense to Aisha Rose, so she wondered if there was actually another reason. She thought that maybe everyone was still a little afraid of them, especially of her.

In any case, she was happy to eat with Jason, with one or the other of those two, the boy and girl who looked alike, guarding the door.

Dessert was dried fruit, mango. Aisha Rose liked it more than the coconut she'd opened, though nowhere near as much as the fresh mangos that had grown outside the Naro Moru house.

Before they took the plate away, Aisha Rose put some of the dried mango in the pocket of her new dress. You never knew when—or if—you'd find something else to eat.

WHEN THEY WERE finished, Shapiro came back with a few others, including a man, not that much older than Aisha Rose herself, who seemed to think he was in charge, too. Not as in charge as Shapiro, though, of course.

Aisha Rose didn't listen to his name. There were too many names.

"Okay if we ask you some more questions?" Shapiro said. Aisha Rose saw that this itself wasn't really a question, so all she did was shrug. Sitting beside her, Jason shrugged, too.

Now he was looking as tired as she felt. She was also a little dizzy and hot, with aching muscles like she'd been climbing.

But that didn't seem to matter to Shapiro and the others. For the first hour or so, they talked to Jason. Aisha Rose listened to some of it. The rest of the time she dozed or thought about what she'd say to Kait when she finally saw her again.

So even though Aisha Rose didn't always hear the words, she loved the sound of Jason's voice, the deep rumble so different from Mama's. Even more she loved the feel of his strong hand, which she kept captured in her own whenever she could.

Not that she needed to pay attention. Everything he told them about the slave camp she either already knew, had guessed at, or didn't care about.

The rest, the way the camp worked, how many people were there, how it had started, what the ovens were for (though she and, she imagined, everyone else had guessed *that*), all of it didn't matter much to her. All her life she'd seen the stain and witnessed its spread, and that was all she'd needed to know.

When they asked Jason why he hadn't been enslaved, though, she started to focus. She'd been wondering that, as well. She could see him only with her eyes, not inside, so she knew that he was untouched.

"First of all," Jason said, "I *was* a slave. But if you're asking why they didn't pump me full of toxins? Because I was useful."

"Useful?" someone asked.

He nodded. "The ones they drug, the ridden ones, they're slow. Stupid. Useless for anything but menial jobs."

"And battle," someone said. "Like the last-stage ones."

Jason nodded. "Yeah. And the young ones," he went on. "The ones born . . . since? You saw them."

Shapiro nodded.

"They're born to it. Slavery. It's all they know."

"Are they educated?" she asked.

Jason's sudden, hard-edged laugh surprised everyone, including—it seemed to Aisha Rose—Jason himself. "Educated?" he said. "You think we had schools in the camp? An apple for the teacher every day?"

No one spoke.

So Jason said, "They're educated in tending the fields and taking care of the host animals. They're educated in feeding themselves and following simple directions. Is that what you meant?"

Aisha Rose knew that wasn't really a question, either.

When he was done speaking, Shapiro said, "Do they have language?"

"Sure, but it's minimal." He shrugged. "One more generation, and I doubt there will be any."

"Because it won't be necessary to talk to communicate."

Jason looked into Shapiro's eyes, and Aisha Rose thought they understood each other just fine though she couldn't tell exactly what they were communicating.

"THE FORT," SHAPIRO said a little later. "The camp. Do you think it's the only one? The only one on earth?"

Aisha Rose heard Jason make a sound in his throat. When he spoke, his voice was like wire. He was angry, but she didn't know why.

"Well, I really couldn't say," he said. "We didn't have telephones. Or Wi-Fi. We weren't exactly hooked into the World Wide Web."

But then the anger seemed to drain out of him, leaving only exhaustion and, Aisha Rose thought, sadness.

"Are there other camps?" he asked. "I'd guess there are, but I don't know for sure."

"I do," Aisha Rose said.

* * *

THIRTY-ONE.

There were thirty-one other slave camps. Aisha Rose counted them on her fingers. All looking in her mind the same as the one at Lamu Fort. The same kind of light. The same stain.

When she told them this, she saw them all sag, like plants when the rains were late. They hadn't known. They hadn't even guessed.

After that, it was such a challenge to follow what they were talking about. Especially Shapiro. She talked so fast, so much faster than Mama ever had, like she didn't care whether anyone could understand her or not. If you couldn't keep up, that was *your* fault.

But Aisha Rose knew she had to try. She had to try to understand because she knew things that they needed to know.

"Can you tell where they are, these other camps?" Shapiro said to her. "Where they're located?"

Aisha Rose shook her head.

"Not at all?"

Aisha Rose just looked at her. She wasn't sure what she was being asked.

But Jason understood. "You're asking," he said, "if there might be a slave camp near where your colony is located. What did you call it?"

"Refugia," Shapiro said.

"Yes. Refugia." He shook his head. "And the answer is, of course there might be. In fact, I'd say it's likely. Wouldn't you? They'd establish one nearby, far enough away to avoid being seen. Bide their time, build their strength, till they were strong enough to attack."

No one in the room spoke until Aisha Rose said, "Like those big red ants do before they attack the black ones. I've seen that."

"Not just ants, all slavemakers," Jason said. "Ants. Parasites. Fungi. Why should thieves be any different? They're still just bugs."

Shapiro's scary eyes flashed. "Yeah, just bugs. So how are we going to stomp on them?"

Everyone else looked at each other, and Aisha Rose kept her mouth shut.

AT THE VERY end, Shapiro asked Jason something else, something that Aisha Rose thought she'd been holding on to the whole night.

The most important question. The one Aisha Rose had been waiting for her to ask.

"Malcolm," she said. "Our friend who was taken."

Jason said, "Yeah?"

"Back onshore, you said he would likely be dead by now."

Aisha Rose saw Jason open his mouth to reply. But she saved him the effort.

"Dead?" she said. "Of course he's not dead."

After that, things got noisy, just the way she'd expected it to.

Still, to Aisha Rose it all sounded like the honking of geese or hornbills. Even though she knew they were asking her questions, she responded the same way she would have if they really were birds. She stayed silent and waited for them, in Mama's words, to pipe down.

She didn't need to say anything, not yet. The fact that they *were* being so noisy meant that things were going as she wanted them to.

EVENTUALLY, THEY DID pipe down, and Shapiro took a long look at Aisha Rose and asked, more quietly, "How do you know this?"

Aisha Rose shrugged. How could she describe what she saw to people who couldn't even begin to understand it?

But Shapiro surprised her. "Somehow you can see those who have been infected," she said. "Right?"

Aisha Rose nodded.

"For example, you can't see the people of Refugia— our colony. Or at least we hope you can't."

None of that had been a question, not quite. Aisha Rose stayed quiet.

"So then . . . how can you see our friend? How can you see Malcolm?"

Aisha Rose did not answer.

After a moment, Shapiro's hand went to her mouth. "The same reason you could see Kait. Because he's been infected. Because . . . he's being used as a host."

Aisha Rose gave a little nod. Shapiro's cobra eyes were coming back, but at least right now they weren't aimed directly at her.

"But he wouldn't infect himself, like idiot Kait did.

And I know he was protected." Shapiro's face had turned very pale. "Which most likely means the vaccine stopped working."

Jason said, "No. It was working. We all saw it."

She closed her eyes for a moment. "Yes, but all it takes is *one* thief that's immune, and you know there will be more. That's how it goes."

Aisha Rose, drifting away from the talk again, found herself thinking about white ants. If you knocked a hole in their mound, they came flooding out at you. Every time.

Yes, that was how it went.

Beside her, Jason leaned his back against the wall. "Without your force field," he said, "you'll be dead in what, thirty seconds?"

He spread out his palms. "So . . . get out of here. Go home. Maybe there it will still be safe."

Aisha Rose saw him take a deep breath. "Just take me ashore before you go."

Shapiro's eyes on his face were like a cobra's. "Why?"

"Because I won't leave Chloe behind."

"Even if," Shapiro said.

Aisha Rose was amazed to see him smile. "Yes," he said. "Even if."

Equally amazing, Shapiro smiled back at him. "Just like we won't leave Malcolm. Even if."

Then she swung around and looked up at the faces of the others standing there. Aisha Rose couldn't tell what Shapiro saw—faces were too hard to read—but whatever it was, it made her smile again.

Then she turned back to look at them. "Go get some sleep," she said, "while the rest of us talk."

SLEEP? NO.

Aisha Rose was lying in the bed in the room they'd given her, had been for hours. It was so strange, that bed, too soft, and the room was so small it reminded her of one of the deeper caves at Hell's Gate. She hadn't liked those caves, and she didn't much like this room.

She knew she was supposed to sleep, but her hand hurt and the boat moved in strange ways and by now she was so past tiredness that she wondered if she'd ever sleep again. So when she heard footsteps in the passageway outside, and then someone rapping on her door, she was completely awake.

Just as she was wondering if she was supposed to say something, the door swung open, and Shapiro came in and sat on the edge of the bed.

Aisha Rose felt nervous. She was glad that the light— from a lantern out in the passage—left Shapiro's face, and those cobra eyes, in shadow.

"How are you?" Shapiro said, sounding . . . nervous. Not at all like a cobra.

"I'm well," Aisha Rose said.

"Good."

She paused, and now Aisha Rose was certain of it. This loud woman was jumpy, more antelope than lion.

"And how are you?" she said, as Mama had taught her to do.

She heard Shapiro make a little snorting sound. "I've

been better," she said. Then, "I'm sure you know we've been talking all this time, me and the rest."

Aisha Rose nodded.

"Well, as you probably could have guessed, we decided to go back in the morning. At dawn. To try to rescue our friend—and his daughter."

Aisha Rose hid the wave of relief running through her. This was what had to happen. This was the decision they'd had to make.

She heard Shapiro draw in a breath. "We know our chances. But without you, we won't even make it to the top of the stairs, much less to the cells where they're holding Malcolm and Chloe."

Aisha Rose was quiet.

"You've done so much for us already," Shapiro said. "We know we can't ask for more."

Again she made that snorting sound, which Aisha Rose recognized as a laugh. "But I'm going to ask anyway. So . . . will you? Will you come with us?"

Aisha Rose said, "Of course I will."

"Good." There was a pause, and she felt Shapiro's hard, bony fingers give her arm a squeeze. "Thank you."

She explained the plan—what there was of their plan. It took only a few sentences. Then she rose and walked away.

But at the door she hesitated and looked back. A dark, hunched, backlit form.

"Aisha Rose," she said at last.

Aisha Rose waited.

"There are others out there like you, aren't there?"

Ah. At last she'd thought of the right question. Aisha

Rose had been expecting it, preparing for it, all evening. But even so, having to answer it filled her with the strangest mix of exhilaration and terror.

"Yes," she said.

"And you can see them, just as you could see Kait? As lights?"

"Yes."

Constellations. Galaxies.

"And you keep referring to someone else, someone stronger than you, someone you've learned from. '*He.*' That's one of them, one who is like you?"

Aisha Rose was silent. She wasn't sure how to answer that question.

"Born like you, I mean?"

"Yes."

"Can he help us?"

That wasn't the right question, and after a moment Shapiro seemed to realize it.

"Will he help us?" she asked.

"I don't know," Aisha Rose said.

THIRTY-FOUR

THE GREEN LANDS. The small streams that trickled up from underground springs, flashed and shone during the spring melt, turned to muddy trickles by midsummer, and trickled under the silvery ice in winter.

The patches of forest, such rich hunting grounds in the spring and fall, and so dense with underbrush in the summer that hunting grew lean . . . but not as lean as during the hungry winter months.

The ponds and lakes. Some gradually filling in as the years passed, until they were little more than round patches of lighter grass that oozed under his feet. Others calm, covered in tiny bright green weed in early summer, smelling of rot and life later, always filled with turtles and frogs and fish. And one so big that its waves turned white when winter storms swept across its surface.

The hills and gullies and tumbledown buildings scattered through the forests and fields. And the life there, the squirrels and scrawny cats and deer and otters and muskrats, and the lions that had chosen the boulders beneath the boy's ruined castle as their den.

The places he'd spent nearly his entire existence, whose every square inch he knew as well as his own hands, his scars, the sound of his voice as it echoed inside his head. The green lands.

His home. His only home.

The boy walked away from it for the last time without looking back.

HE HEADED SOUTH. He'd been this way before. He'd been everywhere on the island before. During the sojourns he'd taken early on, when he still dreamed that there were others out there, others like him. Others who'd been lost, abandoned.

But he'd never found anyone. Anyone alive, at least. So, long ago, he'd decided that he was, in fact, entirely alone, and he'd learned to be content with this fact.

Until *she'd* appeared, the other one, and changed everything.

HIS DESTINATION WAS a building, the tallest in sight. Amid the countless ruins, this building still stood, comparatively undamaged, like a gigantic silver finger pointing at the sky.

The boy had never gone near it. He'd known that a piece falling from its heights would end him, and something about the building's completeness had also kept him away. He hadn't wanted to see what was inside.

He still didn't, but now he had no choice.

HE PICKED HIS way over the rubble that filled the plaza surrounding the tower. The sun dipped behind some clouds, and the whipping wind was cold.

He'd wondered as he approached how he'd find a way in, if that would even be possible. But the building's wide front doors lay shattered on the ground, and all he had to do was keep walking.

Taking care with the glass and sharp metal, though not as much care as he once would have.

The floor inside was of the slippery polished stone that he'd seen in the ruins of other buildings. Big slabs that must have been brought in from elsewhere though the boy couldn't imagine how or why.

Slippery stone floors and pieces of furniture lying here and there. Some bones as well. All in better condition than he'd expected because the building itself was so unbroken and had protected its contents.

He found rows of rectangular metal doors on the bottom floor, some closed, others split in two to reveal small chambers inside. Some of these had bones in them, too.

He'd seen them often enough in other buildings, though not in such numbers, to guess what they'd been designed for: carrying people up and down. But now they were useless, even dangerous. What he was looking for were stairs, steps, and eventually he found them, hidden away in the center of the building.

They were crowded with bones, whiter, cleaner bones than he'd seen in years. Disordered piles of the stronger, bigger ones, the jaws and hips and long arms and legs. But even the fragile, tiny ones, fingers, toes, that usually returned to the earth most quickly.

The boy had to clamber over a huge pile of bones near the door at the bottom of the stairs, but he found many fewer as he ascended.

IT TOOK HIM a long while, this climb. Much longer than it would have taken him just months earlier. He felt weak, weary, breathless. The way he'd let his body waste away was obvious with every step.

But that was okay. He knew he'd be strong enough to accomplish what he needed to do.

AT FIRST HE'D planned to climb to the very top, a flat expanse that had once held a tall, metal spike, slender as a pine needle from a distance. The boy had seen it, still upright, on his earlier journeys, but at some point the wind or rain or simply time had brought it down.

But his physical weakness—and his realization that it didn't matter—made him change his mind. Not that far from the top, he reached an open door that revealed an uncluttered floor and, beyond it, glassless windows. He'd climbed high enough.

Not even noticing the familiar detritus, half-rotted by

the weather that had swept through, he made his way to the edge and looked out. Then, suddenly dizzy, grabbed hold of the edge of one of the windows and looked again.

Far below, the rivers on either side glittered silver-blue in the sunlight. The harbor, with its rusted hulks of wrecked boats and that strange green figure, and beyond the harbor more ruined land.

Above him, the sky was of such an infinite, depthless blue that he could barely breathe when he looked at it.

So he looked straight across into the distance instead, into the great world beyond. The *curved* world.

He'd never known till he stood up here that the world was curved.

HE WAS ALMOST done. He'd found his place, he'd climbed to his last aerie, and now he was ready.

Just one thing left to do.

Usually when he played the game, he closed his eyes. But he didn't want to stop looking at the sky, the glittering water, the curved earth. So he kept his eyes open this time, unblinking. The steady cold wind bit at them, dried them, but he didn't care. It didn't matter.

He reached out.

THEY WERE FAR away this time. Hiding from him.

That didn't matter, either.

Just as there was nowhere on the curved world where he would not be aware of *her*, there was nowhere they could hide.

He reached out farther until he found one. Just one at first, but that was all he needed.

And then he did two more things: He drew it toward him, and he reached out through it.

Just as he'd always done. How he'd always played his game.

But with a different goal this time.

LYING IN HER uncomfortable bed, Aisha Rose could sense it, feel it, the unease, the alarm, spreading from every direction. A new kind of spreading stain.

She thought she knew what the boy was doing, but not why. Not his goal.

And unless she did know that for sure, she would have to continue with her plan.

All the way to the end.

SHAPIRO WAS NOT the only one to visit her in her cabin during the endless hours. At some point later on, the boat rocking gently in the tidal pull, the gleam of the moonlit ocean coming through the cabin's porthole, she heard someone else at her door.

Without even realizing, she'd managed to fall asleep, and she heard the tapping from the midst of a gentle dream that disappeared as soon as she came awake. As always, she was instantly, fully alert. It was how you had to live on the earth, the real one, if you expected to survive the night.

Even this night.

She sat up. "You may come in," she called out, as quietly as she could.

She knew who'd knocked. She'd known from the instant she awoke.

The door swung partway open, and a dark, slender form slipped in. When the door closed again, it left the room in near darkness.

But Aisha Rose wasn't afraid. The darkness was unimportant. She was accustomed to seeing by moonlight and starshine, and in any case, Aisha Rose would have been able to see Kait no matter how dark the room was. In all the ways that meant anything.

Kait sat on the edge of her bed. Tentative, like a little bird.

"I attacked you," she said. "I—scratched you."

Aisha Rose didn't bother to reply. Instead, without thinking—and not knowing she was going to do it—she leaned forward and took Kait into her arms.

Kait, thin, as thin as Aisha Rose, and taut as a string, stiffened. Stiffened into wire . . . and then relaxed. After a moment, her arms came up and went around Aisha Rose's shoulders.

Kait smelled of medicine and soap and her own odors, and of the familiar bitter smell of the *majizi*. The smell that she would never lose, that no one who'd had a thief inside ever lost.

But that was unimportant as well. Aisha Rose held on to her. "You are like me," she said, whispering so only Kait could hear it. "Like Mama."

Kait's arms tightened around her. Then, after a few more moments, she pulled back a little and looked into Aisha Rose's face.

"Am I?" she said. "Am I like you?"

Aisha Rose was quiet for a few seconds. Then she said, "Kait, tell me what you see."

Now it was Kait's turn to be still. The silence stretched on, but Aisha Rose didn't care. She'd waited a long time to ask this question, and she could wait a little longer for the answer.

Finally, Kait said, "I wanted to see . . . what Trey saw. What my father saw."

Aisha Rose nodded. "Do you?"

Again a pause. Then, "I don't know. I think he saw . . . real things. I think he saw through their eyes, at least sometimes. I don't."

"Not yet," Aisha Rose said.

"But I'm aware of . . . movement," Kait went on. "Movement everywhere."

The tone of her voice changed, from wonder to something that sounded like fear. "Are they, Aisha Rose? Are they everywhere?"

Aisha Rose debated how to answer. "No," she said at last. "Not everywhere. But the mind is."

She took a breath. "As long as it can reach between them, one to the next, yes, it is everywhere."

"On our voyage, we were blown far south by a storm," Kait said. "Shapiro believed that the thieves . . . were disconnected then. Until we came closer again to the land."

"Closer to other *majizi*," Aisha Rose said. "Yes."

"But if they *are* everywhere—or as good as—that means we can't possibly reach them all, defeat them all."

Aisha Rose didn't speak.

Kait was silent for a long time after that. Finally, she seemed to relax a little. Maybe it was acceptance.

She said, "And you?"

Aisha Rose said, "Me?"

"What do you see?"

"Lights." She answered at once, without hesitation. "So many lights. It is like—" She paused to search for the right words. She had never been asked to describe it before, not in any detail.

Even Mama had never asked. She hadn't known to ask because Aisha Rose hadn't told her. It had been Aisha Rose's one big secret, the secret of who she was. What she was.

"Now it is like the stars," she said, "but always changing, always shifting."

"And each is someone like you. Someone who's been . . . touched . . . by the hive mind."

"Yes." She reached out and touched Kait's cheek. "Like you."

Kait was quiet for a while. Then she said, "Are they beautiful, the stars?"

"Yes." Aisha Rose paused. "And ugly. A stain. Uglier and more beautiful than anything."

Unexpectedly, Kait leaned forward and hugged her again. Equally unexpectedly, Aisha Rose found that her eyes were filled with tears.

"I wish you could meet my father," Kait said. "Trey would have loved you, Aisha Rose."

Aisha Rose held on to her.

"He would have loved the *mystery* of you," Kait said.

A LITTLE LATER, Kait said, "They told me what you did yesterday, at the fort. And also that you're coming with us in the morning."

Aisha Rose nodded.

Kait was holding her injured hand gently in both of her own. "But you're—"

"It doesn't matter."

"No," Kait said. *"It does."*

Aisha Rose just shook her head.

"IT'S ONLY A few more hours," Kait said a little later. "Can I stay here the rest of the night?"

"Of course."

Aisha Rose lay down on the mattress, stretched out, her back against the wooden wall. Finally, she was comfortable. This was a little more like her perch in the big tree in Hell's Gate.

Kait lay down next to her, on her back. Aisha Rose could see her eyes reflecting the light coming through the porthole. Then Kait closed her eyes, and all that was left for Aisha Rose to look at was her profile, so much like Mama's, so much like her own.

They were quiet for a long while. Aisha Rose was awake—she knew she would not sleep again—but she thought that Kait must be dozing.

So Kait surprised her by saying, "It's all going wrong, isn't it?"

Aisha Rose didn't reply.

"I don't mean here." Kait's voice bore no trace of panic, of fear. "I know it's hopeless, our fight. Trying to reach Malcolm. I know we're going to die there. All of us who go ashore."

Still Aisha Rose was silent.

"I mean . . . back home. Back in Refugia. It's hopeless there as well, isn't it?"

Aisha Rose thought of the lights, the stars. The new stain that had begun to appear in just the past day. But again she didn't answer.

"It's all going wrong," Kait said, and this time it wasn't a question.

Aisha Rose put her palm against Kait's cheek. Kait's eyes opened at the touch, but after a few moments, they closed again. Soon after that, she was asleep.

Beside her, Aisha Rose watched the lights and made her plans until she heard the sound of voices and movement from other cabins and the passageway outside and knew that the day had begun.

THIRTY-FIVE

NIGHTTIME. SOMEWHERE DOWN below, hidden by the boughs and thick rain-forest foliage and the rising mist, something was moving around.

Something or someone. Mariama wasn't sure.

But that didn't matter. All that mattered was that she and Sheila were up here, that the rest of the survivors of the onslaught, the massacre, were scattered around the forest, and that the thieves and their slaves now had control of the ground. The ground and Refugia and time.

Time most of all.

MARIAMA LOOKED DOWN at her meager arsenal and sighed. It was still not enough. Not nearly enough.

She went through it again, as if somehow she might have missed something. As if there might be a dozen canisters of tear gas, or a dart gun, or even a pistol equipped with a silencer, hidden in the small locker in the corner of the blind where she and Sheila were still holed up.

Mariama had never thought about that term. "Holed up." It always had seemed to her to have a positive connotation, as if it meant you'd escaped a threat and were now regrouping, planning, plotting your counterattack.

But that wasn't what it meant at all. Holed up was what your enemies wanted you to be. Holed up meant being stuck in a hole, giving *them* the chance to regroup, plot, plan. To fill your hole with smoke, or pour poison down it, or send down some invading predator that would tear you apart as you cowered at the far end of your hole, trying desperately to fight back.

Or they could just wait. Let the clock tick down while they went about their lives and didn't even have to lift a finger to ensure your death.

Being holed up meant you were trapped. *Treed*.

Treed like a bear or a mountain lion or one of the other animals people used to hunt with dogs and horses. Back in those ridiculous days, when survival was so easy that people had the time to stage competitions for which they trained animals to tree other animals, then rode up at their leisure for the kill.

So here they were, Mariama and Sheila.

Sitting there, waiting for the hunters to ride up and finish the job.

LAST NIGHT, AT dusk, the air had turned unusually chilly, with a stiff breeze blowing in off the ocean. Weather systems like this—Trey had called them *friajes*, though that was a South American term—were rare over Refugia, but hardly unheard-of. They were never severe enough, or lasted long enough, to harm the crops. And though they suppressed the activity of protein sources like birds and small mammals, in a well-run colony this had been no more than an annoyance.

Mariama, sensing the *friaje's* arrival, had thought that the cold might even work to her advantage, especially just before dawn. The chill, wet hour before the sun rose and warmed the earth and sent the heavy mist spiraling up through the trees.

The hour that diurnal mammals were most deeply asleep. And nocturnal ones, at the end of the long, perilous night, at their weariest.

And not just mammals. Thieves, too. Because mammals, at least, could generate their own heat, while wasps could not.

Giving her a chance, at least, to see what had happened down there. Maybe help some of those who were imprisoned.

Or, at the very least, to die on her own terms. Not just sitting up here, treed, waiting for her immunity to wear off and the thieves to feast on her.

SHE CHOSE TWO knives. The first, her bayonet, she wore on her hip. The other, a smaller, double-sided, slightly hooked blade, went into a sheath on her right ankle.

And one more weapon. Something she'd never seen

as she was growing up, even though her childhood had been spent in a war zone. Brass knuckles.

She had no idea where Malcolm had found it, this set of ridged metal loops that fit over her four fingers and nestled in her palm. With her thumb wrapped around it, she knew she'd be able to deliver a strong blow, strong enough to disable a human, and perhaps even a last-stage host.

That might be useful.

Then she straightened and looked across to the other end of the platform, where Sheila, wrapped up in the jacket Mariama had included in her cache, was finally asleep.

The other reason that Mariama had waited till now to leave the platform. So she wouldn't have to say good-bye.

Moving in silence, she climbed down the ladder.

THE WATCHER-THIEF WAS perched on a broad, dew-slick leaf of a philodendron vine spiraling up the kapok's trunk. It was hunched over, resting low on its legs in the early-morning chill.

Mariama picked it off the leaf and squeezed its thorax. Its mandibles gaped wide, its stinger slid out, and the wasp writhed between her fingers.

She squeezed a little harder. Some liquid welled between its jaws, and a drop of thick venom pulsed from the tip of its stinger.

Even in its final moments, it turned its head to look

up into her eyes. Passing information on to the hive mind. But Mariama didn't care. She had never expected to return to Refugia unseen.

One more squeeze, and the thief died, dripping from both ends. She tossed it to the ground. The ants and bacteria and fungi were welcome to it.

Mariama sniffed her fingers. The thief's odor, as familiar to her as her own, made her feel more alert.

No. That wasn't it. The smell ignited her anger. It was the anger that made her fully awake.

SHE WENT OVER the wall at a spot she knew would be at least somewhat screened from view. Located near the southwest corner, it allowed her to drop to the ground behind a row of equipment sheds that hid her from the main plaza and the rows of residences.

Even so, she'd expected to be met on this little patch of bare ground between the walls and the row of sheds. Even at this dead time on a cold morning, she'd expected the hive mind to have planned an attack to greet her arrival.

Deep down, Mariama had thought she'd die right here.

Instead, there appeared to be no one around. The compound was silent, as if it had emptied out overnight.

No: a different kind of silence. A waiting silence.

It was so strange, so inexplicable, that for the first time Mariama felt cold. The chill of the unknown proving that *she*, at least, hadn't become immune to fear.

But she wasn't crippled by it, either. She went on.

* * *

THERE WAS A man out past the sheds. No rider on his neck. A guard? It was impossible to know.

Nor did it matter. Not to Mariama as she came up to him silently through the shadows.

No. That was a lie. It did matter.

That had been the most intolerable revelation about the invaders, Mariama thought. That among them were some who were still human. Men and women who had traded in their freedom for survival.

And who had killed out of choice, not by command.

Ridden slave or human? Yes, it *did* matter.

THIS ONE, WITH no rider, was just turning toward her when she clubbed him with her brass-knuckled fist.

She felt his skull crumble from the force of her blow, and he fell straight to the ground without making more than a tiny moan swallowed up by the cold, still air.

Mariama was impressed. No wonder Malcolm had added this weapon to the stockpile.

The man on the ground was still alive for now, still moving his legs and arms in uncoordinated motions. Mariama stood above him for a moment, thinking. And then, reaching for her belt, she squatted and completed the task with a knife. Showing mercy he didn't deserve.

Then she headed into the shadows once more.

But she was still possessed by an eerie sense of confusion. The expression on the man's face in his last instant had revealed shock, fear, and—most of all—surprise.

He'd had no idea she was coming, and the continued absence of anyone who *would* have known made no sense at all.

But while just a few moments before, this bizarre lack of response, of awareness, had spooked her, now she felt a new emotion ignite inside her. Hope.

Something had changed. Mariama didn't have a clue what or why, but she didn't need to. She didn't need to know what was going on to take advantage of it.

She moved forward, knife in her hand.

THE PRISONERS WERE being held in the Refugia's community center. Where else? It was the only space where more than a few could be kept together.

The door was guarded by four of the invaders. Mariama, across the plaza, thought that they were a mix— last-stage hosts, ridden ones, willing slaves—but at this distance, she couldn't be sure.

That part didn't much matter. Whatever they were, they'd all die the same way, and just as quickly, by her hand.

When the time came.

KNOWING SHE HAD only a few moments before the rising sun made her transit obvious to all, she slipped behind the building. The windows had all been boarded up, but the job had been done quickly and roughly enough to leave plenty of gaps—none big enough to climb through, but easy enough to see into.

Bending to get the best angle, Mariama got her first look at the prisoners. Then she closed her eyes for an instant, not in shock or horror at what she'd seen but to quell her anger.

Taking a deep breath, she looked again at the slave quarters straight out of ones she'd seen elsewhere, on Gorée Island north of here, and at Cape Castle in Ghana. Places where many of her own ancestors had been taken, less than two centuries before the Fall, and where some had died.

The room had been designed for twenty people at most, but there were dozens packed into the small space. Eighty? A hundred? She couldn't tell.

She saw young, old, children. *Babies.* All people she knew. All she'd considered *hers*, under her protection.

Some were standing upright with no place to move, not even to take a single step. Others were lying in the corners in small piles where they'd fallen. Mariama couldn't tell if they were dead or still barely alive, or if that even mattered.

Heat from the living bodies inside the room emanated through the gaps in the window. So did the smells: vomit, urine, shit, *thief.*

MARIAMA HAD SEEN enough. Full daylight or not, she knew what her next destination would be: the front of the building. The four guards. Undoubtedly, she would lose the battle, and her life, before she could open the door to let the slaves escape, but at least she would die trying.

But when she straightened and turned, she found

herself looking directly into the eyes of a last-stage host.
A second one was coming up just behind it.

THE BATTLE, FOUGHT in near silence, was quick, but not
quick enough.

Mariama plunged her bayonet into the closer one.
She'd aimed for the eye, but at the last instant it twisted
away from her and the blade struck its neck instead. The
eruption of blood slowed it, but also blinded her.

And as it went down, it took the bayonet with it.

Scrubbing the blood out of her eyes with the back of
her right hand, Mariama bent, reached—losing the brass
knuckles—and got her other knife out of its sheath.
Before she could straighten, though, the second host
was on top of her, its hands like claws tearing at her back,
its jaws snapping somewhere just above her head.

At the same instant, she felt a fierce pain in her right
calf. The crunch of teeth through her flesh as the dying
host below fastened onto her.

Mariama knew she was very close to losing this battle,
to forsaking those she'd hoped to rescue. With a last,
violent effort, she pushed off the ground, headfirst. The
leap dislodged the jaws of the fallen host, and at the same
instant the top of her skull made contact with the second
attacker's chin. She felt and heard the bones of its jaw
shatter, and it released her and fell back.

Her vision was blurred, the pain in her leg intense as
an electric current, but she still had the knife. One quick
step forward, and she'd put the blade in the throat of
the second host, tearing upward and sideways. Blood

spurted and flowed, and it went down. She stepped out of the way as it rolled and spasmed beside the other, whose own movements were already growing feeble.

MARIAMA TOOK A deep breath. How long had the fight taken? Fifteen seconds, perhaps. Long enough for three of the guards to come around the corner of the building, to hesitate—even then, Mariama wondered why—before coming for her.

Three was too many, and more were joining them with every moment. She turned and ran. No, tried to run, only to have her injured leg almost go out from under her.

She forced herself to overcome the agony and move, half dragging her leg, already planning her next strategy. She would lead them away, around to the rear of the building, then double back and—

But it was hopeless. Before she'd gone a dozen strides, they had her surrounded. Contained. Four of them, no, six now. And still more coming.

The sun rose above Refugia's eastern wall. Touched by the sudden warm light, mist writhed upward from the dew-drenched ground. As the nearest two reached for her, Mariama drew a breath, steadied herself, and raised her knife.

Then a cloud obscured her vision, and a high-pitched screaming filled her head.

THIRTY-SIX

THEY'D COME ASHORE at dawn, not because there would be any element of surprise—of course they'd be seen, of course they'd be expected—but because possibly, just possibly, attacking during those chilly, dead hours might have given them the slightest advantage.

The thieves, with their cold blood, would be sluggish. And even the slaves might be at low ebb at that hour, either not yet fully awake or tired after a long night.

Kait remembered Mariama explaining all this around the fire one night. Mariama, the one among them who knew the most about fighting, about killing. Even more than Malcolm did, and Malcolm knew just about everything.

Kait, who knew nothing about killing, and didn't want to learn, hadn't listened when the topic had turned in that direction. But she did remember that part. You attacked at dawn.

Even when you knew you had no chance anyway.

* * *

EIGHTEEN OF THEM, using both dinghies. Sixteen crew members, plus the two newcomers, Aisha Rose and Jason. The two who knew better than anyone how hopeless it was yet had decided to fight beside them anyway.

Eighteen here meant that a crew of ten had remained on the *Trey Gilliard*. Most likely that would not be enough to sail the ship back to Refugia if the others never returned, but at least it might be possible.

A little hope. The best any of them could do.

THIS TIME THEY got all the way up to the plaza before the slaves attacked. Three dozen of them? Four? So many that it was all a blur to Kait, a blur of bodies battling hand-to-hand, accompanied by the whipcrack sound of guns and the screams of the wounded and, above all, the whirling hum of the thieves in their masses, their clouds, above.

A blur with moments of great clarity. Shapiro with her back against a stone pillar, discharging her shotgun once, twice—flesh and bone and blood flying in the misty gray air—and again.

Dylan Connell, who'd insisted on accompanying them this time, but not for very long, as he fell under the onslaught. Kait glimpsing his shocked expression, his wide eyes, lifeless already as the attackers tore apart his body.

Jason seeming almost to fly through the crowd of attackers, his machete swinging so rapidly that its blood-smeared blade left a crimson afterimage in the air, like the smear left behind by thieves' wings.

Kait herself, infected, safe, invisible to the attackers. Not to the human ones, Jason had warned her, but only to the slaves and their thief masters. But no one, slave or thief or human, seemed to be paying her any attention, because—invisible or not—she seemed like no immediate threat. Weaponless, half-hidden from the melee by a pile of coral stone where a section of wall had fallen, she stood so still that she might have been a wraith, a vision.

Standing beside her was Aisha Rose, face bone white, skin translucent. Far too weak to repeat what she had done on these stairs the day before.

Aisha Rose's eyes were closed, and she swayed on her feet. But it seemed to Kait that she was seeking something. Questing.

PERHAPS TEN FEET away from them stood the twins. Today they were armed with handguns, and though Brett had his out, Darby had already lost hers. A group of slaves surrounded them, shouldering closer as they stood side by side, awaiting death together.

Kait looked at the two of them, knowing there was nothing she could do to save them. She had never been any sort of a fighter, and she would not leave Aisha Rose's side.

And then, in that instant, she felt a shift in her brain. Like a key turning, and something new opening.

And, at last, she saw. Saw from within what Trey had witnessed all those years and kept secret from her. Her own place in the mind whose shape shifted with every instant, whose horrifying, overwhelming consciousness was built from countless eyes, countless senses. Including her own.

She understood how weak, how unimportant, the human mind was by comparison, with just one slow, incomplete, individual response at a time. How could it match up against a million visions all channeled effortlessly into the whole? A million visions creating a million responses, reactions, commands, followed by another million, and another?

And now she had become part of that whole.

At the same moment, she understood something else. The thing that Trey had discovered when he saved Malcolm's life in the helicopter, the night the Last World fell. He'd saved Malcolm by shouting out a warning—a false warning—to the thieves, and by doing so had allowed Malcolm to save his life in turn.

Kait understood that amid the ebb and flow of information that threatened to overwhelm her, to drown her, she could discern individual thieves' responses. She could see through their eyes.

See through their eyes. See that every nearby thief was avoiding Shapiro, the twins, everyone who'd taken the vaccine. Echoes of alarm that translated into a "stay away!" call transmitted instantly.

Transmitted by every nearby thief . . . but one. One was different.

Kait detected it, that one thief—and was immediately inside it. She saw that it was focused on Shapiro but, instead of adding one more alarm note to the endless stream, was registering something quite different.

It saw Shapiro, and it saw her as a threat. A threat it could eliminate.

Kait knew what it was. The new kind of thief, the one that had developed an immunity to the vaccine. The kind that would, without effort, cast all free humans—the ones whose lives had depended for all these years on their fragile vaccine—into slavery or extinction.

Starting with Shapiro, whom it unerringly recognized as their most powerful fighter.

Kait, simultaneously watching the thief and looking through its eyes, saw it, felt it, rise in the air. Such a familiar motion, the one that preceded the dive, the fatal sting.

As this thief, this new thief, reached its apogee, it paused. This was the instant when Kait's hand would have darted into the air, fast as a blur. When she would have snatched the wasp, rendering it suddenly harmless and easy to kill. If only she'd been close enough to reach it.

Except . . . she was.

Closing her eyes, she threw herself, her consciousness, her thief awareness, at this individual fragment of the hive mind. Feeling it shudder in the air, seeing it lose contact with the whole for an instant.

Just for an instant, but long enough for Kait to commandeer it, to send it spinning to the ground. To the ground at her feet.

Or had she done it alone? Had she done it at all? She didn't know because when her vision focused again, Aisha Rose was looking up at her. The glimmering light in her eyes was very strong.

They both looked down at the wasp, quivering on

the ground. Still alive. Until, with an efficient little movement, Aisha Rose reached out with her right foot, clad in one of the bright blue sandals that Kait had found for her, and squashed it.

It might be the first of a new horde, a new conquering army, but it was not going to be present at the conquest.

Aisha Rose straightened, looked up at the sky. Suddenly she seemed to stand taller, more erect. All of her exhaustion seemed to disappear in an instant, and for the first time Kait sensed her true power. And understood that Aisha Rose was also the beginning of something new. The point of the spear.

But at that moment something happened, and Aisha Rose cried out and crumbled to the ground. That was the last thing that Kait saw—Aisha Rose falling—before something pulled her inside out, and she fell, too.

Reaching out with the last of her strength, and gathering the girl's still, slight form into her arms.

IN HIS DUNGEON, Malcolm, sick, drifting, had been listening to the battle outside. Hearing the gunshots, the screams, thinking as he listened that he recognized who was in agony, who was dying.

Waiting to hear the sound of Clare Shapiro's death.

They'd come back for him, Shapiro and the others. He knew that. They would have been long gone if he hadn't allowed himself to be captured. If, at the last moment, he'd turned his gun on himself. If they'd seen his blood flow, if they'd seen him die, they would have fled and never looked back.

Their deaths were his fault.

The smell of blood came through the small window high on the far wall, the hole in the stone showing only a patch of gray dawn sky gradually turning the palest eggshell blue. That pure, beautiful African sky he'd always loved so much, tainted forever for him. Tainted by the smell of death and the black cloud of thieves whirling above the carnage he could not see but could hear and imagine. Imagine too well.

Soon enough, he knew, the screams and other sounds of battle would die down. The whirling thieves would settle once again, and the slave camp would resume its normal activities. Growing, spreading, until it covered all of Africa. All of the earth.

Would that take one year? A hundred? A thousand? It didn't matter. Eventually, the planet would be one giant slave camp, and no one would remember the glories that humanity had once been capable of, or the atrocities.

He heard someone cry out and thought, his heart shattering, *Kait.*

And then, *Trey.*

Trey, I'm so sorry. I promised.

But I couldn't stop her.

And then he was shouting, cursing, filling his cell with his bellows as he tried to tear its stone door apart with his bloody hands. His unbridled rage at first causing him to miss the change in the sound the thieves, the slavemakers, were making.

It was the sound of their wings, a million wings, rising in pitch.

Malcolm stood still, looked back at the tiny window

high in the far wall. Through it he saw an enormous knot of thieves form against the blue sky. Then they broke apart in confusion, came together, fragmented, rejoined again.

And they were screaming.

MARIAMA KNOCKED HER attacker's hands away from her neck. It wasn't hard to do: The hands had lost all their strength, her attacker all its will.

Six of them there were now. Six clustered around her, who would have slaughtered her where she stood.

But now, when she stepped forward and cut the throat of the creature nearest, the one whose hands had been on her, it simply fell straight down. Its life gurgling away into the soil at her feet.

And the rest did not seem even to notice. They were standing there, unmoving, as if thunderstruck by the sight of the thieves spinning in confusion above Refugia.

Four of them were, at least. Two last-stage hosts and two who until a few moments before had been thief-ridden. Paralyzed by whatever was possessing their masters above.

And the fifth? That one was human. Mariama could tell that, had been able to tell even as the attack unfolded. It had moved faster, had quicker instincts. Less brute force, but a more developed sense of self-preservation.

Now it was staring up at the spectacle above them, then shifting its shocked gaze down to Mariama's face.

It. *He.*

Mariama felt a powerful revulsion blossom inside of her. She leaped forward, and a few moments later this human, this one who had made his own choice, was dead anyway.

The four who still lived stared upward. Their faces showed . . . fear? No, loss.

As if they'd been abandoned.

Mariama, taking a breath before finishing them as well, looked up at the screaming mass whirling above her and felt something she hadn't experienced in decades.

An emotion so unfamiliar that at first she didn't even recognize what it was.

THE BOY STOOD on the edge of his perch, the wind enveloping him, blowing so strongly that he thought it must be passing through his emaciated body. If he leaped, he wondered for a moment, would the currents carry him? Would they bear him gently to the ground? It was so tempting to find out, to take that leap and see what happened.

No. It wasn't time.

Not yet.

Below him, above him, inside him, all was darkness. The sky above covered with clouds and the curved earth below not illuminated by a single flame.

Had this place once been lit? Had it once glowed? He knew it had, but standing there in the utter blackness, he could not imagine it.

But that wasn't true, not entirely. The world wasn't entirely black. She was still there, inside him, as she always was now. Crouching behind her pitiful walls and in danger. In more danger than she'd ever been before.

But so far out of his reach that he had no way to protect her.

No way but one.

He was nearly done with his game. He'd pulled the net taut. They were all inside it. Every one.

The net was full, and he was the one holding its mouth.

The boy stood in the darkness and sent out the command. It wasn't even hard to do. All he had to do was begin, and one by one, million by million, they would do the rest for him. Do the rest, and end themselves.

And then his job would be done, except for the last, most crucial part. The part that he'd been training himself so relentlessly for, all these recent weeks and months.

IT WAS A wave. Kait could tell. A wave as big as the world, as the universe, coming toward her. Purifying the earth as it came, sweeping the stain before it.

She saw it coming and knew that she was standing directly in its path. It towered over her, and she understood that in a moment, she, too, would be swept away, along with the rest. The rest of the stain.

That was okay. She *was* part of the stain now.

It was only right.

"I LOVE YOU so much," Mama said, "that I would stand between you and a bullet, a lion's jaws, a tsunami."

Aisha Rose knew that. She knew how much Mama loved her. She'd always known.

She also knew, now, that Mama was truly gone. That

her soul had ascended when the vultures took her body up on the mountain. And that, regardless of Aisha Rose's daily recitation, neither of them—neither Mama nor Aisha Rose herself—was human. The thief inside Mama had changed her into something else and had made something new of Aisha Rose as well.

She, and the boy, and all the other lights, had been wrought out of new clay.

But none of that was important, not anymore. The only important thing was that Aisha Rose's plan had worked. The boy had unleashed the tsunami, and no one, not the slaves, not Aisha Rose, not the hive mind, not even the boy himself, could stop it now.

Already it was spreading across the earth, and all who belonged to the mind would be swept away. The stars, the galaxies that had accompanied Aisha Rose on her journey, and of course, Aisha Rose herself. New clay and old.

And Kait. Kait, too. The newest, and the only one that mattered now to Aisha Rose.

But then, as the wave towered over them, she saw that it wasn't what she'd expected. And she understood: He was choosing to save her. He was choosing to keep her alive.

So only the two of them would remain. The two of them standing on a cleansed earth.

That was his dream.

Her heart broke then. *I'm sorry,* she told him, though she never knew if he heard her. *I'm so sorry.*

The wave broke. And Aisha Rose Atkinson, human being, something else, something more, stood in front of Kait, so she could be swept away in her stead.

* * *

"NO," KAIT SAID, her arms around Aisha Rose.

She thought of all the people in her life who had fought for her, protected her. Her birth mother and father, who had never seen the Next World. Her grandmother Mary, who'd brought her to Refugia. Trey. So many dead, and she hadn't been able to save a single one of them.

No.

Not this one. Not this time.

IT WAS OVER.

The boy stepped forward into the darkness and let the wind carry his fragile body away.

THE SCREAM OF wings had built to an impossible crescendo. Followed by . . . silence. Complete, utter silence.

Malcolm awoke. He had no idea he'd been asleep, unconscious. At first, he didn't even know where he was. He didn't understand a thing.

And then he did.

His belly hurt. He noticed that. And, when he pulled his ragged, stained shirt up and looked down at his flesh, he saw for the first time what had been done to him.

The tiny swelling. The pinprick of an airhole.

And, half-emerged from the pinprick, the minuscule larva. Newly hatched from its egg yet already dead, hanging limp in the midst of its hopeless attempt to escape.

Revolted, Malcolm pulled it from the hole.

Then he looked back at the window, at the patch of blue sky. There was not a movement there, not a single black dot, no shimmer of bloodred wings. Nothing but silence.

A silence broken by the sound of voices. Familiar voices.

Shapiro's voice.

He stood, head spinning, but somehow maintaining his balance. Four steps across the slick stone, and he stood beneath the window.

"I'm here," he called out. But it was only a whisper. No one would hear him.

He took in a deep breath, and when he tried again he shouted more loudly than he ever had before, or ever would again. *I'm here.*

He heard answering shouts from outside, then another voice coming from much closer. A familiar voice, one he recognized right away even though he hadn't heard it for so long.

Calling his name.

THE GROUND WAS carpeted in thieves. Normally, this would have been the most dangerous time, dying wasps desperate to sting or lay their eggs in anything warm-blooded.

Only . . . not this time. Not now. These thieves were still, unmoving, not even a twitch or quiver, much less that rhythmic pulsing of their abdomens, the jagged, mindless punch of the stinger.

Unmoving. Shriveled. Again, and for the last time, just bugs. Harmless, finally and forever.

A scene repeated across the world, Kait thought. All was silence inside her head as well. The hive mind was gone.

Taking most of the slaves with it. The last-stage hosts and the ridden ones, all the ones that had ever been infected, had been struck down. Kait could tell this, too.

All except Kait herself, and she knew why. She knew what Aisha Rose had done for her, and for all those other lights she saw in her mind. The other ones like her, scattered across the earth.

What Aisha Rose had done to protect them all from the wave, and what Kait herself—far too weak and new to save them all, but strong enough to protect just one— had done in return.

Kait looked down at the girl cradled in her arms. As she did, Aisha Rose opened her eyes and looked back up at her.

"Mama?" she said, her voice a breath. Then, a little more strongly, "Kait."

"I'm here, Aisha Rose."

"They're still there," she said. "I can still see them."

"See what?"

Though she knew. Constellations. Galaxies.

Aisha Rose, smiling, burrowed more deeply into her embrace.

EPILOGUE
Kait

Nova Refugia
Year 5

IT TOOK THE dinosaurs ten thousand years. *At least* ten thousand.

I remember learning that from Carl, a friend of Jack Parker's at the American Museum of Natural History back before the Fall. I was . . . God, I was ten, and I'd never been to the museum before, and Carl took me on a behind-the-scenes tour of the dinosaur department. It was so cool, that huge old building with shiny floors and hidden rooms filled with shelves and drawers and old wooden crates containing fossil bones and teeth and who knew what else. I remember they had one fossil that had come from a uranium bed, and it was still radioactive.

And Carl was easy to talk to, kind of like Jack. So I asked him how quickly the dinosaurs had gone extinct after the earth had been hit by an asteroid. (I'd read that in a book.) And he shook his head and told me they'd never gone extinct—that modern-day birds were dinosaurs, too.

"That pigeon you saw sitting on Theodore Roosevelt's head on your way in . . . that's a dinosaur," he'd said. "Dinosaurs are everywhere, even now."

I saw him smile at the expression on my face. "Oh," he said, "you mean the *nonavian* dinosaurs? Well, paleontologists have been arguing about that for a long time, and we still don't know. Some believe it took as long as a million years, but others think as little as ten thousand."

I remember he snapped his fingers, and said, "Ten thousand? A million? Both of those are nothing. Gone like that!"

But I'd thought they'd both sounded like a long time. An incomprehensibly long time.

And I still do, and always will.

You want "Gone like that"? Forget dinosaurs, even "nonavian" ones, and look to humans instead.

Because it's possible that the human race won't last anywhere close to a hundred years, much less ten thousand.

Only . . . not if we have anything to do with it.

And not if we're willing to tweak the definition of "human" a bit.

IT TOOK US eleven months, but we finally made it back to Refugia on the *Trey Gilliard*. Forty-one of us, in the end: twenty-one from the original crew and twenty more who hadn't taken the outward journey.

Twenty strangers, even though it's hard to remember now, five years on, that they were ever strangers. They're woven into Refugia's fabric now. Part of Nova Refugia.

A strange section of the weave, admittedly, but a section nonetheless.

Twenty of them then, many more now, five years in, and we hope for still more in the future.

There are no guarantees, of course, but someday we might even get past the point where we'd have to worry about minimum viable population for species survival, one of those subjects that can keep people like Shapiro arguing all night. You see, back in the Last World, some scientists believed the minimum number was *this*, and others believed *that*, and . . .

Never mind. We'll just see what happens.

What a relief to be able to say that.

WHO WERE THE twenty newcomers on the voyage home? Well, Chloe, of course—and how weird was it to see Malcolm as a dad, with a nearly fifty-year-old daughter who looked almost like his clone? Their arguments were—still are—fierce because they're nearly as alike as the twins. Just noisier.

We also picked up two actual children, a three- and a five-year-old, left behind in the carnage at Lamu Fort. Feral children. Not feral anymore, and loved here, though I don't think they'll ever really get over those first unimaginable years of their lives.

We brought no other adults back from Lamu, though. The ridden ones died when their masters did, and the natives and human slaves all disappeared into the ruins of the town as soon as the tide of battle shifted our way. We never saw any of them again.

I suppose I understand that. They must have thought they'd be killed on sight if they returned. After all, they knew we were human, too, and wasn't that what humans do? Take an eye for an eye?

I can't swear that we wouldn't have, either, if they'd dared to show their faces.

SO . . . THREE FROM Lamu. And then, not long afterward, two more.

Early on our return journey, in what had once been Tanzania, we saw an enormous flock of vultures circling near the shoreline. We moored offshore, went to check it out, and found—as we expected to—the remains of another slave camp.

Piles of bodies everywhere, so many even the vultures were sated, the remains in a condition where it was impossible to tell whether they'd once been human, ridden, or born into slavery. Not that it mattered by then.

But just as we returned to the boat, these three came running toward us. Two adults and a baby boy who couldn't have been more than a year old. All three shaking with such fear that they were hard to look at.

There was some debate, but in the end we took them with us as well. The father died of a fever after just two weeks—the kind of fever that explorers have been "gifting" to native peoples since time immemorial—but the other two survived to land in Refugia with the rest of us.

* * *

BUT, REALLY, THOSE weren't the important ones. The important ones were those that Aisha Rose brought to us. The Newcomers.

Her lights. Individual stars in the galaxies she saw.

It didn't start right away because we almost lost Aisha Rose early on. The infection in her hand and arm didn't require amputation, but Fatou had to perform one surgery after another and use up most of our supply of antibiotics. (No one would have had it any other way.)

Still, she was close to death for days, and in great pain for weeks, but she bore it all with her usual calm, bright-eyed stoicism. Of course she did.

Her left hand and arm have never been much use since then—too much nerve damage—but she's never complained about that, either.

Anyway, it was soon after she finally got well that she, quietly, and to me alone at first, suggested that she could bring others like her to us. That she could call to them, and some might make the journey to meet the ship if we'd be willing to stop for them and pick them up.

Call to them how? I asked.

She just shook her head and said she didn't have the words for it. Not speech, she said, or mind reading. A deeper connection.

"They'll be so scared," she told me. "Many of them have been alone for a long time. But I think they'll come, some of them, anyway. It's hard to be alone."

Well, when I broached it, THAT idea caused quite the discussion on board. Some people were against it, afraid and wanting to press on home. But Malcolm, who knew what it was like to be separated from someone you loved, and Shapiro, who was fascinated by the science of it all, and Chloe and Jason, of course, argued strongly in favor, and their arguments carried the day.

So Aisha Rose, our beacon, reached out, in that way that none of the rest of us could begin to understand, and some of them—the others like her—did respond.

And in that way, over the months, we added to our crew, one or two at a time.

The Newcomers. Human?

I'm not sure. Something different, I think.

Members of an evolving species. Same clay, new mold, as Aisha Rose put it.

Ross and Trey would both have loved to meet them. I wish they'd had the chance.

WE MADE IT back to Refugia to find a colony grievously altered. Nearly a quarter of the residents had been killed during the invasion and its aftermath, and more died of injury and disease, shock and heartbreak, in the weeks and months that followed. If not for Sheila's medical expertise—and tirelessness—and Mariama's leadership, many more would not have made it through.

Still, everyone lost someone they loved. I won't list them here. Death, regardless of where it comes from or when it happens, isn't usually worth recording anyway. It isn't very distinctive or terrifying. It just is.

We all know that too well.

But we also know how to go on.

* * *

AS SOON AS we got home, Malcolm gave the order to start building new ships, two at once, following the same design as the *Trey Gilliard*. It felt like we barely had a chance to take a breath and mourn our dead before we were back at work. All of us, even the kids, even the new ones.

It made sense, as Malcolm well knew. He gave us all something to do, to focus on, and by doing so helped bring the community together in its new shape.

Now, after five years, we have three ships, and we're ready for further forays. (It's amazing how fast you can build a sailing ship when your whole colony pitches in.)

We're planning the first attempt at a transatlantic voyage, and another ship will head (at last!) for the island of New Guinea, to make contact with the colony—the truly human colony—that Sheila, at least, insists still thrives there.

Someday, one of our ships won't return from a voyage. We know that. It's inevitable.

And we'll mourn, and hope for another miracle, and go on.

AISHA ROSE WON'T be on board any of these voyages. Her damaged arm, for one thing, would be a hindrance . . . but she's also had enough of hejiras.

That's good, because it's crucial that she stay here, in Nova Refugia, to greet the new arrivals and help with their transition. Which is almost always very difficult, as she'd known it would be, since most of them had been on their own for years, and that's not something you just get over.

But it turns out that Aisha Rose—I think because Mama was with her for so long, telling her about the Last World, making her perform her recitation—*is* the most human of all her new species. Much more than the other Newcomers we've brought in, though, as time passes, the distance between us all narrows.

I think it's the colony's young people, the natives, who deserve the most credit for the meeting of cultures, of minds. People like Jack Gilliard, my brother, who, not really belonging to any world except this one, serve as a conduit between us. They're invaluable.

Plus, Jack really likes Aisha Rose. And even though she treats him with a kind of amused tolerance, as if he's just a child—I imagine I'm hearing Mama's voice when she chides him for something—in truth he's only about three years younger than she is, and in most ways much more worldly.

It turns out they're both human in some important ways. Go figure.

AS I'D GUESSED, whatever happened that day at Lamu Fort was the end of the thieves. The true end: the asteroid impact that carried them into extinction.

The tsunami, the gigantic wave, swept them away.

To be honest, our assumption—that they're extinct—is based purely on empirical evidence. For example, we saw so many on our journey home, dried husks flying in the breeze, piling up amid the ruins, and floating in uncountable abundance in the sea, that it seemed impossible that every last one hadn't perished.

And no one has ever seen a living thief since, while the primate population has rebounded everywhere we've looked.

Even so, these observations don't come close to proof. Nor, in truth, do Aisha Rose's assurances that the *majizi* are gone forever. It's hard to have complete faith in someone who claims to hear voices in her head, no matter how much you love her.

But I have another reason, though I know it's just as much a leap of faith: I'm certain that the thieves are extinct because I'm still the same. Still healthy.

Whatever dragged Trey, Aisha Rose's mother, and others like them—the hosts who survived infection—into irrevocable decline, and killed them when they were young, has left me unaffected. I think I understand why. It was the mind that was slowly destroying them, and now that the mind is gone, the fact that I once had a thief larva growing inside of me, pouring its chemicals into me, changing my own chemistry . . . it's inconsequential.

Who knows? But I'm still here, and the thieves and their hive mind are gone. Of course, this means I will never see everything Trey saw. My lifelong dream, the dream I was willing to die for, has been denied.

That's fine with me. I've seen enough. I'm ready to stop seeing.

AND THE OTHER one? The one who unleashed the tsunami that swept the thieves and their slaves away? He died that day, too, Aisha Rose says. She's certain about this, and I have no reason to doubt her.

She can't know how he died, or where he lived—except that it was a park in a big city—or anything about him other than the face he'd showed her, the fact that he was damaged in some way, and that no one else on earth had the power he did.

And—she told me late one night, in our cabin, when no one else could hear—that she thought he died for her. Out of love for her.

This broke her heart, she said, but at the same time left her filled with relief. His power had really frightened her.

But where had it come from, this power? Shapiro speculated that something had happened to him, some injury, that had unlocked his brain, making it (in her words) even noisier than your typical Newcomer's.

"Even with all our toys in the Last World," she said, "there was a whole lot we didn't understand about brain function. People would awaken from head injuries, from comas, with strange new abilities. When you add the brain remodeling of the kind that's gone on in all of them . . ."

Then she laughed and turned her palms up in an elaborate shrug. "Oh, who cares how it all happened? It just did."

She's come a long way, has Shapiro.

THE LAST TIME I wrote in this journal was right before we headed off on the *Trey Gilliard*. The first voyage of the Next World.

That wasn't so long ago, but it feels like an age. An epoch.

The invasion, the final destruction of the thieves, learning that we were not the only humans left on earth, the arrival of the Newcomers . . . it's a different world, and we're a different colony today. Different forever.

So many changes, but sometimes I think that the biggest one is that we took Refugia's walls down. Yes, we needed the wood for new housing and shipbuilding, but it was more than that.

I think it showed that we'd finally accepted our place in the world. Not the Next World, just the world. The real earth, as Aisha Rose calls it.

You take walls down when you understand both life and death—even extinction—and face them all with open eyes.

When you know where you stand on the totem pole . . . and embrace it.